JOHN MACKENNA was born in 1952 in Castledermot, County Kildare.
His books include:
The Fallen and Other Stories (1992), which won *The Irish Times* First Fiction Award, *A Year of Our Lives* (London, Picador, 1995), *The Last Fine Summer* (London, Picador, 1998) and *Things You Should Know* (New Island, 2006).

the River Field

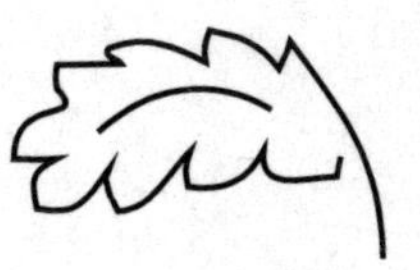

For Ewan MacKenna

the River Field

JOHN MACKENNA

NEW ISLAND

The River Field
First published 2007
by New Island
2 Brookside
Dundrum Road
Dublin 14

www.newisland.ie

ISBN 978-1-905494-78-1

British Library Cataloguing Data. A CIP catalogue record for this book is available from the British Library.

Printed in the UK by Mackays of Chatham Ltd, Chatham Kent.
Book design by Inka Hagen.

New Island received financial assistance from
The Arts Council (An Chomhairle Ealaíon), Dublin, Ireland.

10 9 8 7 6 5 4 3 2 1

Contents

1958

It's a twelve-acre field. Triangular.

A narrow country road sidesteps along one ditch, nodding in a deliberate and gentle hollow as it passes the wide opening framed by two cut-stone pillars that hold the corroded hinges of a fallen gate like fruit in the golden afternoon.

At the far end of the field, the second boundary edges the bank of a slow, shallow river, as the headland tumbles gently into the shadowed water where two oaks bend as they have bent, slightly towards each other, for almost two hundred years. A young boy swings out and back, his hands tight around a rope that hangs taut as a line, his feet racing on the low, unhurried river.

The third side of the triangle is strung with a broken necklace of smaller granite pillars on a rabbit-warrened mound, glinting like diamonds in the sunlight, rusted wires arcing slackly between them.

And the meadow that draws these sides together is deep and bountiful with the shining flowers of July.

The Low Terrace

It was the breathing that made us realise something was wrong, something beyond the ordinary, more a warning than a possibility. A rasping, uncertain, caught-in-the-throat breath that was a statement of intent, that said this was it, there was no going back, no recovery, no hope.

Each time I stepped into her hospital room I'd hear the laboured breathing. And each time I left, it followed and died when the door was closed. The corridor was always a relief after the endless hawing.

And sometimes there was the rambling talk about my brothers. I didn't have any brothers. I'm an only child. But she went on about them and about how we were to take care of them and not let them get cold.

'Keep them warm,' she'd say. 'Make sure they're warm.'

My father would lean across the bed and pat her hand and assure her and sometimes, when I was alone with her, she'd tell me to check that they were warm and I'd do my best to reassure her and pat her hand and massage her temples. And then she'd stop her rambling and, for a while, there'd be quietness.

We'd sit with her in shifts. My father through the day, my aunt in the evenings and myself through the night, sleeping in that hard armchair, a blanket tucked around me.

On the Saturday morning, at four o'clock, I walked the length of the corridor, while the nurses turned my mother.

Outside the day was white and fresh. Summer without the heat. A washed-out day. I walked right to the end of the glass-panelled mezzanine and looked across the car park, with its tarmac boxes and their dinky cars.

And I knew when I walked back, even before they said. I knew by the way the nurses were standing outside the door.

'She's gone,' one of them whispered softly.

I nodded.

'Would you like to spend a few minutes with her?'

I nodded again and the nurse opened the door for me and I stepped inside. She stood a moment watching me, the lemon skin of daylight like an aura around her, before she quietly closed the door and left me alone.

The silence in that aching, tortured room.

I stood at the window with my back to her, waiting for some movement, the slightest noise. I couldn't believe that death could be so still.

I remembered us packing the string shopping bag and climbing out through the back ditch and heading for picnics in the River Field. And I remembered Tommy MacMahon.

Jesus, Tommy MacMahon! What put him into my head? There was no silence when he died. When was it? July. Yes, it was July, but what year? Nineteen fifty-nine? No, earlier. Fifty-seven? Fifty-eight? Yes, fifty-eight. He was eight years younger than me and I was ten when he was killed. Tommy and Geraldine and Mr and Mrs MacMahon. They lived in the next cottage from ours. The gardens ran a full acre side by side. Twenty-four semi-detached cottages in a cul-de-sac. The Low Terrace, a village all on its own.

You were in your element that summer and then the world came tumbling down.

And the radio blaring all day long. What the hell was it? *All I have to do is dream*. But who sang it? I can hear you singing it.

I can make you mine, taste your lips of wine,
anytime, night or day,
Only trouble is, gee whiz,
I'm dreamin' my life away.

Who was it?

'The Everly Brothers,' my mother says. '"All I Have to Do is Dream." God, they're gorgeous. Your father says they can't sing, not in Mario Lanza's class, but they're gorgeous.'

And then she leans across the fence between the gardens.

'Do you like them, Mrs MacMahon?'

'Who?'

'The Everly Brothers.'

'Do I know them?'

'*Dream, dream, dream...*' my mother sings.'Oh yeah, yeah, they're good. Geraldine likes them. Don't you, Geraldine?'Geraldine MacMahon, sixteen, lying in the sun, rarely bothering to speak, even when she was spoken to.

'What?'

'You like them fellas that sing *dream, dream, dream.*'

'They're all right.'

Mrs MacMahon gives up on her daughter.

'I see she's still knocking around with Liam, that looks like a strong line,' my mother says.

'He's a very nice lad.'

'And very bright.'

*

Later, I overhear my mother and father discussing Geraldine and Liam.

'She has one aim in life and it isn't books. She's fella mad, anything in trousers.'

'So long as he stays in the trousers, things'll be all right,' my father laughs.

My mother looks at me and then back at my father.

'Ssshhh,' she says.

'He's ten,' my father grins. 'The bould Geraldine is another matter. And a grand-looking young one with it.'

My mother puts her arms around him and wrestles him against the sink, laughing.

'Don't you even think about that or you'll be out on your ear.'

When I look back, life seemed like that all the time. All happiness and laughter and light. Black and white is how childhood seems from this distance and that summer was all whiteness, all light, all sunshine and my parents laughing in the back garden. It was a summer of finding them kissing in the kitchen. A summer of my father spinning me on the swing, and my aunt coming to stay, and my parents dolled up to the nines for a midsummer dinner dance and waking, the next morning, to three bars of Fry's Cream on the bedside table, and the sound of my mother and my aunt giggling in the back garden and the sight of them on the garden seat, sipping tea. And then watching as my aunt drove away, waving, before going with my mother to pick lettuce and scallions for a salad for the tea. And my father's car in the yard and my parents hugging at the back door.

But there must have been another side.

And the corner-boy voices reassure me, the chorus of watchers, the ranks of seers:

Course there was another side.

We saw.

Of course we saw.

Everybody saw.

We all knew.

The whole Low Terrace knew.

The whole town.

We saw the MacMahon one and the Master's son at it.

Conniving under the streetlight was one thing. Going into the River Field was another matter altogether.

No light there!

Never a truer word.

Ha ha!

Never.

The long hot summer.

Long hot young lad.

Young wet wild one.

Sure we all knew.

She wasn't laughing at nothing.

I saw them.

And I saw them.

And so did my brother, saw them down the Back River.

Kissing and their mouths wide open.

And him feeling her.

And her with her hand inside his trousers looking for the long lad.

Ha ha!

*

And then one evening, is it the same evening that my aunt drove away or is it another? No, I'm sure it is that evening. We're walking between the strawberry beds at the side of the garden and Mrs MacMahon comes to the fence and calls my mother.

'Mrs! Mrs!'

'What is it?' my mother asks.

'Jesus, Mary and Joseph ...'

'What's the matter? What's wrong?'

'Sacred Heart of Jesus.'

'What is it?'

'It's Geraldine.'

'Is she sick?'

'Four months gone. Jesus, what am I going to do?'

'When did you find out?'

'Half an hour ago. They came and told me, her and Liam. They're gone to tell his mother. What are we going to do? He's all on for marrying her, getting a job, but what age is he? Seventeen. And her only sixteen.'

'How did it happen?'

'She says she doesn't know. And now I have to tell her father. She'll be a laughing stock. Young Tommy is only two and now his sister is having a child. What will I do?'

'God is good.'

'She told me she tried jumping off a wall early on. But too late to hope for it stirring now, it's well and truly settled.'

'God is good,' my mother says again.

'I better go and get Martin's dinner ready.'

And she walks away, her back bent, her head shaking.

*

Later, my parents are whispering in the garden.

'As though Martin will say anything to her!' my mother says. 'Geraldine's the apple of his eye. He dotes on her.'

I sway quietly on the swing.

'It's not the first time it's happened,' my father says, 'and it won't be the last. They'll get along all right. He's a bright young fellow. He'll get a job. They'll make out.'

'How can he? Isn't he waiting for the Leaving Cert results? He has prospects, the guards or a call to teacher training, something worthwhile. His father isn't going to let a thing like this destroy Liam's possibilities. I know the MacMahons are grand people, but they're hardly the same cut as Liam's people. Farm labouring is hardly the same thing as teaching!'

'It's not the fathers that are in trouble. They're not the ones wanting to get married,' my father laughs.

'Don't be smart,' my mother says and she's not smiling. 'Do you imagine, if you were in Liam's father's boots, you'd want your son marrying a little trollop like Geraldine MacMahon?'

'At least she'd tango,' my father grins, 'and that takes two!'

'Oh, for God's sake. She was never done chasing fellows. We saw her ourselves at the marquee, going outside with three different fellas.'

And, even now, I can hear the chorus behind my mother.

She did.
By Jasus she did.
Couldn't keep her legs together if she tied them.
A whore to go.

But sure, her mother was the same in her heyday.
Doesn't know how it happened, she says.
Doesn't know what it's for!
Or where to put it.
She'd milk an ass!
And come back for more.

A week later, Mrs MacMahon and my mother are at the fence again. Tommy MacMahon leaning against the wire, watching me dawdling on the swing.

'Young Liam was up last night. He says he wants to marry Geraldine as soon as she'll say yes.'

'And what does his father say?'

'I don't know. I'm afraid to go and talk to him. What would I say to a schoolteacher? Martin says they'll come and see us when they're ready.'

'And what does Geraldine say?'

'Little or nothing. She's cool with Liam but I think she's putting that on. Would you talk to her? She'd listen to you. She thinks you're great.'

'If you want me to, if you think it'll help.'

'Do, do. Good woman. Geraldine!'

Mrs MacMahon calls and calls again. Eventually Geraldine slouches from the house.

'Come here a minute,' her mother says. 'Talk to Mrs. She could tell you, advise you on things.'

She sweeps Tommy into her arms and leaves my mother and Geraldine at the fence.

'How are you?' my mother asks.

'All right.'

'You're not showing yet, anyway.'

'No.'

'Your mother says you weren't too sick either.'

'No.'

'That's good.'

'Yeah.'

'So what are you going to do?'

Geraldine shrugs her shoulders.

'What do Liam's parents say?'

'Dunno. His mother just said she'd have to talk to his father. I haven't been back there since.'

'How long ago was that?'

'Two weeks.'

'And what does Liam say?'

'He wants to marry me.'

'You're young.'

'So?'

'Do you love him?'

'Suppose.'

'Something'll happen.' My mother smiles and pats Geraldine's arm.

And it does. But my parents only hear about it second-hand.

Liam's father puts his foot down. No marrying. You have a career, he says. You'll get your call to teacher training. You'll be a teacher like me, he says.

And the voices leak from under doors around the parish.

I'll marry Geraldine, the young lad says. Over my dead body, the ould lad says. The mother screamed. He walloped the young lad.

He was always a dab hand at that in the school. Ha ha!

You've brains to burn, you'll do your training and you'll qualify, the ould lad says. You won't keep her from me, the young fella shouts. Well, by Jesus, I'll keep you from her then, the ould lad says. And he did!

By God he did!

Yahoooooo.

By Jasus, did he what!

Every night, over the kitchen table, my parents talk in riddles.

'I heard all guns are firing on the Western Front.'

'And what about the good woman over yonder?'

'Not a word, she says there's not a word at all. She says they may be moving the young soldier to another camp.'

'I heard otherwise. A reliable source tells me the Right Reverend has been called in.'

My mother frowns. 'Is that so?'

My father leans forward and speaks very seriously. 'Both as spiritual adviser and as manager of the school. He wants the fire brought under control as quickly as possible.'

'And what about the young soldier himself?'

My father runs his tongue around the inside of his mouth and shrugs.

'There's not a word to be got out of her ladyship,' my mother says. 'She just sits out there in the garden sunning herself. But I don't see him about at all.'

'I'd say he's still holding out for married bliss,' my father grins. 'The fool.'

My mother leans across the table and slaps him with the rolled-up newspaper and they both laugh out loud.

After that, everything seems to settle. There's talk of

Geraldine going away and having the baby and then coming home and giving it to her mother to raise. And Liam is to go to teacher training college and complete his course. They'll wait and see how things turn out. They won't see each other for three years and then the situation can be looked at.

My mother knows all this because, out of the blue, the parish priest sends for her and asks her to help.

'He brought me down to the kitchen,' she tells my father. 'The table was laid for afternoon tea. The housekeeper must have done it before she went out for her walk. He sat me down and told me the whole story. It was Geraldine's doing! I thought as much. He told me straight that she'd insisted on Liam doing it.'

Her voice drops to a whisper so that I have to strain to hear from the corner where I'm playing with my soldiers.

'He wanted to pull out but she held onto him. A proper little vixen.'

'Isn't it great the way the parish priest has all this inside information,' my father mocks. 'Like he was there, overseeing the whole thing, making all the calculations. Would he not have caught Liam by the legs and pulled him out?'

'Are you saying he made it up?'

'I'm saying nothing.'

'She had her claws in him,' my mother says, and the words come out hard and sharp. 'Anyway, there's more. As the PP pointed out, Liam has a career. It's all well and fine for him to talk of love now, but ten years down the road, when he's stuck working at the bacon counter in Browne's and she's off gallivanting, and there's six or seven children, as there's likely to be with that one, he won't thank anyone for letting him make a fool of himself. The PP put it perfectly. "Youngsters, given the freedom to pursue their passions, are given a loaded gun." If they can't control themselves now, they'll hardly control themselves when they're married.'

'Is that his expert view?'

'You're making a mockery of the whole thing,' my mother says. 'He's right too. Ten years from now Liam will have a house full of children without a mother. He'll be a frustrated and thwarted young man with his life in ruins, and she'll be at it with every Tom, Dick and Harry.'

'And where do you come into the picture?'

'He explained that, as manager of Liam's father's school, he's in an awkward situation. He wants me, as a neighbour, to talk to the MacMahons.'

'And you told him to feck off with himself.'

'I talked to them this afternoon. I explained his side of it. He'll arrange a place for Geraldine and she can decide, when the time comes, whether she wants to keep the baby or give it up. Mrs MacMahon says she'll look after it for her.'

My father shakes his head and says nothing.

A week later, my mother is back in the Parochial House. By the time she gets home she's fuming.

'I can't believe it. He can't be so stupid as to throw his life away on that one.'

'They're gone to Gretna Green,' my father smirks.

'Oh, stop being so smart, you. They were caught. Together. At it. Again.'

Ha ha!

No stopping them.

Like an ass's tool, big when he's out.

Can't get enough of it.

Up she flew.

And where do you think?

In the long grass behind the chapel. Broad daylight. Knickers around her ankles. Stretched to the limit. Driving right into her.

Ha ha!

The sacristan saw the sun glinting on the young fella's arse.

The parish priest met them and they sneaking around by the bell. You're a prostitute, he says.

He never did!

He did. By God he did.

And rightly so.

'"No further discussion," the PP says. She goes next Friday and there's no coming back if she decides to keep the baby. And he's gone already, he was sent to his aunt in Blackrock. "Enough is enough," the PP says.'

My mother is standing at the kitchen sink, as my father sits looking into his teacup.

'And he should know,' he says, angrily. 'He should know exactly what to do in this kind of situation. He's the man to put things to rights because he's the man that knows what the world is about. He's God's deputy-vicar on earth. He's the boy to put us all in our places.'

'I'm going to talk to Mrs MacMahon,' my mother says. 'I see her in the garden. I'm going out to talk to her. I feel sorry for her, but Geraldine brought this on herself.'

'Is that what the PP says?' my father asks before he turns on the radio and my mother goes out through the open back door and into the garden. I give her ten seconds and then follow, quietly.

'Will he not think twice?' Mrs MacMahon asks. Her voice is a beaten whine.

Geraldine is standing beside her, gazing over my mother's shoulder to the figures on the distant football field.

'He says it's all arranged,' my mother says.

'I know what she did was wrong. And, God, behind the church! Why did you do it there?'

'The grass was long,' Geraldine says lightly.

'Would he not think again, Mrs?'

'He thinks it's for the best all round. He says they need time apart.'

'But wouldn't he think about changing his mind about Geraldine bringing the child home? She wants to. Don't you?'

'I suppose so.'

'It'd be someone for Tommy to play with,' Mrs MacMahon says, as if my mother has the final say-so. 'There'd only be two years, two-and-a-half years between them. How is she going to live away from home with a baby? Would he not consider that?'

'I think he believes it'd be best for everyone if Geraldine gave the baby up.'

'But she doesn't want to, do you, Geraldine?'

Geraldine shakes her head.

'Well,' my mother sighs. 'Unless you go and talk to him yourself.'

'But what could I say?' Mrs MacMahon asks. 'What

could I say to a priest if he has his mind made up? And after him seeing them in the chapel grounds. What would I be able to say?'

'You could tell him to fuck off and mind his own business,' Geraldine says and she turns on her heel and walks away.

Afterwards, as I get ready for bed, I hear my father laugh and say, 'Fair dues to her, she has a point.'

And my mother sighs in exasperation.

'I'm not listening to you. It says everything about her and how she got to be the way she is. A young one of her age and in her condition having the gall to talk like that. Can you imagine the merry dance she'd lead that young lad for the rest of his days? Imagine it! He's lucky to be shut of her. The sooner she's gone, the sooner it'll be mended. Can you imagine her with children streeling out of her? You cannot!'

The following afternoon, I'm kicking football in the garden. Mrs MacMahon is pulling stalks of rhubarb. Geraldine comes down their garden and stands beside her mother. Her voice is breaking.

'Don't let them do this to me,' she says. 'I won't go near him. Honest to God, I won't see him. I'll keep away from him when he's home. I won't even go up that end of the town. I swear, Mam, I swear.'

'There's nothing I can do,' her mother says. 'I can't change the way things are.'

'It's nothing to do with Liam, I swear. I don't want to be shut away for the next four months. I don't want to be with people I don't know. I don't want to be away from you and Daddy. How'll I make out in Dublin? Just let me stay here, please. Please. Don't let them send me away, Mam, please.'

'What can I do, girl?'

'Please, Mam.'

'He said it'll be the best thing in the long run. He said he's seen it a hundred times before. He said it's the only way. And Liam's father says the same.'

'Let me talk to Daddy about it.'

'What can he do?' Mrs MacMahon asks and she puts her arms around her daughter. 'There's nothing any of us can do. Bear with it, child.'

'Please,' Geraldine says and she buries her face in her mother's breast.

I seen her getting on the bus.

Ha ha!

The mother walked her down.

I seen them on the Square, waiting. Stood there with the mother and the little brother, Tommy. Bold as brass.

Her belly like a little hill.

Three little hills, I say three little hills.

Ha ha!

Was the PP there to give them his blessing?

The teacher slipped her a fiver.

Ha!

And his young lad slipped her another.

And a tenner for the ride!

Some whore. I wouldn't go with her if you paid me.

Neither would I.

And neither would my brother.

That's not what I heard.

Ha ha!

*

Geraldine MacMahon leaves in the middle of July and I have my mother to myself. Mrs MacMahon is there in her garden but she and my mother do nothing more than pass the time of day. She seems never to be at the fence when my mother is about. I'm relieved, glad to have my mother's full attention again.

Now and then little Tommy wanders into our garden and my mother lifts him and swings him around.

'He's a wanderer,' she says. 'There'll be no stopping him when he gets older.'

Apart from that, there are no other interruptions and the days are mine and, in the evening, my father's car is in the yard and my parents are kissing in the kitchen and the three of us are around the evening table.

'Any sign of Mrs MacMahon these days?' my father asks one evening.

'She seems to be avoiding me,' my mother says. 'Maybe she blames me for siding with the PP.'

'I hope not,' my father says. 'Didn't you say she seemed to see the sense in it, if there was any?'

'That's what I thought. But you never know.'

'I met Martin down the town and he was as friendly as ever.'

'He has no say in anything, one way or the other, as far as I can see.'

All those summer days. We play cards in the garden, we laugh together in the shadows of the gooseberry bushes, we go on a picnic to the River Field and I swing on the rope that dangles from one of the giant oaks leaning across the water. Swinging out and back, my bare feet rippling the river of the sky turned upside down.

Until the first day of August. Another sunny day, like all the other sunny days that summer.

We're in the front garden, weeding. Children on the terrace road, the sun shining, the coal lorry turning at the far end of the terrace and reversing into Hayden's gateway, Tommy MacMahon standing, watching as he always does, two dogs fighting in the Church Field, the high lob of a football in the sky. A game and voices in the air.

'Queenie eye oh, who has the ball?'

Another game.

'Ring a ring a rosy, a pocketful of posies, atishoo, atishoo, we all fall down.'

And another.

'No walking! No talking! No laughing!'

Four o'clock on a summer afternoon, on a peaceful street. The Low Terrace going about its childish business. Children sing-songing, dogs barking, a lorry turning, my mother and I weeding.

Afterwards, there are versions of what happened. All of them, more or less, accurate.

Easy does it, back her up easy.

Two bags of coal for Dinny Smith, a bag of turf for Harringtons, three bags of blocks for Dessie Hayden.

The paraffin. Did he load the paraffin for Whelans?

Easy does it, look behind.

He must have put it in with all the rest, he'd never be that thick as to leave it behind.

He swore to God that he never felt a thing. And then one of the children began shouting.

*

We hear someone shouting. My mother drops her trowel and starts running. I have no idea why. Children are always shouting. And then I hear a wail and the summer sun and the blue sky can do nothing to check the coldness running through me. I realise the wailing sound is coming from the mouth of a man and his voice is high and lost.

Oh Jesus, Jesus, Jesus.

And my mother is running towards him and there are children everywhere and I run after her, through our open gate, along the road. And I see my mother, on her knees, under the lorry and the driver is kneeling beside her, talking to her, crying, shouting at her.

'I never seen him, I don't know where he come out of, he must've stepped under the trailer. I never seen a thing. I'd have seen him if he walked in front of me. He was that small. I never felt him. What can I say, Ma'am, what can I say? Jasus, I wouldn't wish this for all the world. I'd do anything to bring him back.'

A small boy turns to the girl beside him and giggles.

'He was under the trailer. He never heard it starting. The axle caught his head.'

And, out of nowhere, Mrs MacMahon is on her knees beside my mother, driving her fists into the clay-covered road. And then my mother lifts Tommy out from under the axle. He doesn't look dead to me. A small bump on his forehead. The lorry driver looks as if he is the one about to die. His face is the colour of ashes, the colour of sand. He goes on whispering.

'I never seen him, I never seen him at all, I swear to Jesus, I never felt a thing.'

'We'll take him home,' my mother says to Mrs MacMahon.

And the children follow at a distance. My mother with the dead child scooped in her arms and Mrs MacMahon beside her. We follow them up the terrace. Near MacMahon's gate, I look back and the lorry driver is talking to one small boy who stands with his hands on his hips, nodding. And then the festival of children stops and my mother and Mrs MacMahon pass through the gateway and around the side of the house. I hesitate, unsure of what to do.

'Go in,' someone says. 'Your mother's gone in, you can go in, too.'

And so I do.

The days are one long funeral. The wake, the church, the burial. The neighbours, the town, the priest at the graveside.

'We have no words that can repair the hurt,' he says. 'Only prayer and the love of the Almighty God.'

I stand with my parents, beside the MacMahons, and the voices drift in the afternoon heat.

'Sorry for your troubles.'

'You have our sympathy.'

'He was a dote.'

'You have an angel in heaven.'

And the priest's voice, again.

'In the name of the Father and of the Son and of the Holy Ghost. Amen.'

Walking home, my father is angry. 'You'd think they'd have let Geraldine come back for the funeral. She was his sister, for Christ's sake.'

'Would it have done any good?' my mother asks.

'She's his fecking sister.'

'It'd only open wounds.'

My father starts to say something but thinks better of it and steps away from my mother, quickly making small talk with someone else.

Once, and only once, after that, do I remember my mother and Mrs MacMahon talking at the fence. It must be a month or more after Tommy's death and autumn is setting in.

'It's not only that I miss him,' Mrs MacMahon says. 'God knows I miss him. But to think of her little baby growing inside of Geraldine and my little baby buried in the graveyard above. Tommy gone and Geraldine gone and her baby to be took from her as soon as it's born.'

'I know,' my mother says. 'I know.'

'No one knows, Mrs. No one.'

'I know,' my mother says again and her voice is dark and breaking. 'I do.'

Some days, that September, I come home from school and find my mother in the garden, crying, and when I ask her if she's sad because of Tommy MacMahon, she nods.

'For him, for them. For all of us.'

Geraldine's baby was born in Dublin and she never came back home. I lived beside the MacMahons until I left the Terrace. I'd see them at Christmas and Easter. And then they died. First him. Then her.

And then my mother died.

That long bleak night and the church and the Mass and the burial. And clearing out her clothes and coats and shoes and my father in the doorway of their room, unable to step inside. And visiting the graveyard and him stopping for a moment at MacMahons' headstone.

'They were nice people,' he said. 'Good, decent people.'

'I remember the day Tommy was killed,' I said.

'It's a long time ago.'

'That was a strange summer, with Geraldine and all. It was a nice summer for me, until he was killed. And then it was like no one recovered. I remember that autumn I'd find Mam crying in the garden.'

'For the boys,' my father said.

'What boys?'

'At least Tommy got a proper burial. A Mass and a grave up here.'

And then the whole sorry story came out. My brothers, dead at birth. Unspoken of, unblessed. A burial in the garden at dawn. My father wrapping them in towels. Their small, still features resting on the grass while he dug deep.

My mother lying inside, in their pale room, waiting for the rasp of the spade in clay. It all came back when Tommy MacMahon was killed, and then again in that hospital room. Children about her bed, Tommy MacMahon and my brothers.

And I hear the voices trickling under the doors again.

That's the way it was.

We all went through it.

Dark mornings and summer mornings.

Gardens and ditches and fields.

The dead are dead and buried and it's best to leave them lie.

*

And then I hear my mother's voice at my bedside, praying with me. Outside, the sun is going down and I can hear my father closing the shed door and cleaning his boots on the back step and spring is everywhere and that long, bright summer is before us with the promise of picnics in the River Field.

1920

An autumn day and the field is empty, the last of the summer grasses flattened by a wind that has blown without stopping for more than a week. The rain is gone but the sky is the pewter grey of a biding storm.

The oaks which still hold their leaves dance a deliberate and gentle dance, one bowing, one stepping as far as the wind and its roots allow. They dance to a silent music, to strains that no one hears, to something quieter than the wind.

Frank and Ellie

'When I think of him, I think of someone dead still, lying there pale and still. That's the way I picture him. I know full well it couldn't have been like that. Of course I do. But that's the way I think of him. The way I choose to think of him, for my own peace of mind.'

That's what his mother says to me. We're sitting in the garden behind the cottage. It's an evening in the high summer and they're both gone. She's lying in the graveyard up the hill and he's buried under the muck of Ypres.

'I think of them more and more these times,' I say. 'I suppose when you're faced with your own mortality, it's natural to think of theirs.'

That's when I hear him giggling and then I hear her shushing him. Sitting there, in the garden at the back of his mother's house, with the slow August sunshine spattering the grass under the trees. Sitting there, talking to his mother, I hear them.

They'll hear you, Ellie says.

Not a chance.

They might.

Well let them, he says and then he turns on me. *Feck's sake, Matty, don't be getting all highfalutin with your mortality.*

I try to ignore them, to listen to his mother as she attempts to draw some consolation from the past. I know she wants to find a place for Frank in the parade of history, a way to preserve his place.

'We were ever a family of soldiers and poets, Matty. A great people in this part of the country. All this land once belonged to the Ledwidges. I told him that. I made sure he knew that.'

And then I hear Frank laughing, a big belly laugh.

Now she's getting as bad.

She's your mother, Ellie scolds.

I know who she is. Anyone would know that, anyone could see – mother and son.

And his mother goes on talking to me.

'I told them all, all the children fanning out from my arms. Paddy, my husband – you don't remember him, Matty, do you?'

I shake my head.

'He told the history to me, back in the days when we were digging this cottage garden and I sang it to the children, told it to them in bedtime stories, whispered it at night.'

And Ellie is whispering to Frank.

Did she?

She did.

I watch Mrs Ledwidge's face, wondering has she any inkling of their presence, but she goes on talking, hearing only the things she's saying, not their voices beyond her.

'The corn mill was ours, Matty. And the woods as far as Kilcairne. Paddy told me, in the evenings when we sowed the half acre, told me by firelight, told me at night in bed when we lay in each other's arms.'

I look at the old woman, but whatever embarrassment she might once have felt was buried, a year ago, with her son.

She goes on about him now, Frank says, *but whenever I asked her about my father, her eyes said no, said not to talk about him, and I learned to leave well enough alone.*

The old woman looks at me.

'I think of Paddy, dead. And of Frank, dead. And of young Ellie Vaughey, dead.'

See, Ellie says brightly. *She does think of me!*

I want Frank to stop his giggling. I want to tell his mother about me and them. Frank and Ellie and me but how can I, with their voices thrumming faintly in the evening air?

He's getting too serious, Frank sighs.

He has to, Ellie says and I can almost see her pouting, putting Frank in his place with a look.

And then I hear the sulk in his voice.

Why?

Because he doesn't know. He knows it all, but in the end he knows nothing. About now.

So?

So let him be, will you?

All right, Frank says. *For you.*

And his mother goes on talking and I'm half-listening but I'm thinking about how far we went back, Frank and me. He told me once that I was a *master fiddler*, said it with that slow Slane drawl that us boys living nearer to the metropolis of Navan used to laugh at. He said I was a *mighty footballer*. He said the cherries in our orchard were the best in the world.

I knew he was a bloody fine poet.

His mother loved Ellie.

'There's a clearness in her laughter,' she told me once.

I'd cycled over to Slane, but Frank had gone walking with Ellie so I sat in the kitchen with his mother and we drank tea.

'I can see they're in love,' she said. 'She breaks his seriousness. You and him can get fierce serious, Matty, but she's always making the pair of you laugh. I like to see him laughing. I like to see anyone laughing. Laughter is a great thing. And there's a lovely cleanness about her; she has a light in her face and good health in her hair.'

I remember that and I hear Ellie laughing now. There's pride behind her laughter.

See, now! She's right. That's what you missed.

And the rest of it!

'I always know when he comes back from seeing her. He brings some of that light inside himself,' his mother had said.

I imagined Ellie laughing uproariously on such evenings. Telling Frank that his mother knew a lot more about her than he did, reminding him that women have a sense of things, that they fathom a lot more than he could ever imagine!

'I was half in love with Ellie Vaughey myself in those days,' I tell Mrs Ledwidge. 'I'd watch her and Frank together, leaning over a stile or walking the headland of a field or dancing, and I'd be envious.'

'Well, there's a thing I never knew. You had an eye for her.'

The summer evening draws on, his mother still dressed in black, a year to the day since his death.

'But Ellie was taken with him, Matty, wasn't she?'

'She was.'

'Why wouldn't she be? I told her stories about him. Like the time he was working in Lady Conyngham's kitchen and the cook had a slate listed out with the dishes on it for that night's dinner. Frank rubbed it clean and wrote instead – Pig's feet, cabbage and spuds. That was the end of him there!'

She smiles a rich, warm smile, remembering.

'And then he was off to Dublin, shopkeeping,' she says, telling me the story as if I didn't already know it. 'Home in less than a week, hiding that last morning from the postman in Slane in case the word got home before him. And when he came in here it was like him and Joe hadn't set eyes on one another in a year.'

She looks at me and then she looks away.

'Sixteen. And Joe was twelve. You should have seen the light in their eyes.'

A blackbird whistles a rich, round note from the foot of the garden

'I think of him and her, dead,' she says and I can hear Frank giggling again.

I sit with her for another while and then I get up to go and she walks with me to the side of the house, to where my bicycle lies propped against the gable wall.

'Do you remember the evenings, Matty, when he'd dress up and cycle over to see Lord Dunsany. They'd talk about the poems they were writing. He was always at Frank, encouraging him. "Bless us," I'd say, "there's you up there with the Lord and look at us down here." And Ellie was always worrying about his head getting turned, but there was only Ellie.'

'He talked to you, that was the great thing,' I say.

'Always, all the time.'

And the blackbird sings out his solitary note again.

'You'll come and see me again, Matty, won't you?'

'I will.'

'You're one of my own.'

I hug her and pull on my cap and glide, one foot on the pedal, through the gateway, between the box hedges.

Out on the open road for home, and I think of another summer evening, an evening I'm supposed to know nothing of, an evening Ellie told me about, an evening when Frank had left her house and gone off in a huff.

'I wanted him to kiss me,' she told me. 'Do you know what I wanted to say to him, Matty? I wanted to tell him not to be just standing there like a young fool. I wanted to say, "Kiss me. Your tongue makes words for your mouth to say, but all I want is for you to kiss me. Tempt me. Whisper words in my ear. Whisper words in my mouth." I wanted to tell him that when I'm working I think of him, young and strong and laughing. I wanted to remind him that I made him laugh, that I took the serious look off his face. I wanted to remind him of the Sunday in your orchard. The three of us, watching the bees fall drunk from the cherry trees. I was drunk on him. He tempted me and I wanted him to tempt me again. Do you know, Matty, sometimes I fancy myself by that name. Ellie Ledwidge.'

Then she said it again, twirling it round a time or two, trying it out like a new dress.

'I like the sound,' she said. 'Do you?'

And I nodded.

I'm coming out of Slane now, freewheeling down with the castle to my left and the night is thinking about falling but there's time enough and light enough for me to get home before it does.

*

Another evening, maybe two weeks after, and the long day is drawing in and I'm sitting on a form against the back wall of my own house. There's a heat haze coming down over the orchard and I get that feeling again. Then they're here, the two of them.

Somewhere among the trees I hear Frank giggling.

'For Jesus, sake, Frank, stop it,' I shout.

There's silence, a deep unreal silence that goes on for a long time. In the end, it's Ellie who speaks.

He knows we're here.

How?

He must be dead, Ellie says. *Are you dead?*

'No, I'm not dead. But neither are you. Either of you.'

Ellie laughs. *Of course we're dead.*

'Not to me,' I say. 'Not yet.'

Can you really hear us? Frank asks.

'Stupid question.' I nod my head. 'Stupid question.'

I don't like this. Ellie's voice is subdued, serious.

'It's all right,' I tell her. 'I just knew you were there, once I started thinking of you. Will you come back here?'

Can we?

Where would we be going back to? Frank asks, ever practical.

'I don't know,' I tell them.

Back to the days when God forgot us? he asks and his tone is suddenly bitter. *Back to the days when my brother was dying? Back to the clots on the pillow, the wrack of his cough in the room, the bailiffs and the police at the door, the way he wasted to nothing, the voices outside while he was dying? Him laid out in the room, the parish burying him, the silence in the morning after he died. If there's any call for going back, go back to that?*

Sssshhh, Ellie says quietly

Hah!

'Ssshhh,' I say.

Don't you try to shush me, Matty.

Ellie starts praying, the words tumbling out fast, like a song, and it takes me a while to know what she's saying.

OurFatherwhoartinheaven, hallowedbeThyname,Thykingdomcome, Thywillbedoneonearthasitisinheaven...

Hah, Frank says again.

I want you to kiss me, Ellie says.

They're silent again and the silence makes me uneasy.

'When did you notice Frank first?' I ask Ellie, for something to say.

I'd see him speeding on his bicycle from some football match to home, from the Conyngham Arms to God knows where, always speeding on that bicycle.

Pegasus, Frank laughs.

His face was tanned and his eyes were bright and he always waved when he was passing. I wanted him to stop. I went to the places he went, in the hope of seeing him there. Sometimes I was lucky and sometimes not. He wasn't like some of the others I knew. He was always neat and clean.

You're embarrassing the man, Frank says.

'I can talk for myself,' I say.

Touchy!

Am I embarrassing you? Ellie asks.

'Not embarrassing. Saddening me a little bit, more making me envious.'

I'm only telling him what he knows, she says.

Well, why tell him then? You're getting worse than my mother.

Because I like talking about those times. I like remembering you all dressed up, washed and fresh after a day working on the roads. I like thinking about the nights I went to see you in plays in the hall, you and Joe and the rest of them. Do you remember the way I'd hang around and hope to see you afterwards?

It's as well you didn't know me when I worked in the copper mine, you'd have had a thing or two to worry about then.

Sometimes, there'd be a rumble in the afternoon and the whole village would go silent, waiting on word to come. And men would be taken out, pale as death, and laid on boards. Pale as death under coppered skin. Dead men were dragged out like wagons of coppered clay. Dead men dragged out and left. Mourned, talked about and waked and buried while the work went on.

I didn't talk to you enough, Frank says to Ellie. *Not enough about your soft skin and your laughing face.*

All three of us are silent. I stand and walk a little into the orchard, hoping against hope that I might catch a glimpse of them, but the voices always come from somewhere just beyond where I can see, a place that marks the minutes between the sun going down and the start of night coming on.

I remember the first night you came to our house, Ellie says gently.

'I feel that she will come in blue, with yellow in her hair and two curls strayed out of her comb's loose stocks…'

I knew your tricks, coming late of a Sunday night and asking me to bring your poems to Drogheda for the paper.

It took you long enough to notice me beyond the messenger you made of me.

I want them to stop this conversation, it has nothing to do with me. It's not a conversation I should be hearing. I can't listen to coffined pillow talk. I've lived through it once, I can't do that again.

It did, Frank says.

Those were the days when he had his eye on her but never a word.

I'd rise him. 'You like her, don't you?'

And he'd just shrug.

It took you long enough. I'd almost given up hope and then I was that happy. And the poems you brought were for me – they were mine.

'I feel that she will come in blue,
With yellow in her hair, and two curls strayed
Out of her comb's loose stocks, and I shall steal
Behind her and lay my hands upon her eyes,
"Look not, but be my Psyche!"
And her peal of
Laughter will ring far ...'

I'd hear her laughing. She had a laugh that made you want to laugh with her. Frank's mother said her laughter was a song.

Once, one summer evening, the three of us sitting in a field, Frank trying to read a poem and Ellie laughing and he with that look that said, *I'm hurt.*

'Can you not stop laughing?' he asked.

And she said, 'I can't. I swear to God. I'm sorry. Now read me the poem.'

'"And the blue of hiding violets watching for your face / Listen for you in every dusky place."'

And then there were laughing tears dancing in her eyes. 'I'm sorry, Frank, I can't help it.'

Sometimes, I thought there'd be no end to their happiness. The two of them, walking together, him rushing off on a Sunday to see her.

'There's always a reason,' he told me.

'I know his knock,' she said.

She laughed less.

'I don't need to laugh at everything,' she said.

They're quiet. They might be gone, but I don't believe they are.

And suddenly Ellie is talking again and something in her tone has changed. It's like she's meeting me as a confessor, as if Frank is no longer there.

I knew he was in love with me, she says and I imagine her blushing. *My love was as tense as my body, ready to spring, ready to wrap him up inside me. Would that have been so wrong, Matty? It would have been the right thing to do, wouldn't it? It might have saved our lives. To have him inside of me, safe. To let our bodies say what our mouths couldn't. I say it now when it's too late, too far away.*

We were in love, Frank interrupts.

But Ellie isn't listening to him. She wants to talk to me and I want her to. I want her to be mine, if just for this one conversation.

Too late, too far away. Do you know what we've become, Matty? Ghosts meeting in a church at night. Ghosts before we were even dead. November nights, All Saints, All Souls. What about the other nights? Spring nights. Summer. What about the chances come and gone?

Don't, Frank says.

And now she's talking to him and her tone changes and there's anger in her voice.

You were buried with your books. What did I have? Half-remembered chances, half-taken. Whatever I took I took because I needed it and that was all. Look back whatever way you like, Frank Ledwidge, but I needed more than words.

And I'm thinking about the times when Frank and myself talked about Ellie. I think of her sitting in this very orchard, watching the bees. I think of her and the time when everything changed between them. I remember how Frank tried to make light of it.

'That's the way the world turns.'

'Things'll work out!'

'No, you were right when you said not to get too serious.'

'I never said that.'

'You did and you were right.'

His first Sunday at home in months. His mother asking if anything is the matter?

'No.'

'Is Ellie not well?'

'She's well.'

'Are you not going over, then?'

'I might go out for a cycle with Matty.'

Sunday and the ticking clock.

'I might.'

The day dragging on towards darkness.

'I might.'

Afterwards, we took the bicycles out and cycled fifty yards down the road and sat in the ditch, out of sight of his mother.

'Ellie said she had something to tell me,' Frank says. 'And I told her, "Tell me."'

He was quiet for a while.

'And she said, "I have to." And I said, "Tell me." And she said, "I can't see you again." And I said, "Can't?" She said it was no good. That's all she said, Matty. Nothing about the acres her family have, nothing about the hard words in the night. Nothing about the things they said of me. They've talked her out of it and the only reason is because I work on the roads. They have half the Hill of Slane and we have a half-acre garden.'

There was silence again and then he said, quietly, 'And she listened.'

There was disbelief and desolation in his voice.

'Maybe because she loves you, Frank,' I said.

'What?'

Maybe because she saw no hope for you, I thought. Maybe you never told her where the hope was.

But I didn't say it.

And now Ellie is talking again, to me, to Frank, to herself.

I might have been stronger, but it was too late. You want to know what got in the way. Land, family, money? Yes, all of them, but mainly hope. Or the lack of it. I waited for words, real words, but nothing came. Only verses. Had you no way of saying anything that wasn't in a verse? Had you no way of leaning your head to mine the way you did with others? Did you think I'd always be satisfied with that? You loved me but you never said, never touched me the way I wanted you to touch me. And when they sat me down, the family, and pointed out the rest of it, rich and poor, landed and penniless and all that goes with that, I couldn't find a word to say in your defence. All I saw was the gap between us, between what you gave and what I needed, and that had nothing to do with money. It had to do with need. Love, touch, kisses, soft words whispered in the dark.

She falls silent and I'm relieved that this confession is over. But, suddenly, she's whispering to Frank, and I know I shouldn't be hearing, but her whisper is insistent and nothing will block it out.

Love, touch, kisses, soft words whispered in the dark, she says, and now, again, *Love, touch, kisses, soft words whispered in the dark.*

And on she goes, her words becoming a seduction.

Love, touch, kisses. Love, touch. Love, touch. Touch, touch. Touch me. Touch me, Frank.

And a silence like the silence after lovemaking.

See, nothing about land or money.

I try to block her voice from my head. I go back to that Sunday afternoon, sitting in the ditch and Frank confessing everything.

'She said, "It just won't work." And I said, "Is that what your family says?" And then she said, "Just hold my hand, will you?" But I wouldn't.'

He told me she'd put her hand on his shoulder. They were in the garden at the side of her house, under the lilac hedge and there was a full moon rising.

'There was a calmness about her. Her eyes were full of sorrow, real sorrow, and then she folded her arms and I swear I heard wings fluttering and I asked her, "Is that all?" And she said, "You never know." And I said, "Will I hear from you?" And she said, "Soon, maybe soon." And her white teeth were biting down on her lip and I walked to the gate and the last thing I heard her say, while I was wheeling my bike out from under the hedge was, "Maybe."'

He went home in the rain, he told me, and bolted the kitchen door and went into his silent room and lay on the bed. But sleep only wearied him. He said he dreamed about mortar and bricks and sheep in rich fields.

I heard the clock chiming all night, Ellie says. *Your mother told me once, long after, that you were bent on keeping me, that you never gave up hope.*

Hope is a great thing, Frank says and all the anger and uncertainty is gone out of him. *And I had hope. It was there in everything I did and said. If the sun rose up resplendent, there was hope in it. If it crept along the shoulder of a field, there was hope in that. I drew life from the sun and hope, and hope is the greatest thing, the one thing worth talking of. Oh, I had hope that I could make you change your mind, that we'd find a way round the ditches thrown up in our path, that love would out. I had more hope than I knew what to do with. It set my head singing and my heart racing ahead of me.*

But that's not how I remember it. The rumours started, that Ellie was walking out with John O'Neill, a handsome man. I met Frank's mother in the village.

I asked because I had to.

'Did you hear that Ellie is seeing John O'Neill?'

'Does Frank know yet?'

I shook my head.

'Someone should tell him,' she said, 'before he meets them on the road.'

'Will I tell him?'

'Do,' she said.

And I did.

John O'Neill who played the fiddle, danced and sang. John O'Neill who knew there was more to love than words.

And the following Saturday evening I met Ellie on the road.

'What was I to do, Matty?' she asked. 'I'm tied in on every side by my family and Frank's coldness. John is a handsome man. He lifts me round the dance floor, my feet off the ground, head spinning, heart racing, eyes closed, kisses my hair. Tells me how beautiful I am, how beautiful ...'

I wanted to tell her that I, too, thought she was beautiful, but I didn't.

I tried to lose myself in others' eyes, but nothing came of it, Frank says, matter of factly. And then the war.

And then the war, Ellie says.

The people that knew me least thought I joined for high ideals, Frank says, as if he's trying to persuade someone – me, or Ellie, or himself – of something. *I joined because the British army stood between Ireland and an enemy of our civilisation and I wouldn't have it said that we were defended while we did nothing.*

'But there was another reason, Frank,' I say.

What was I to do? Everywhere I went, their shadows fell in front of me.

I heard the stories, Ellie says, and if a voice can be pale and washed out, her voice is just that. *Snipes in the street at John and me. Slane is a small place.*

And I remember the letters coming from Frank, saying all was well, saying he missed the Conyngham Arms, words about summer nights in Slane.

But I was drifting far away, he says.
And I had no way of knowing.
I kept remembering the little things.
They were the things I couldn't forget.

And then I saw it, in the paper Matty sent to me. I learned it off, like a mad alphabet. 'O'Neill and Vaughey in St Patrick's RC Church Slane. By the Rev. F. Fagan, CC, Slane. John O'Neill (Rossin) to Ellen Mary (Ellie), only daughter of the late John and Mrs Vaughey, Hill of Slane, Co. Meath.'

What did you expect? Ellie asks, as if she's never asked the question before.

I expected to go back to you when the war was straightened out.

They're both silent and I think back on that time.

He came home on Christmas leave but things were changed. He was changed. The spark was gone out of him and all the coaxing in the world wouldn't bring it back. The same week that he was home, young Jack Tiernan, a neighbour's child, was killed. There was nothing left of that black year. He wrote a verse for the boy.

*

'He will not come and still I wait,' Frank says quietly. 'He whistles at another gate / Where angels listen. Ah, I know / He will not come, yet if I go / How shall I know he did not pass / Barefooted in the flowery grass.'

'That was it,' I say.

How was I to know? Ellie asks.

I missed the bog in Wilkinstown. Every time I heard a blackbird singing, I wanted you to think of me.

I did.

I remembered the crows flying from Wilkinstown to Slane. I saw all the old landmarks when I was crossing the fields in my dreams.

And so did I, from a single room in Manchester.

That's how it was. Frank gone back to the war and Ellie gone with John O'Neill to live in Manchester.

'Go where the work is,' John O'Neill said. I heard him say it. But her step was less light there.

I thought of men planting spuds in Carlonstown and I was back there in my head, back in the kitchens around Slane.

And so was I, far away from the black streets of Manchester.

Again the silence. I walk to the gateway at the foot of our lane. And then Frank speaks, but not to me.

I had a dream that night. There were white birds flying above the sea and I was on the ground, watching. The dream haunted me. I knew there was something wrong. I had a feeling that there was something wrong.

I died, Ellie says, as if he didn't know. *In a back street in Manchester. It all went wrong for me. Unhappy in my marriage. Away from Slane. Pregnant. Sick. I wasn't cut out for housekeeping. I couldn't keep a house. I fell out of love. Unhappy and sick. The colour gone from my face, my teeth decayed, my daughter born while I was dying. I called out for you.*

I went to see you, Frank says, as if she didn't know, *laid out in that room in Manchester. I was on leave and I went to see you, but it wasn't you, it was someone else. You were gone. Escaped.*

You wrote me a poem.

I did. And then I went back to Gallipoli and the smell of dead corpses and I lay in a trench, remembering Slane. I put you out of my mind when I could, to keep myself from going mad. I passed the time thinking of ordinary things, wondering whether the cow with timber tongue survived or died.

He came back home with me, followed my spirit from Manchester – did you know that, Matty?

I shake my head. I hear Frank laughing, a dry laugh.

And I brought you with me to Egypt and back to England on leave and on to France and I spent my birthday in a little red town, in an orchard with a lovely valley below me. There was a river that went gabbling down the fields, like turkeys coming home, an idle little vagrant that did no work for miles and miles. I slept there with you and, in the morning, the cuckoo came to a tree nearby and called his name and I thought of Slane Hill, blue and distant.

And of me there, with a blue ribbon in my hair.

For Christ's sake, stop, I think. You're wounding me.

Can you hear me, Matty? Frank asks.

'What?'

Can you hear me?

'I hear you.'

It must be beautiful out on the bog now.

'It is.'

Out in France the land was broken up with shells and the broken woods were like winter armies of skeletons. I used to think of the bog and the silence of it. I used to long for silence before I had it.

I nod.

But once I heard a bird singing in the middle of all the killing and I stopped and listened. And that was all I could do, listen.

I hear the weariness in his voice, despair almost.

And his heart lifted with hope, Ellie says quickly.

'Hope,' I say.

There's hope for us all, Ellie says. *My heart is lifting Frank's heart, lifting with it.*

I hear Frank sighing, that sound that I haven't heard for so long, that sound I can never forget.

A terrible rainstorm swept over us, he says and his voice is low and hard, without life or light. *The place was grey, land and sky. We stopped our work and sat in the half-dark shelter, drinking tea.*

Thinking about me, Ellie laughs, but he doesn't respond.

I tried to remember that single bird singing amidst the killing and the other birds, in Slane. And I tried to remember Ellie laughing. But I could hear nothing. Only the rain rattling on my tin mug. The rain on my helmet. The rain on my sodden boots. The rain on my coat. I watched the rain sliding down the handle of the shovel I was holding.

Ssshhh.

It was the last day of July.

He knows.

It was the last day of July. I was on a digging party, resting between trench digs. The shell exploded beside us. Seven of us were killed. What did the letter say? 'Francis was killed at once. He suffered no pain.' That's what it said. As if anyone knew what pain any of us did or didn't suffer, then or anytime in our lives. Who lives without pain, Matty? Tell me one person that lives without pain?

Frank! Ellie says and her tone is sharp.

All right, all right. But I want him to know.

'I know,' I say. 'And there's something I want to tell you, Frank. The night you died, I was locking up the print works; it was after two, and, as I was turning, I could've sworn I saw you on the far side of the street. I called you. I thought you were home on leave. But you just kept walking, so I thought it must be someone else.'

He was looking for me, Ellie says.

I heard you but there wasn't time, Matty.

I was waiting, Ellie says, and I can tell they're walking away from me.

I follow them to the gable end of the house and look down the orchard and I know where they are; I know which tree they're sitting under, but I don't go down. I'm happy to know they're about the place.

There were times afterwards I'd be sitting at home, winter nights by the fire, or long evenings, pulling on for dusk, in the orchard, and I'd imagine they were there, the pair of them. It was just something I sensed. I'd open the back door and stand in the darkness outside, listening, but there was never any sound, not even a whisper. But I never gave up hope of seeing them. I often told the pair of them not to give up hope, when they were drifting apart. I loved them both. All I could do was tell them never to give up hope.

Sometimes, I nearly gave up hope myself, and then I'd remember things. Frank flying along on his bike, gabbling that fast I could hardly understand what he was saying. Or Ellie laughing. I never forgot that laugh. The sweetest laugh.

And sometimes, out of nothing, there'll be a reminder there before me, out of absolutely nothing. A field I passed one time, down in Kildare. It was the autumn of 1920. I was travelling down to a funeral in Carlow and the hackney man stopped at the gate of a field to put petrol in the car. And sitting there, I caught a glimpse of these two oaks at the far end of it, leaning towards one another, nodding in the wind, like they were laughing, like the breeze was a secret that only the pair of them could share.

1864

The river is the shade of the last day of the old year. Its colours washed away to somewhere else, to the sea or oceans beyond the sea, to waters where the sun remembers to shine. Night has hardly lifted its darkness out of the pools beneath the oaks before it starts to fall again.

A rabbit scuttles down the sandy bank that cuts this field off from the next one and the next. The animal nibbles the lank grass, stops, raises its head and listens, and then nibbles again.

A crow is blown slowly across the sky, leaning into the bite of a winter wind that arcs above the water and the grazing rabbit and the trees that will be its home when darkness falls.

For miles around there is silence, the stillness of a season that is sleeping.

The crow rises and dips and rises again, holding itself against the wind.

The rabbit goes on grazing.

The trees forget to move.

Deep Midwinter

The pair of us came from opposite headlands of a long field that dipped at one end. Only when we were twenty yards apart did either of us have a clear view of the other. Heads bent, hands on ploughs, slack reins about our shoulders, we worked in contrary directions. The only sounds were the cut of blades through clay, the jingle of horse brasses and an occasional word of encouragement from one or other of us. Halfway down the field we passed, yet neither one raised his eyes from the earth unfolding before him. Only the heavy clouds of breath from the horses' nostrils met and compounded in the sharp October air.

We passed each other time and again as the afternoon light sharpened the tree branches that slashed the kingfisher sky and sods folded over, closer and closer, until only a narrow strip of unploughed ground remained between us.

'I'll do the last couple,' I said. 'You can get him into the shafts.'

George Greene worked his way to the headland, loosed his horse from the plough and put him between the shafts of the low cart. As he did, he watched me work down the field.

The spit of his father, I could almost hear him think.

George, who had known me since childhood. Carried me on his back to and from harvests in the forties, the bad forties. Seen me bury both parents in the one year. Watched me sink and then straighten myself out again. Observed the changes about the farm. Two new heavy horses bought. New ploughs. Work done on the house, painting and the like. Five thousand daffodils put down along the avenue, all good things.

Bending to plough the last furrow, I smiled at the figure waiting at the other end of the field. My horse stepped brightly, ready for home. The plough skated through the clay, turning the final sods. Around me, the long day's earth glistened red and blue after the fallen sun. Behind me, a sheet of gulls lifted into the air.

Driving home in the low cart, we talked about Christmas.

'I'm going to have a party, George,' I said. 'Like the ones my parents had, with lanterns along the avenue and food and music and a band from the town. What do you think? The week before Christmas, wouldn't that be the thing to do?'

'It would.'

At two o'clock on the morning of Monday, December 19th, 1864, I watched George Greene and Peter Clarke, a boy whose right leg was shorter than his left, drive a herd of cattle down the avenue in front of my house and onto the road that would take them to the fair at Castledermot. The sky was stabbed with stars, the fields were white and ghosted.

Once the pair had turned off the avenue, I went back inside. Wandering the house, I opened doors, allowing my lamp to light the rooms momentarily. Already they were set for the midwinter party. The drawing room was empty, apart from chairs that lined the walls and a small stage for the musicians. In the dining room, four tables were laid end to end. The sitting room had three sideboards already stocked with drinks. The stable housed five dozen home-made lanterns that would hang on the boughs of the avenue trees.

Tomorrow, young Clarke would spend the day decorating the doorways and mantles and mirror frames with holly. Three women would come up from Ballyadams to start the cooking. On Wednesday night a band would strike up the music at nine o' clock. Supper would be served at eleven. Afterwards, the dancing would continue into the small hours. Everything would run like clockwork.

It was still dark and bitterly cold when I left for the fair. On the Castledermot road, a handful of late jobbers drove their beasts ahead of them. Beyond Kilkea Bridge, I stopped to rest my horse, hunkering out of the bitter wind coming off the side of Mullaghcreelan Hill, shivering and sweating at the same time. A blade of light slashed the black night sky and the stars were fading. The early birdsong was loud and clear, but my heart was racing and my limbs suddenly ached.

A pair of heifers trundling over the bridge disturbed me and, getting up from my shelter and taking the horse's reins, I climbed slowly into the saddle.

George Greene was standing in McDonald's yard as I rode in. I could see that he was shocked at the change that had come over me in a couple of hours, my forehead damp with perspiration and my eyes bloodshot and sunken.

'You're not well,' George said.

'I feel terrible. It just came on me this past half-hour.'

'A fever?'

'Yes.'

'Well, you can rest up and break it now or you can be sick for a week.'

'Things to do,' I barked. 'The cattle and a new mare.'

'I know all that. Most things I can do.'

I half-nodded.

'You're coming with me,' George said. 'To Rice's. I'm going to ask Anne to give you a large brandy and a bed and you're going to stay there till I come back for you. I'll sell the cattle and I'll have a look for a horse.'

I woke the following morning to the sight of George Greene dozing in a chair just inside the bedroom door, his forehead collapsed in a frown.

I shook the old man awake.

'You're better?' he asked.

'I'm better, thanks to you. Now, get into that bed. I'm going downstairs for something to eat.'

'What time is it?'

'Half-past seven. I'll call you at eleven. You can eat then and we'll go home.'

'Have a look at the mare in McDonald's yard. She's in the stall next to your own. I didn't say you'd buy her, but she's yours if you want. I told Dan D'Arcy we'd let him know today.'

'Young Clarke?'

'He got a lift home on John McHugh's cart.'

The barroom of the public house reeked of the previous night's pipe smoke and porter. In another room, pots rattled. I threw a few turf sods onto the fire and stretched myself, feeling grateful for the pleasures of good health and life. Anne Rice appeared at the other end of the bar.

'You're up and about.'

'I am. I gave my bed to George.'

'He wouldn't take another room.'

'That's him. Thank you for your hospitality.'

'You're more than welcome. Now, you must be starved. I'll send Sarah down with your breakfast. You'll have a good feed.'

'I will.'

While the breakfast was cooking, I walked to McDonald's yard and looked at the mare. I knew at once that I'd buy her. We'd borrow a saddle from McDonald's and I'd take the mare and George would take my horse. Two gentlemen of leisure, riding home for Christmas.

Back inside, the barmaid was talking to a bearded man who had taken a seat by the fire and laid out a cloth with silver rings on it. She looked up as I came in.

'Your breakfast is near ready,' she said before returning her attention to the rings, lifting one and holding it in the light, then replacing it on the cloth and lifting another.

'They're lovely but too dear for me,' she finally said, walking away into the kitchen.

'May I see them?' I asked.

The man laid the cloth on the table between us.

'They're silver?'

'They are and I'm a silversmith and if you want something scripted I can do that, too.'

I picked up one of the rings, a delicate swirl of narrow bands.

'This one, I'll take this one. No inscription.'

'You're sure? Won't cost you.'

'I'm sure.'

When she came with my breakfast, the barmaid asked if I was feeling well.

'I am. I missed the fair. But there'll be others.'

'There will, of course.'

'Were you busy?'

'Busier nor ever. Still, it's over now and done.'

'You didn't buy a ring?'

The woman blushed. 'Did you buy anything?'

'I did,' I said, taking the ring from my pocket.

'It's beautiful,' the barmaid said, trying it on her finger.

'For a friend. For Christmas,' I said and we both laughed.

Anne Rice appeared at the other end of the room.

'Your breakfast is ready, Sarah,' she called.

'I better go,' the young woman said.

'Bring it in and eat here with me,' I said. 'I'd enjoy some company.'

We sat together and I told her about the Christmas party. She said it sounded lovely. She was inquisitive. Who'd be there and how many and what would we have for supper and how good was the band and who was cooking?

'You could come.'

She blushed again. 'That's not why I asked about it. I wasn't rooting for you to invite me.'

'I never thought you were.'

'In any case, I'll be working.'

'Tell me about you, I don't even know your name.'

'Sarah,' she said. 'But I hate the name.'

'Sarah what?'

'Sarah Dowling.'

'From?'

'Mullaghcreelan Hill.'

'You don't give much away, do you?'

'There's not that much to give.'

'Tell me about what you did yesterday.'

'I worked, here.'

'It's Christmas week, Sarah Dowling. It's the best time of the year for telling secrets to total strangers. Tell me everything.'

'Like what?'

'Tell me about who came in here, the smell, the noise.'

She sighed deeply. 'The place was full from early on, the way it always is. Jobbers. Eating their dinners at breakfast time. It was like that all day.'

'What time did you come to work?'

'Half-three.'

'Did you walk?'

'Of course. It was bitter cold, but there was lamps lit in every house along the way and jobbers on the road. And cows and the smell of cow shite. That's the smell of the fair. On the road and in the square and on the jobbers' boots in here. That's why I can never enjoy Christmas till the fair is over. Too much cow shite.' She laughed.

'And what else did you do?'

'I looked in on you a few times. You were dead asleep.'

I smiled. 'And what did you do last night?'

'I stayed here and went to bed about half-two.'

'Do you dance?'

'Sometimes.'

'I'm a terrible dancer. I'd like to be good but I'm not. It'll be a purgatory to me tomorrow night, trying not to stand on people's feet. Trying not to stand on my own.'

Sarah laughed at the notion.

'I've done it,' I declared. 'I've stood one foot on the other and fallen over. Sober as a judge.'

'You haven't!'

'I have. In Athy, at the harvest ball.'

I stood up and, putting my right boot down on my left, slowly keeled over, only at the last moment putting my hands out to save myself. Sarah screamed and Anne Rice came running from the kitchen.

'Jesus, Mary and Joseph. You put the heart crossways in me. Are you all right?'

'I was just showing Sarah how bad a dancer I am.'

'I thought he was split,' Sarah said, laughing and shaking.

It was midday before George and I were ready to collect the horses. The sky was a smooth, stony blue and the frost had lifted from the open spaces where low sunlight scratched the street.

'Safe home, now, and I hope your party goes well,' Sarah said.

'A very happy Christmas to you.'

'And the same to you.'

George and I stepped onto the square.

'You go ahead,' I said, 'I'll catch up with you in McDonald's.'

Sticking my head back around the public house door, I saw Sarah sweeping the floor.

'What would you have called yourself, if you'd had your way?'

'Susan,' she said, without a second thought.

In Kilkea, we stopped to pay Dan D'Arcy for the horse. In Athy, we stopped at the Hibernian for a hot whiskey. When we reached Ballyadams, darkness was falling but we could see the house lights shining through the winter afternoon.

The kitchen was a cloud of steam. Louise Meredith, my neighbour and lifelong friend, was running up and down the hall, with Peter Clarke limping in her wake, cautiously carrying bundles of holly.

I stood watching her until she saw me.

'Peter told me you weren't well.' She hugged me. 'Are you better?'

'Not only better, never better. Thanks to George. And you, young fellow,' I said, turning to the boy. 'I hear you did a powerful job with the cattle.'

As dusk fell on midwinter's evening, Peter Clarke lit the lanterns and took them down the avenue, hanging them from tree branches on both sides. The kitchen door stood open, and inside a huge fire roared in the range, welcoming visitors from the frosted darkness.

'None of them will ever forget tonight,' Louise said when she and I finally had a quiet moment together. 'It's the best party that's ever been thrown in this parish.'

'Mostly your doing,' I said.

'And George's and Peter's and yours.'

'I had very little to do with it.'

'Why do you think people came?'

The band played the closing dance at twenty past five in the morning.

'Well, now, was that the longest night of the year or what?'

The fiddle player stretched himself as the last of the guests reluctantly left.

'You earned your money,' I laughed.

'We had a good time. Same day, same place, next year?'

'What do you think, Louise?'

'Why not?'

On Christmas day, I rode down to Meredith's of Ballintubbert for lunch.

Late in the afternoon, as the extended family of cousins from Athy and Stradbally arrived for music and cards, I made my excuses for leaving.

'You're more than welcome to stay,' Mrs Meredith told me. 'You're one of our own.'

'I know that,' I answered, 'and thank you. But George is coming for his tea and I want to have the fires lighting before he arrives.'

'We'll be here well into the early hours. Come back, if you have a mind to. And bring George, if he'd like.'

'Thanks.'

Louise walked me to the stable. 'Are you all right?'

'Of course I am.'

'Why are you leaving so early? That stuff about George is nonsense.'

'Is it?'

'It is. George told me Wednesday night that he was spending the day with his sister in Carlow.'

'Well, there you are then.'

'Are you really all right? Would you like me to come down with you?'

'Honestly, I'm fine. I have some cattle to check. If I get finished in time, and the weather holds, I'll come back after tea.'

'Which means you won't. So long as you're all right.'

'I'm really well, Louise. Honestly. And a very happy Christmas to you.'

I handed her a small box. Opening it, she saw the silver ring and slipped it onto her finger.

'Thank you,' she said.

'You're welcome. And thank you for your friendship.'

'I want you to be happy,' she said.

'I will be.'

The rain swinging in against the windowpanes comforted me. Drawing my chair closer to the open fire, I turned my attention to the pages on my lap. It was a question of how much to send. I must send something, there was no choice about that. But I had already written more than I could reasonably expect her to accept. I had changed her name, both names. Taken her from the familiarity of her own home and carried her across the Barrow into the Queen's county. I had shown her the rooms of this house.

Dipping my pen in the inkwell, I began again.

Monascreeban,
Ballyadams,
Queen's County.

December 25th, 1864

My dearest Susan,
This is Christmas Day and the happiness of the feast is made even happier for me by the memory of you. Today, I have baptised you again, with the water of the winter rain. You were destined to be called Susan. And you were destined for many other things, too. Your laughter was meant to be heard beyond the walls of Rice's public house. Your smile was intended to grace other rooms. Your beauty was created to be loved and worshipped. Since Tuesday, I have thought of little else but you.

The party passed almost without my noticing. I waited in the wild hope that you might arrive. How could you? You had work to do. I had work to do myself but I could barely manage it for thinking of you.

If you have room in your life for my affections, then you must tell me. If not, then tell me that. Any word from you would be a light.

William Dunne

On New Year's Eve, George Greene arrived in the yard. I was preparing the mare for a journey.

'I'm bringing the saddle back to McDonald's in Castledermot. Will you find something for young Clarke to do when he arrives?'

George nodded. 'You'll be back tonight?'

'I will, and we'll see the old year out together.'

Crossing Kilkea Bridge and facing the mare up Mullaghcreelan Hill, my heart began to pound. Sarah lived in one of those houses on the hill, but which one? Might I pass her on the road, making her way to work this Saturday morning? What if I met her walking arm in arm with someone? Would my heart still beat as loudly or would it stop altogether?

Trotting up the Barrack Road into Castledermot, with Rice's public house in front of me, my heart began to sink. The letter in my pocket was a pale representation of what I had felt. Christmas Day was over and the possibilities engendered by the season were already diluted by the wintry light.

The square was empty. I wheeled the mare around and walked her into McDonald's yard. The yardman came to meet me.

'Well, did you keep Dan D'Arcy's horse?'

'I did,' I said. 'But I couldn't keep your saddle as well.'

'You come all the way from Ballyadams just to drop this back?'

'I had a few other things to do in this direction.'

'Did you want to see Mr Mc?'

'No, no, I'm just going to stop into Rice's and have a bowl of soup before I go about my business.'

I pressed a coin into the yardman's palm.

'Happy New Year, Mr Dunne.'

'And to you.'

*

Rice's public house was empty but for an old man seated just inside the door.

'She's below in the kitchen,' he told me as I stood at the fire. 'Give a rap on the counter.'

'I can wait.'

'It's a cold one.'

'It is.'

'But then it's the time of year for it. If we don't have it now, when would we have it? Better December nor May.'

There were footsteps in the passageway. I looked at my boots, not knowing if I wanted to see her. She'd know somehow I hadn't come this far on New Year's Eve just to deliver a saddle.

'I didn't expect to see you back here this soon.'

Anne Rice stood behind the counter. My heart sank, then soared with something like relief.

'Did the Christmas go well for you?'

'It did, very well. I was just delivering a saddle to McDonald's. I thought I'd have a bowl of soup, before the road home.'

As I paid for my meal, I asked after Sarah.

'Not here today, she'll be back tomorrow.'

'Give her my regards.'

'I will.'

In McDonald's yard I enquired if the yardman could give me directions to Dowling's of Mullaghcreelan.

'I can,' the man said. 'But there's three of them. The Light Dowlings, the Quigley Dowlings and the Stone Dowlings.'

'The daughter works in Rice's,' I said.

'Ah, the Stone Dowlings. Mrs and Sarah. Take the old road at Lambe's corner and up the hill, you'll come to two houses straight again you. Theirs is the one to the hill.'

Opening the garden gate and walking up the path, I looked neither left nor right. Rapping on the door, I waited. It opened to reveal a woman in her fifties, a slight woman with a tight face.

'Good afternoon, I was looking for a Sarah Dowling, if I have the correct house?'

'Oh, you have the correct house, all right,' the woman said, and I was sure she put an emphasis on the word correct. 'But she's not at home.'

'Will she be absent for long?'

'If I knew that, I'd know more nor I do,' the woman curtly said.

'Right,' I stammered. 'Well, I'll go on then.'

'Will I give her a name because I wouldn't know you from Adam?'

'William Dunne.'

'And will that mean anything to her?'

'It might. It should.'

'Fair enough,' the woman said and she closed the door.

I allowed myself a smile, doubting I was the first to have encountered such a reception.

I had just put my boot in the mare's stirrup when I heard footsteps behind me and turned to see Sarah running along the roadway.

'I thought it was you. I was in Quigley's, did my mother not tell you?'

'She just said you were out.'

'She would,' Sarah said.

I knew she was waiting for me to say something but I was watching her, taking in the half-remembered features. She was truly beautiful.

'I was leaving a saddle back to McDonald's,' I said at last. 'I stopped in to Rice's and Anne said you were off today.'

She nodded.

'So, I thought I'd call and see how the Christmas went, as I was passing so close.'

She nodded again.

'And I wanted to give you this.' I handed her the envelope.

'What is it?'

'A letter I wrote you over the Christmas. Take it with a grain of salt if that's what you want.'

'Will I open it now?'

'If you like. Maybe I'll just graze the mare up the road.'

I didn't particularly want to stand there watching her read, so taking the reins, I walked the mare along the old road. The grass was frosted and limp, curling backwards into the hedges. I thought I'd wait until I reached the next fence post and then steal a glance, but as I drew level with the post, the mare snorted and I was afraid to look. Instead I walked another ten yards and still no word, no sound of Sarah. I moved on to the wood's edge and stopped there, looking out across the expanse of the valley, across the low, winter-worn hedges, following the drift of a crow above a field in the distance, where two naked oaks dipped their toes in the freezing Lerr.

She must definitely have gone home, but stealing a glance behind, I saw her standing where I'd left her, the letter in her right hand, her left hand against her mouth. Finally she looked up and began to walk slowly towards me.

I waited until she was beside me before I spoke. 'Whatever you have to say, I can hear it.'

'What can I say?'

'Something. Anything.'

'It's a beautiful letter.'

'But there's someone else in your life?'

'No, there's no one else in my life.'

'Apart from your mother,' I laughed, relieved.

She smiled and then the smile was gone. 'Is it the way you really feel, what you writ in the letter?'

'It's the way I really feel. You don't have to say anything now. I know this came out of the blue.'

Sarah nodded.

At the bend, where the old road and new forked, I put my hand on her arm.

'Why don't you think about it for a while? I can come and talk to you when you've done that.'

'You probably think I'm not grateful.'

'I don't think that at all.'

'When I said, a little while ago, that there's ne'er a one in my life, I wasn't telling the truth. My life is full of people, too many people.' Looking up, her face brightened into a broad smile. 'But there's room for you.'

'May I come and see you, or will you write to me?'

'I'll write to you.'

'Is that a promise?'

'That's a promise.'

I put my foot in the stirrup and swung into the saddle.

'The address is on the letter.'

'I know. I read it.'

'Well then, black-eyed Susan,' I said, smiling. 'I'll see you in the next year.'

'You will. And I'll write.'

I turned the mare for home.

'William!'

'Yes?' I wheeled the animal again.

'I knew you'd come.'

Snow was falling on the morning of January 6th when I saw the postman on the avenue.

'That's a hardy day.'

'And getting worse. We're in for a storm.'

He handed me my letters.

'You'll have a cup of tea?'

'I wouldn't say no.'

Walking up the yard, I glanced through the envelopes, checking the postmarks. There it was. Leaving the letters on the kitchen dresser, I made tea, cut large slabs of Christmas cake and called George and the boy from across the yard. The four of us sat together, discussing the weather. We all agreed the snow would be heavy.

Only when I had finished my evening meal, washed the dishes, banked the kitchen fire, shovelled a path through the snow from house to byre and checked the cattle did I take the letters from the dresser and sit down before the open door of the range. The first was from my aunt in Dublin, inviting me to her son's wedding in March. The second was a catalogue from a seed company. Finally, I opened the third envelope, this being the moment I'd anticipated since the year's turning. Late Christmas cards, New Year greetings, reminders, invitations had all poured in, as if the world knew I was waiting and had decided to taunt me with an avalanche of post. Sitting back, I took the sheets from the envelope and unfolded a neat copperplate.

Mullaghcreelan,
Castledermot,
Co. Kildare.

January 4th, 1865

Dear William,
You probably won't be pleased with the first thing I'm going to write. When you were here Saturday I couldn't think of anything to say and now that you're not here I still can't think of anything to say. I was pleased to see you at the house. I'm sorry you had to cross swords with my mother but she'll always be like that.

I have read your lovely letter a dozen times here at home and walking to work. I've brought it everywhere with me. I wish I could write like that but writing isn't much a part of me. I want to explain to you what I said about the people in my life. You're going to find this hard but I'll do my best. There was always a lot of people that kept coming into my life and they all seem to think that they're the ones that matter. They do it out of kindness for the most part but they don't leave me time to make my mind up. Did you ever have people trying to tell you what is best for you? Well, that is the way there with me. But I'm not talking about you and I know most of them do it for the best. Anne Rice looks out for me and James Rice and my mother does. But sometimes I wish they could let me make my own mind up. There's a lot of things I'm not very good at, mostly to do with myself and the like.

See I've filled two pages and I'm still rambling. I thought it would be easy to write and now I think it would be easy to talk if you were here or I was there. I can't even remember all the things you asked me. I was so flustered when I saw who it was that I remember hardly nothing. I know it's a long way from there to here but I would like to talk to you. You could write me a letter but I'm not good at writing things down but I would try.

I would like to see you again if that's what you want. Maybe you'll let me know. I hope this is not all strange and I hope you are well over there on the other side of the Barrow.

Susan (because you said it)

I woke several times during the night and peered through the blinding mesmer of falling snow that flicked against my bedroom window. I tried to convince myself that a thaw might set in and the clouds turn to rain by morning, but daylight brought more snow, and a battered snowman in the shape of George Greene tramping thigh-deep across the hill field.

I saw him from the window and had the door open and towels waiting when he staggered in.

'Christ, George, what are you doing out in this, you could've been killed.'

'You'll need help with the cattle.'

I said nothing, but going upstairs I sorted out some of my father's clothes and brought them for the old man to change into.

'Is your own place locked up?'

'It is.'

'Well you'll stay here till this is blown over. I'm not having you risking life and limb going over and back every day, and I wouldn't trust you to stay there even if you did get home.'

While the snow continued to fall that week, George and I fed the cattle and cleared the drifts around the house and the sheds against the thaw and the flooding that would follow. Each day I tried to bury my frustration in the shovelled snow. And each night, after we had played cards and George had gone to bed, I wrote to Sarah and waited for the time when I could deliver the epistle.

A second letter arrived from Mullaghcreelan on the afternoon of Friday, January 20th, the first delivery of post in a fortnight. The snow had been followed by days of frost, which locked the drifts into place. Almost nothing had moved in the countryside. Those who found it necessary to travel did so on foot.

When a thaw then set in, the land had begun to flood. We had done enough work the previous week, moving the snow out of the yard and into the haggard to save the house and the cattle sheds from damage. But the dykes were bursting with torrents of melting slush.

And then, on the Friday afternoon, the postman arrived with a bundle of letters.

'Where were you?' I joked. 'On holiday?'

'Oh aye, taking it easy. Enjoying life. A long winter's holiday, the only way to do it.'

Sauntering up the yard, I searched through the letters until I recognised the handwriting and checked the postmark. This time, I didn't allow myself the luxury of waiting. Once inside, I threw the other letters on the table and tore open Sarah's envelope.

Mullaghcreelan,
Castledermot

Friday, Jan. 6th, 1865

Dear William,
It's hard to get used to writing the new year date, isn't it? You should have got my other letter today. After I posted it I thought it wasn't much of a letter. Like I said when you were here, I couldn't talk and when I write I feel it would be easier to talk. Could you come next Saturday or Sunday, I'm off work Saturday after dinner and all the Sunday, if that's agreeable. I would love to see you and we could try to talk then.

Sarah

*

That night, after I'd seen George safely home, I wandered the house, imagining Sarah there. I whispered her name in passing, glimpsed her through the open door of the sitting room, saw her framed in the faded night of the drawing room window. I stood on the turn of the stairs and spoke to her. Tomorrow we would talk.

The countryside through which I rode was shabby with slush and melting snow. The fields were vast lakes. Lumps of melting ice, broken from the sides of ditches, floated slowly across the face of the water. It would be March before the land dried out. Ploughing and sowing would be late. Easter would have come and gone before the countryside was back to its best, before spring even sign-posted summer.

I prepared myself for Mrs Dowling's curt reception as I knocked on the cottage door, but instead was met by Sarah's smiling face.

'I was hoping it'd be you,' she said, opening the door wide and touching the side of my face with the back of her hand as I stepped into the kitchen. It was only a momentary touch, a caress hidden from her mother's view by the open door, but my face flushed and my heart sang.

For her part, Mrs Dowling was as taciturn as ever.

She didn't know this article nor my seed, breed and generation, as she told Sarah, and she wasn't at all sure she wanted me under her roof. If Sarah wanted to flit around with me then on her own head be it, but her mother wasn't going to have any hand, act or part in it. All of this information was relayed in short bursts of dramatic whispering in the pantry, intentionally pitched just loud enough to reach my ears. Furthermore, she wanted to remind her daughter, in case it had slipped her mind, that this was still her house.

When I suggested we might walk in the woods for an hour, before I escorted Sarah to work, Mrs Dowling sighed deeply, banged several saucepans off the table, and sighed again.

'Would you like to walk with us?' I asked.

'Are you trying to rise my dander, young fellow?'

'No, I just thought you might like to.'

'I don't need no one coming in here asking me if I want to walk in my own woods, thank you, not you nor anyone. I've lived here fifty-seven years and I walk as I please, where I please, when I please.'

Once outside, I reached quickly into my coat pocket and handed Sarah the letter I had written over the previous three weeks.

'You don't have to read it now,' I told her. 'And I want to talk to you, while we have the time.'

'I'd like to read it. I've waited this long for it.'

Stepping away from her, I buried the toe of my boot in a bank of snow, twisting and lifting it until it crumbled. Then I turned and watched Sarah, her head bent, the red locks falling over her face.

'Your hair is a great temptation,' I said.

She blushed.

I took her head in my hands and kissed her, my fingers soaking in the warmth of her skin.

'Is it too soon to talk about falling in love?' I asked.

*

A sharp wind through the first fortnight of February sucked the wetness from all but the lowest fields. By the end of the month, the countryside had wrung itself of most of the winter's flooding and daffodils poked their heads above the grass. As the evening light stretched beyond six, the rope of work left undone since January slowly shortened. And in spite of the long hours and the backbreaking labour, my energy and high spirits were inexhaustible.

On Sundays I rode to Mullaghcreelan to visit Sarah.

As February slipped into March and the dry spell continued, wildflowers shoved aside the rotting leaves. Banks swelled with primroses, and along the river secret shoots of irises danced on the clear coolness of the water. I planned to go to Dublin, to my cousin's wedding, at Easter. I wanted Sarah to come with me.

'I couldn't.'

'Why not?'

'I just couldn't.'

On Easter Monday morning, I attended the wedding in Dublin, where I met again the uncles and aunts and cousins I hadn't seen in years.

'And can we expect a big day from you sometime soon?'

'I'll do my best for you, Bridie.'

'Is there anyone in particular I should be looking out for?'

'There might be.'

'And why didn't you bring her?'

'The time wasn't right,' I said, not wanting to tell her the truth.

'Young fellow, my lad, the time is never right. Don't be like me and die wondering!'

*

Late that night, I sat in my hotel room and wrote to Sarah. I was drunk. I wrote to her about the day. And I wrote the things I truly wanted to say.

Spring opened into summer and each time I saw Sarah her skin had darkened like the crops ripening in the fields. Headlands thickened with dandelions and hedges hardened with new growth. By early August, people had forgotten the shapes that clouds make. Days began and ended with a blue cloth over everything. Men worked stripped to the waist, the sun dyeing deeper their mahogany skin. Children came down the headlands four and five times a day with cans of cold tea. The harvest was three weeks early.

'Who'd have thought it?' George Greene said.

He and I were sitting beneath the spread of a red chestnut on the headland of a cornfield. Around us, harvesters stretched in the shadows, sleeping off the morning's work.

'Did you ever imagine back in January we'd have an early harvest? This field was a lake then.'

'Things turned, no doubt.'

And then, in the last week of August, with the harvest done and autumn already scattering the hedges with scabs of rust, I sat down and wrote what I hoped would be a confession and a temptation.

My darling,

If I trade my own pain for the pain you have suffered, will you marry me?
If my sadness can come close to your terror, will you marry me?

If I can love away your dread, will you marry me?
If I can trade my darkness for your anguish, will you marry me?
If I can hold you long enough to set your heart free, will you marry me?
If I can be your angel of God, will you marry me?
If I can burn the past and find the future, will you marry me?
If you can say yes, I will marry you.

William

'There's only the one way to be sure,' George told me when I asked his advice.

We were slating the roof of one of the cowsheds, perched on the ridge, looking out across the near fields. The autumn sun was still shining, but there were clouds building from the west and the wind was no longer warm.

'Go and see her. If she's there, you'll know. If she's not, you'll know that too.'

'Her mother isn't the easiest person to get past.'

'It's not her mother you're going to see.'

'I might try it.'

'As long as you're prepared for what she might say. It could go one way or the other, you know that?'

'I do.'

Late the following morning, I saddled the mare. George was there to wave me off, handing me a satchel of food, as I was about to leave.

'You might need that.'

'You won't be worrying if I'm not back tonight.'

'I won't. And this place'll be all right, I'll look after things.'

'Decent man.'

'Good luck.'

I tethered the mare to a tree and stayed in the shelter of the woods until I reached a spot opposite Dowling's garden. The wind smelled of rain. I sat in the sanctuary of a sapling grove. A knot of children grumbled by, bickering over marbles, wrestling in the dust, laughing. A woman came down the lane. I recognised her as Mrs Quigley. I thought she had seen me but I stayed very still, squatting on my hunkers, back against a tree, as she knocked on Dowling's door and stepped inside. An hour passed before she reappeared.

Dusk began to fall and I took some food from my satchel and drew my coat around me. And then the rain came, a steady drizzle through the lightly covered branches. I went to check on the mare and, when I returned, the lamp had been lit in Dowling's kitchen. Another hour passed. I checked my pocket watch by the light of a match. Twenty to eight. There were footsteps and a lantern on the lane and then the lantern was in my face and I was caught.

'I brought you some soup, you must be perished there.' Mrs Quigley handed me a can. 'I seen you and I coming down and going back. Are you stopping the night?'

I laughed. 'If I have to. I'm hoping Sarah's in there. Is she there?'

'She might be.'

'I thought her mother might be going out some time.'

'And she might be, too. She might be going up to my house for a hand of cards.'

'And, if she was, how long would she be there?'

'Well, I never seen her shut our door before eleven.'

'Thank you. And thanks for the soup.'

'It's not my place to say, but Sarah isn't happy. I'd like to see her happy. Now, I'll go and get Mrs Dowling and get on about my business. You can leave the can there after you.'

'I asked you not to come after you last wrote,' Sarah said when she saw me outside the door.

'I couldn't not come.'

'You better stand in out of the rain.'

The kitchen was warm and tidy.

'How did you know my mother was gone?'

'I saw her.'

'How long are you out there?'

'Seven hours.'

'You'll get your death. Take off that coat, I'll dry it.'

'What if your mother comes back?'

'She'll have to like it or lump it. You're here now.'

She spread my coat across the sheila hanging above the fireplace and then she sat opposite me at the table.

'I can't tell you I'll make you happy,' I said quickly, 'because no one can promise happiness. But I'll try and if you're not happy it won't be for the want of me trying.'

'There's things.'

'I know all the things. You told me about your family.'

'Other things. When my brother died, I was glad he was dead. It felt like spitting something rotten out of my mouth. But there's more.'

'Tell me and then, if you want, I'll go off and I'll never come back, unless you ask me.'

'Can I have that letter?' I asked when she said nothing. 'The last one I sent you?'

Sarah blushed and took it from her pocket.

I left the sheet on the table and searched in my pocket until I found a pencil. Then I wrote a line of words beneath my signature and pushed the letter back across the table. Sarah turned it and read what I had written.

If I swap my madness for your madness, will you marry me?

She looked at me, with my hair spiked and drying and my eyes shining. I thought she was going to say yes but she didn't.

'I don't know, William.'

'But you're not saying no?'

'I can't say anything.'

'But you're not saying no.'

In early November, I told Sarah I was going to have a Christmas party and I wanted her to come. She promised she would.

'Your mother can come, too, in case she has any worries about you.'

'I doubt she'll want to.'

'Well, I'll ask her, nearer the time.'

'You're a brave man.'

*

Sometimes our conversations were sharp. Sarah knew my calmness was a cover for something deeper. My letters told her that.

He wondered what it was she wanted. He waited for her to say, to tell him. He knew she'd tell him about the sea, where she'd never been, and he dreamed of that, too. Of the water lapping below them and the sand still warm after the heat of the day and the moon lifting its head out of the ocean, big and yellow.

And then he thought of how the trees in the wood sounded like the sea. And he knew there were other things in their lives, other people, other problems, but, more than anything, he knew he loved her and wanted her and was content when he was with her and he hoped she felt the same way.

When we were together, my talk was much more measured and I know she found herself caught between the words she was hearing and the words she'd read.

'I want to be able to say yes to you,' she told me. 'I really want to.'

'You don't have to.'

'I know that, but one thing follows another, that's the way it is with people.'

'Not necessarily. Because you kiss me doesn't mean anything more is going to happen.'

'But you want it to.'

'Why don't we let what happens happen.'

'It's not just words that matter.'

*

I made my preparations for the Christmas party on the 21st. Nothing must go wrong. Successful as the previous year's celebration had been, this must be even better. I went to Duthie's, the jewellers, in Athy and bought a locket for Sarah. And then I bought a ring because I wasn't sure the locket said enough.

I read the note in the kitchen, while guests flowed through the open doorway.

> *I hope your party goes well. I'm sorry I cannot be there. We will talk after the Christmas time. I will try to explain everything to you then. I'm sure everyone will enjoy thereselves tonight. Sarah.*

On Christmas Eve, I went to great lengths to let George off at midday. In the afternoon, I saw to the cattle and made sure I was noticed about the yard. As soon as darkness fell, I started drinking and by ten I was asleep on the half-landing, too drunk to get to bed.

Rain came in the night and it rained all Christmas Day. I stayed in the house, drinking and sleeping and drinking again. In my drunken state, I was convinced that there was more whiskey in the stable. Staggering across the yard, I stumbled through the open door of one of the sheds and fell asleep on the floor. I woke long after dark to find the rain had blown in on me. It was ten o' clock and Christmas Day was almost over. I was relieved.

*

'Do you know how painful it is to be in love with you?'

'Yes.'

'And do you know how good it could be?'

'No.'

'It's like being in the horrors and then it's what happiness can be like.'

It was the afternoon of St Stephen's Day. Sarah and I were standing in the yard of Rice's public house. From inside, I could hear the sounds of singing and laughter.

'I've had enough,' I said. 'I'm not asking you to forget things or change things, but I've had enough of being lifted and dropped like a corn sack. Tell me what kind of future there is, if there's any. Tell me what you want and you can have it, but don't treat me like a fool.'

'I haven't.'

'Ah, for Christ's sake, Sarah! I'm not forcing you to marry me. I'm just asking you to tell me, one way or another, what you want. Is that too much for you to do?'

'No.'

'So what do you want? Tell me.'

Sarah said nothing.

'You're going to say you don't know,' I suggested.

'I didn't say that.'

And then the tears came.

'Crying tells me nothing, either,' I said. 'Do you think you're the only one with sadness in your life, Sarah? You're not. I could give you a catalogue. And so could everyone else. Different sadnesses, but just as deep. And I'm not asking you to wipe them away, but I am asking you to be honest with me and to make what you say the same tomorrow as it is today. It's as simple as that.'

'If it was …'

I waited for her to finish the sentence, but the silence hung like a dead branch.

'I've said what I had to say, so I'll be on my way. A very happy New Year to you.'

And with that I was gone through the yard gate. At McDonald's I saddled the mare, swung onto her back and rode up the street, across the square and away from Castledermot.

My satisfaction at this outburst was short lived, however. Reining in the mare, I dismounted and sat in the shadow of the Round Bush. The last time I'd sat there, fifty-three weeks before, I hadn't even known of the existence of Sarah Dowling.

'What did you come for today?' I asked aloud.

'To say my piece and get an answer.'

'And did you do that?'

'I said what I had to say.'

'Did you get an answer, do you know where you stand?'

'No.'

'Well, then, go back and get the answer.'

Anne Rice saw me from the door and pointed to the kitchen.

Sarah was sitting at the table.

'I'm glad you came back.'

'Are you?'

'I'd've had to find my way to Ballyadams otherwise.' She forced a smile.

'I'm sorry for some of the things I said, but most of it was the truth.'

She sniffled, wiped her nose and looked at me. Her face was a terrible white.

'I thought you were gone.'

'If I could be, I would be.'

'That's what frightened me.'

'If friends is what we have to be, Sarah, then let us be that. I'll settle for it. So might you.'

She nodded.

'Is that what we're settling for, then? Is that decided?'

'No.'

'What then?' I was exhausted.

'I would've gone to Ballyadams. I would've found out where you live.'

'Why?'

'When I saw you turning at the end of the road, I thought you were gone. I didn't want you to be gone.'

'Do you love me?'

'Yes.'

'Will you marry me?'

'Yes.'

'Will you tell me tomorrow or the next day that you've changed your mind?'

'No.'

I had no need to say anything to George, my eyes told their own story.

'You have the look of a happy chap.'

'I am. Will you be our best man?'

George grasped my hand and shook and shook and shook it.

'I'd be honoured. I'm terrible glad for you. Good health and every happiness.'

*

It was arranged that Sarah should come and visit the house at Ballyadams on the third Saturday in January.

I had the trap waiting at her gate at ten o' clock on the Saturday morning.

'You're sure your mother won't come?' I asked.

'Another time.'

Mrs Dowling came to the door. 'Drive careful, now.'

'We might be late enough back,' I said.

'It won't be the first time she was in late.'

After we had eaten, I took Sarah on a tour of the house, opening doors on rooms that smelled of polish. On the turn of the stairs, we stopped and I pointed through the window, to the expanse of the Wicklow foothills.

'Some days you can see Mullaghcreelan from this window.'

'Can you?' Sarah looked at me. 'Are you joking me, again?'

I shook my head. 'You can.'

Putting her face to the glass, she stared across the fields and the miles between.

'We don't have to live here,' I said. 'I know it's not home to you.'

'It's a beautiful house. All this many rooms, so much space.'

'Let me show you the rest.'

We continued up the stairs and along the corridor until I opened another door and she found herself standing in a large bedroom.

'This could be your room, if you wanted.'

She said nothing.

We moved on, looking in on three further bedrooms before coming to the most cluttered.

'This is my room,' I said.

Sarah crossed the floor, stopping at the window to peer out over the garden.

'William!' George's voice came from downstairs.

'You wander about,' I said. 'I have to pay George and Peter. Take your time.'

The day before the wedding, George and I arrived at Mullaghcreelan in the trap, sitting in splendour among buckets of sunflowers, whose heads had exploded into golden globes of dazzling brightness. The Quigley children flocked around the trap. Even Mrs Dowling was impressed.

I refused to tell Sarah where we were to spend our honeymoon until the morning after our wedding. Over breakfast, in the hotel in Carlow, I reminded her of the Easter morning she'd walked to the station in Athy to see me off.

'I wished you were travelling with me that morning. So, that's what we're doing. Catching the train in an hour. You and me, husband and wife, together, spending a week in Dublin.'

'I've never been in Dublin.'

She was like a child on the train, unable to sit still, calling out the names of stations at which we stopped. Maganey; Athy; Kildare; Cherryville Junction; Newbridge; Sallins; and Kingsbridge Dublin.

We went to the shops in Sackville Street; stood on the Ha'penny Bridge; climbed Nelson's Pillar; went to shows at night; walked in St Stephen's Green; travelled out to Killiney to see the sea.

There Sarah kicked off her shoes and ran along the strand, chasing in and out of the waves, scandalising the sedate matrons who had come to take the air, running and running until she was clear of the tutting tongues and daggered eyes.

I let her run, laughing as I strolled after her, enjoying the reproach that followed us like a lapdog.

When finally I caught up with her, she was sitting on a rock at the edge of the water, dipping her feet in the incoming tide. The hem of her dress was soaked and her hair had come undone.

We returned to a harvest that was almost in. George had overseen the week's work and only one field remained to be cut. On the last night of the reaping, the workers gathered in the house for a meal and a dance that lasted into the early hours.

'It was like a second wedding,' Sarah said when the last stragglers had left. We were tidying the kitchen and washing crockery. 'They worked hard.'

'I told you, farming isn't easy.'

'And now that I'm here, I'm trapped into a life of farm work, is that what you're saying?'

I laughed. 'Something like that.'

Autumn settled with the falling leaves. Most days, when George and I came in to eat, we found something had been painted or moved or rearranged. The washing line billowed with curtains and sheets. The kitchen walls changed colour and then changed again. The loose board on the stairs was suddenly silent. The sitting room door no longer caught on the saddle. There were dahlias and autumn leaves in vases. The pantry was stripped and scrubbed and repainted. Often Peter Clarke was missing from the yard and inevitably found inside, at one end of some piece of furniture, Sarah at the other, both laughing, manhandling it into this room or that.

And so our lives passed in happiness.

Louise Meredith was a regular visitor that autumn and winter. Together, she and Sarah planned the long-awaited Christmas party.

'I've never had a party,' Sarah said.

'Well, this is your chance to go mad. I'll go mad with you.'

And when the 21st came, together they laughed and danced the night into day.

Spring brought the daffodils cluttering along the driveway. And in the summer we took a train to Waterford and spent a week at the sea. Then, in the first week of August, the weather broke. The harvest was ready in the fields, but there was nothing to be done. Much of the time the harvesters sheltered in the sheds, peering through the dripping rain as Lenten clouds shuffled across the sky.

Sarah paced the kitchen, searching the drab skyline for some sign of light.

'It could be worse,' I tried to reassure her. 'We were lucky we bought in the sheep, as we're not depending on the crops. Once the corn doesn't lodge, it'll be all right. We'll survive.'

'Will they?' She nodded at the workers crowded into the shed across the yard.

'Well, the crops have to be harvested and the workers have to be paid. It just won't happen this week. We'll see what next week brings.'

In the third week, the weather finally lifted as the clouds broke and the ground began to dry.

'It looks like we might have a decent cut after all,' George said.

The three of us were standing in the yard while the harvesters collected their coats and satchels from the shed. An orange moon rose above the fields and the sky was clear, promising a fourth consecutive fine day.

'Looks that way.'

'Will you stay for a bit of supper, George?' Sarah asked.

The old man shook his head. 'Thank you, Ma'am, but no. I'll hit the hay. A good night to you both.'

'Goodnight.'

Sarah waited until George was out of the yard before she spoke. 'Why does he still call me Ma'am? I've asked him to call me Sarah.'

'Old habits die hard.'

'It makes me feel like I'm a hundred years old.'

'You look sixteen,' I said and I hoisted her into the air and carried her down the avenue.

'Where are we going?'

'We're going up to the Sycamore Hill, to watch the moon.'

Only when we'd reached the top of the hill did I put her down.

'See?'

The moon was a marmalade husk, stooping over the countryside, its face smiling down on the work of the day. As it slowly rose in the sky, it brightened the fields below, where every bush and branch and stalk of corn seemed to stand out from its neighbour, and the tree shadows were sharp as blades.

We lay on the hilltop in silence, our eyes moving from the rising moon to the countryside below and then back to the golden globe climbing through the night.

And we made love.

The last week of November brought incessant rain that was followed, in the first days of December, by an iron frost. The basin of the low field that had flooded now froze solid, and we went to watch the local children skating and sliding on it. It wasn't long before we were down among them.

'I'll be careful,' Sarah said, in case I needed reassurance.

'I know you will.'

Soon we were both careening across the frozen water, the wind rushing against us as we screamed louder than the loudest child, trying to hold our balance before shooting off the edge of the pond and into the icy stubble, our laughter echoing across the fields. Eventually, reluctantly, we went home to eat, but after supper I made two torches which we took with three lanterns to the low field, where we continued our sliding. The light drew the children back, and later their parents in search of them, so that by nine o'clock the pond was circled with lanterns and torches, and there were as many adults, as children, on the ice.

*

'I was thinking about the Christmas party,' I said one evening while we were eating supper. 'Maybe we should keep it smaller this year, just have a few friends.'

'Over my dead body, last year's was the best night of my life. Well, one of them,' Sarah smiled. 'Anyway, people would kill you if they thought you weren't having it.'

I sighed a resigned sigh. 'We'll have it. What day?'

'The twenty-first is a Saturday, that'd be good.'

'Twenty-first it is. Will you talk to Louise?'

'I already talked to Louise,' Sarah said.

I planned on selling a herd of cattle at the December fair in Castledermot. Prices were good.

'Will you go over with them yourself?' Sarah asked.

'I will. We should do very well out of them, they're fine beasts. Would you like to come?'

'No, we'll be up to our eyes here. That's two days before the party!'

George Greene and Peter Clarke were in the yard by eleven. The night was bitterly cold and overcast. The cattle breathed clouds that dimmed the lanterns while the three of us inspected them, ready for the journey. That done, we went into the kitchen, stamping our feet and blowing on our hands. Sarah had cooked a midnight meal.

Peter Clarke was dressed in heavy breeches and a gaudy, bright red jacket.

'You won't get lost in that,' George laughed.

'I like it,' Sarah said.

'Do you, Missus?'

'I do. I think it's lovely. It suits you.'

'So do I,' Peter smiled, pleased with Sarah's approval. 'My cousin sent it from America.'

'Every young one in Castledermot will be dazzled by you. I'd be tempted by you myself.'

Peter blushed and drowned his face in a mug of steaming tea.

'Right,' George said. 'We'll hit the road. Thank you, Ma'am, for a lovely meal.'

At five Sarah went down to the kitchen to make breakfast while I shaved and dressed upstairs. She must have heard my footsteps on the boards above her head, heard me moving along the landing, opening the doors to the other rooms and walking about them.

'What were you doing?' she asked when I came down.

'Just mooching,' I said.

'Did you think you'd find your Christmas present?'

'No, I was just looking around the place. I like this house, especially at Christmas time.'

'You're a strange man, William Dunne.' She sat opposite me at the table.'I hope the sale goes well today.'

'It will. You make sure you go back to bed now.'

'Yes, Sir.'

'What time is Louise coming up?'

'Not till twelve. Can we have Peter tomorrow, to help with the holly and the decorations?'

'Of course.'

'Mrs Abbot and Mrs Ryan'll be here in the morning, to start the cooking.'

'Good. You just — '

'Don't overdo it,' she finished my sentence for me.

*

Sarah waited in the stable while I saddled the mare, holding the lantern and leaning in against the animal's warm neck.

Once she was saddled, I took the lantern from Sarah, put it on a shelf and held her to me.

'Black-eyed Susan,' I said and rubbed her belly.

'I love you,' she said.

'I love you.'

'You'll be back safe and sound.'

'I'll always be back.'

And then I swung into the saddle, leaned down and, kissing her again, walked the horse across the cobbled yard and into the blackness. I looked back and Sarah was standing on the gravelled avenue, waiting for the silence to flow back.

I found George and Peter with the cattle at Keenan's Lane. It was Peter's coat that I saw first, resplendent among the more sober garb of the other jobbers.

'Any interest yet?'

'A fellow from Baltinglass was about and went away and come back again. Said he'd see you when you got here.'

'Early enough. We'll hold out for what we want.'

Eventually the buyer returned. His offer was high but not high enough.

'Christ, Mister,' he said in frustration, 'they'd want to be shiting gold to warrant the price you're after!'

I eyed the man. He was shabbily dressed, but his clothes were part of the show. The torn coat and the ragged trousers spoke of hard times, of watching the pennies, but his boots were good. There was money behind the façade.

'Well, now,' I said warmly, 'in a way, they do.'

'They're not doing it today then, their shite looks the same as that from ones half their price.'

'But it's not. I know that and you know that.'

'I'll think about it,' the man said.

'Well, you know the price, but they won't be there all day.'

'I'll be back to you.'

'Good.'

A half-hour later the dealer was there again, eyeing the cattle from a distance.

I pretended not to notice. He walked in a wide circle, sighing and shaking his head, stepping away, feigning disgust.

'Can't be done,' he said, finally.

'Fair enough,' I said. 'We better let them go to O'Toole, so.'

'If Mick O'Toole was interested, he'd have taken them by now. I didn't come down in the last shower,' the dealer laughed. 'I'll give you twenty under.'

I shook my head.

'Fifteen,' the man said.

'Five.'

'Ah, for Jasus' sake, blood from a stone.'

'Ten and that's as far as I can go.'

'You drive a hard bargain.'

'Like you, I didn't come down in the last shower either.'

The man circled again, coming to a stop beside me.

'To be fecked,' he said, spitting on his hand and pushing it into my palm. 'It's Christmas. I'll do you a turn and take the hoors off your hands.'

I smiled.

'You're getting a good herd.'

'And you're getting a fine wad of money.'

He turned his back and, peeling notes from his pocket, he counted them out and thrust them at me.

'And there's something for luck,' I responded, putting a guinea in his palm.

We shook hands again. The man signalled to two young boys who were sitting on a wall nearby.

'Drive them on,' he said. 'And make sure yis count them out.'

'We did well,' George said when the dealer had gone.

'We did. Now, you and Peter go and eat some dinner. Tell Anne Rice I'll pay her later. Are you staying around?'

George shook his head. 'Noel Lambe has the trap and is going to Athy at half-two. He said he'd bring me that far. Young Peter here wants to stay.' He winked.

'Well you can travel with me then,' I said to Peter, who nodded.

'Now, I'm going down the town, there's something I want to get.'

I found the smith at Hamilton Bridge. Drawing a piece of string from my coat pocket, I handed it to the man.

'I want a gold ring, that size.'

The man took a tray from under the stall counter.

'This one?' he suggested.

I took the ring and examined it. 'That's solid gold?'

'Solid.'

'And have you one the same but in a girl's size?'

'What age?'

'A child.'

The man produced another tray and showed me a smaller ring.

'Can you inscribe them for me?'

'I can, but it'll be six o'clock again I have them ready, I'm that busy.'

'That's all right, I'll wait.'

'Write what you want on that,' the goldsmith said, offering me a sheet of paper and a pencil.

I took them and wrote *Black-eyed Susan* on the paper.

'And on the other one?' the goldsmith asked.

'The same,' I said.

By four o'clock it was dark. I sat in Rice's kitchen and drank two hot whiskies and read a copy of The Carlow Sentinel.

'You'll have a bowl of soup and a cut of bread before you go?' Anne asked.

'I wouldn't say no. It'll be a cold journey home. Could have snow yet.'

'God forbid. And you won't forget to give Sarah our best.'

Pushing through the thinning crowds, I reached the goldsmith's stall and handed in my receipt.

'Just done,' the man said and he held the rings in the light of a lantern.

'A fine job. Thanks.'

The goldsmith slipped the rings into an envelope and I put it in my trouser pocket.

'A happy Christmas.'

'And to you and yours.'

*

In McDonald's yard, young boys scuttled between the stalls, leading the animals out, harnessing some and putting them in the shafts of carts.

Peter Clarke was waiting by the mare.

'She's thrown a back shoe, Mr Dunne. The smith said to bring her down, and I was just going to do that.'

'I'll take her. Is there anything you want to do?'

'I might walk on out the Athy road and meet you when you're ready.'

'Will I look out for you on your own or in company?'

'Maybe just me or maybe not,' Peter said, his face brightening. 'I won't be gone no further nor Hallahoise.'

'Go on. Enjoy yourself. I won't leave without you!'

It was after eight when the smith finished his work

I put my foot in the stirrup and sat into the saddle. The town was quiet. Most people had gone home and those who hadn't were in the public houses. The mare walked on, away from the lights of the public house, into the black darkness of the Athy road.

1763

The old man lifts the bare rooted trees from a sack and hands one to the small girl at his side. She slowly waltzes the sapling, which is as tall as herself, to the edge of one of the holes he has dug, lowering it gently until the roots spread out across the rich clay of the river bank. The old man spades the clay around the tree and then heels it firmly into place.

The pair moves along the riverbank and the old man hands the girl a second tree. She holds it straight in position, her face a study in concentration, her tongue protruding between her lips. Again, the old man fills the hole with clay and firms it with the heel of his boot. Then he and the girl stand back and survey their work – two oaks, leaning towards each other – and beyond them the quiet ripple of a river going home.

The woman at the window

This is my window.

Some afternoons the voices of children bolt up from the paths and stir me from my devotions. I don't understand the games they play. I rouse myself and try to make some sense of them, but, to be truthful, I cannot care.

I constantly wander the rooms of this house, my house, forever my house, wishing again and again I could undo the thing I did.

I watch these children about their games. I suck their laughter into my soul and try to smother the gap of loss, but the world will never hold sufficient happiness to still my anguish. It haunts me, as I myself haunt this place. I cannot leave, nor would I ever leave my darling.

By day, I sit watching these other children play, seeing them grow into their lives.

In darkness, I wait for her at the foot of the narrow stairs. I listen for her returning step. I search for her smile and dream her face happy again. I wait in the hope that I may kiss my darling Jane again.

And sometimes, when hope raises its head above the parapet of my regret, I'm inclined to believe I can then go back beyond to the other, warmer times in my life, to love, to laughter, to days spent running in the long meadows, to that other child who was myself.

My grandfather pushes me on the swing that dangles from the red chestnut.

Push me higher, Grandfather, higher, push me higher. Higher, higher, push me higher, Grandfather, higher.

And he does and I swing out above the pasture and then let go of the old rope and my stomach falls and I follow. He tells me I'm wild as weeds. And my words tumble out as I'm rolling.

I was flying, Grandfather. Did you see me flying? Did I fly as far as the birds? I did, didn't I? Will you tell Mama and Papa that I was flying? If we put a swing on Seven Trees Hill and you pushed me as high as you can push me and then I let go, could I fly all the way back to Ballitore? I could, couldn't I? I could fly to our garden and be home long before you.

You'd hurt your feet, child, he says.

Well, I could wear my heavy boots then!

You'd need more than boots to save you.

Well, what if Mama put the mattress in the garden and I landed on that? Will you ask her to put two mattresses out? Will we do that, Grandfather? Will you bring me up to the Seven Trees Hill?

I might.

When?

Soon.

Tomorrow?

Not tomorrow.

When then?

Soon.

And you'll ask Mama to put the two mattresses in the garden, the two big mattresses?

What if it rains?

Well, if it doesn't rain, then?

And I climb onto the wall of the bridge above the Griese and walk carefully, arms outstretched, teeth biting on my lower lip, but I don't stop talking.

Grandfather, why can't we go and swing on Seven Trees Hill on the Sabbath?

Because it's the Sabbath.

But Jesus never said anything about not swinging on the Sabbath. Did He have a swing? If His father was a carpenter, why didn't he make Him a swing? If I was Jesus—

Were Jesus, my grandfather corrects.

—were Jesus and Joseph didn't make me a swing, I'd swing anyway on an invisible swing because if I was God—

Were God!

—were God, I could do anything, couldn't I?

My grandfather listens.

Why are you sighing, Grandfather?

Am I sighing?

Yes, you are. When you die and go to heaven, will you ask Jesus to make me a swing on the highest tree on the Seven Trees Hill?

He nods.

You know the story of Isaac and Abraham, Grandfather? Are you the same Abraham?

He sighs again. *What age do you think I am, Mary?*

I don't know, Grandfather, about a hundred and fifty?

His eyes are shining and his mouth is a crooked grin.

Why are you smiling?

He doesn't answer.

Grandfather, why does Mama say I'm your shadow?

He takes me to see a field he has bought, near Castledermot. We sit side by side and the horse's reins lie idle in Grandfather's palm.

Why have you bought a field, Grandfather?

Because I liked it. Because I want to plant a forest there.

Will you plant that forest today?

Not today, Mary. Today we'll plant two trees, one for thee and one for me.

And we do, close to the edge of the little river that is one boundary of the folded napkin of terrain my grandfather wants to see planted as his wood.

I walk with him the length of the pasture, back to where the horse is tethered, and we stop at the gateway and look back at the pair of oaks, the first and last my grandfather will ever plant in that place.

And then his shadow grows longer and he's more distant from me, and then there's no reaching him at all, he's gone. All I have left are my memories and a faint trace of his expressions. I spent so much time with him in my girlhood that I take and keep parts of his Yorkshire phraseology.

My family laughs at me sometimes; they call me their *Maid of the Dales*. They ask me if I'm coming into the *hoose*.

After he's gone, I refuse to let his inflection go because I don't want that part of him to disappear from my life. I don't want to admit that I will never see or hear him again. And sometimes I frighten myself when I speak and hear his voice in my own.

Sometimes I still do. Grandfather Abraham was a light in the darkness of our lives. He was strict but never severe. Not like the Elders in our meeting, not like James McConaghty, always looking for weaknesses and failings in people, always there to point out the wrongs we had done.

*

It's a summer afternoon. My sister Sally and I are in the garden. The day is heavy with heat. Voices and laughter drift to us from the fair in the Mill Field across the wall. And somewhere in there is John Elsey. Handsome John Elsey.

I'd say there are men riding horses and jumping fences and acrobats and jugglers and all kinds of things.

But Sally isn't convinced.

What if we get caught looking?

We won't get caught, Mother and Father are inside.

They might come out.

Well, I'll look then, let thee watch for Father.

I climb carefully, a foot between two stones, another foot higher up and then another, until my elbows are leaning on the top of the wall and the fair is laid out before me like toys on a tray.

And then a voice from behind me.

Let me see.

Sally pulls at the hem of my dress. I dig my elbows firmly into the wall and tighten my toes in the crevice between the stones.

Stop it!

Let me see.

If we want to see it properly, we'll have to climb into the field. Thou'rt sure Father isn't watching?

Yes.

Come on then.

I take her hand.

Put thy foot in there, on that stone. Now come on, I'll hold thee until thou get onto the wall. That's it.

We perch on the wall, but we can't sit there like two coconuts on a shy.

Let's jump down and walk around the field.

What if Father misses us?

He won't.

Thou'rt sure?

Yes, I'm sure. Now, jump. I'll jump after thee.

Thou won't run off and leave me alone?

Of course not.

My hand on her back.

Now jump.

I push her and she falls through the sunlight, all skirts and arms, and I fly after her.

Look, look at the fire-eater!

And then the sight of John Elsey on horseback, his long fair hair streaming behind him.

Don't let him see thee looking at him.

Yet Sally gawks, as Sally would.

Don't stare, he'll come and talk to me.

I thought thou liked him.

I do, but I don't have anything to say to him.

Well, I'll go and talk to him then!

Don't thou dare! Sally, stop!

Too late. She waves and John Elsey waves back and turns his horse.

Just before he reaches us, I pinch the inside of my sister's arm, the soft bit just above her elbow, keeping my thumb and first finger scissored in her flesh until John Elsey's horse is towering above us.

Hello, Mary. Sally.

My name first!

Hello, John. We came out to see the fair for ourselves.

Your father doesn't mind?

No, not at all.

Good.

We'll come down and see thee jumping, won't we, Sally?

Yes.

Her voice is high and pained; there are tears in her eyes.

Good. I'll see you there then.

He turns the horse, smiles over his shoulder and moves away. Sally slaps my hand.

He's handsome, isn't he? Isn't he, Sally?

She says nothing. Her face is white. And then I see him.

Oh, James McConaghty.

He stands, his withered hand a curled fish against his chest.

Well, now, Mary Shackleton, I'm disappointed in thee. I watched thee, climbing the wall and peering about like a chicken over a pen. And then thou led thy sister here into temptation, bringing her among these God-forsaken heathens. Thy father will not be impressed with thy behaviour and, worse still, of a Sabbath day. I want to hear none of thy excuses. Go and stand at the gate and wait for me and then thou and thy sister can accompany me to meet thy father. He shall not be pleased. Go wait at the gate.

We move slowly. His voice rings across the Mill Field.

Outside the gate.

Heads turn. Mouths smile.

Yes, James McConaghty.

We stand at the gate, a fraction outside the gate.

Why couldn't he mind his own business. He's right, Father will be furious. And we'll have to listen to James all the way home, with his 'Thou shouldn't do this' and 'Thou shouldn't do that' and 'Thy father was ever a man to obey the Sabbath' and 'Young ladies of our society do not do things like this.' Hellfire is too good for him!

James McConaghty, thriving on the misfortunes of others until misfortune struck his own business, but that was years afterwards.

That evening I'm sent to my room, yet I can't resist sticking my head out of the window to catch sight of John Elsey on horseback in the field across the wall.

But the window comes down on me, trapping me, and I'm afraid to call for help, in case John Elsey hears me and laughs at my predicament. In the end my mother finds me and chides me for hanging out of my window *like a common girl.*

When I think of my father, I think of a schoolmaster in his boarding school, a man walking the lines of children, instructing the boys and young men in their arithmetic and geography and Latin. And I think of those same boys sitting in rows, their faces and their accents blending into one.

And I'm sitting there with them, one of his class, all of us lost in his Latin rote.

Mensa, mensa, mensam, mensae, mensa, mensa.

Our voices rise.

Mensa, mensa, mensam, mensae, mensa, mensa.

We gabble again.

Mensa, mensa, mensam, mensae, mensa, mensa.

And I'm watching the boys' faces, the outlines of their heads, the different way each has of bending to his books, the shape of each body, young men from Ireland and France and Norway and Jamaica. And I'm wishing the lesson over so that I can walk the street with them, listen to their laughter as we cross the bridge above the Griese, but the Latin lesson goes on and on.

Amo, amas, amat, amamus, amatis, amant.

Amo, amas, amat, amamus, amatis, amant.

I love, you love...

I love James Skinner, whose fading French accent and dark skin are like the sun to me each morning. I wake with him on my mind and sleep with him in my heart.

I'm fifteen and he's a year older.

Three times we have the chance to be together.

The first is when my parents are away at Yearly Meeting. We walk the length of the Mill Lane, then sit in the shade of a chestnut, where he sings me a song he learned at his uncle's house in Dublin. It's a song I've never heard before and he sings it twice.

Sing with me, Mary, he says and we sit at the millrace and sing it together, though I hear nothing of the water, only the sound of our voices harmonising, convincing me that we belong with each other.

Alas, my love, you do me wrong,
To cast me off discourteously.
For I have loved you well and long,
Delighting in your company.
Greensleeves was all my joy
Greensleeves was my delight,
Greensleeves was my heart of gold,
And who but my lady Greensleeves.

I want to sing that song for my aunt or my parents, but I don't dare. They'll want to know where I learned it *and from whom.*

The second time James and I walk alone together is to meet the stagecoach bringing his little brother David to our school. By now, James has forgotten much of his French and little David knows no English. It's my pleasure to act as their interpreter.

What harm can my father see in this?

I have the two of them to myself and, in my head, I'm a young wife to one and a mother to the other.

The third time is at Christmas and we're walking late from the school to my house and we stop at the gate of Fuller's Court and James kisses me. He takes my hand in his hand and he kisses my fingers. And he presses my hand against the side of his face and I feel the warmth of his skin. And then he kisses my mouth, his lips gentle against my lips.

And happiness is mine.

That January, an epidemic of measles strikes our school and little David Skinner weakens and dies.

Shortly afterwards, James goes home to his parents in France.

I've lost them both.

My memory of that spring is of days spent following my mother about the garden, across the matting of wood anemones and cowslips and bluebells, wanting to tell her how much pain I was in but never able to say. She believed I was grieving for David's death – and so I was – but I was grieving even more for the loss of James and that grief made me guilty.

Is it my imagination, or does death follow death? David Skinner was hardly cold in the ground when another calamity followed on.

We're in evening worship at the Meeting House, each of us in silence and the air is still and the room is lit by glimmering candles and I'm listening to the breathing of the Friends about me. From the Overseers' gallery, I can hear the wheezing of James McConaghty and the strong, even breathing of my father and the short, rasping breaths of John Cooper. I wait, vainly, for some inspiration that will lift me out of this unpleasant eavesdropping and onto a spiritual plane. Outside, through the window with its dozen counted and recounted panes, I can see the leafy branches of the summer trees. It's a still and lifeless evening and then, as suddenly as if a gale has blown open the Meeting House door, a candle gutters and dances and goes out.

Despite the heat of the evening, I believe there is no one in that crowded room who doesn't feel a shiver pass down their spine; it's as if everyone is holding their breath and the silence is complete. No sound of breathing, no sign of any movement from anyone, nothing until, at last, James McConaghty stands and speaks.

The Lord giveth and the Lord taketh away. Blessed be the name of the Lord.

Afterwards, we walk home in silence.

The following evening, my grandfather left us. I was inclined to think God had deserted us, if He knew we were here at all.

*

I'm twenty-six and my father takes me to London, to Yearly Meeting. London makes little or no impression on me, but afterwards we travel to Yorkshire to visit my coosins in their hooses there.

Suddenly I'm no longer the one with the strange way of speaking; I who have been branded *the Yorkshire lass* in Ballitore am hardly understood by my real Yorkshire relatives. They think my accent is Irish and laugh at some of the things that I say. But their laughter is polite and their welcome warm, and they take my father and myself into their homes and make us feel we belong there.

We go from house to house and in every house the coffee pot looks like a replica of the coffee pot in the house before. Only later do we learn that the pot has come from the big house and is on loan to each dwelling we dine in, arriving no more than an hour before us.

I loved Yorkshire and the dales and the way the sky seemed to open up and stretch away forever. Behind my cousins' house there was a particular copse that was wild with honeysuckle and most days we walked through it, taking a short cut here or there. My head was filled with the sweet smell of the flowers and I'd come home with my arms wrapped around enormous bunches of tumbling fragrance and I'd take down every vase I could find and fill the house with them. My cousins laughed and called me *the honeysuckle gatherer.*

Maybe it was a vanity, but always thinking my sisters and cousins prettier than myself, I felt glad to be noticed at all.

That was a bright time in my life and I can't smell honeysuckle even now without remembering that valley and the narrow path that wound down between the flowers and the long grasses and wishing I could go back to that time and that place. A time before everything that happened within these walls had ever been dreamed of.

If I had met someone there, if I had allowed myself to be persuaded by my cousins that I should stay, if David Skinner had not died, if James Skinner had not returned to France, if my dream of him had been reflected in his dreaming of me, if he had come back for me.

If, if, if…

A happier day. My brother Richard's wedding to Lydia Mellor. All the Friends and relatives gather in the Meeting House and, afterwards, our neighbours throng my father's house and music plays and couples dance and children are running everywhere and the tables lean sideways with the weight of food and laughter. And my new sister, Lydia Shackleton, with her hair tied up and her gorgeous face shining and the radiance of love in her eyes and her gaze constantly following Richard, as though she thinks there is no other man in the world.

I watch her watching him and I envy her the love she has for my brother. I wish for a love just like hers, for a face as fair as hers, for hair that shines the way her hair shines, like ripening apples in the sun.

And in the garden, under the old trees where the snowdrops push the winter away, I see them kissing and my heart leaps with delight and sadness both.

In the garden the snowdrops came up year after year, all through my childhood and girlhood. Do the snowdrops still come up at the back of the yew hedge? Do they?

They were beacons of the spring. They were hope. I wish I had hope now.

What about the lilac tree that was outside the pantry door? Is that still there? Is that still blooming? Could it still be blooming after all this time? How much time has passed since then? I know it's a long time, a long, long time, but I have no idea how long.

The days come and then the nights and I sit up here and I walk these floors and I stand on the stairs and I remember and I wish. I wish everything could be different; I wish I could go back beyond the first day we stepped into this house.

I run down a hill with the cold wind on my face. I feel the sweep of a swing, the dizziness inside my head and the giddy sickness in my stomach, the ecstasy of flying. Flying and laughing and smelling the scent of lilac and hearing my grandfather's voice, a voice I love, and taking one last, long look across a woodbine valley before I leave a place in which I'm happy, a place to which I will never go back.

I remember the faces, the names. Squire Keating. Edmund Burke. Peter Widdows. John Pemberton. Hannah Stratford. Thomas Cash. William Cooper. John Duckett. Mick Murray. The Widow Taylor. Bridget Taylor. Abby Boake.

Yes, Abby Boake.

A beautiful girl of seventeen married to William Carter, a middle-aged man. Do I envy her or pity her? I can't decide. Soon afterwards she's carrying William's child and she comes home here to Ballitore, to her father's house, to have the baby. And I visit her and she tells me how motherhood feels, how blessed she is to have a man who loves her, how fortunate she is to be confined in her father's house, how much she wishes me half the happiness she is living.

Little does either of us know, when she says that, how wishes have a way of achieving their own ambitions.

Abby gives birth to a beautiful boy. Her joy is like a shout. Her husband is there, filled with love and pride.

A week afterwards, he goes away on business and a week after that again Abby takes sick and dies in her father's arms. I'm sent for, for no better reason than that I had been her friend. And while I'm there, her husband arrives back from his travels, rushing to see his wife and newly born son, again. Abby's father meets him as he enters the gate and he falls like a shot to the ground.

I watch him as he silently gazes on Abby's cold remains – a wife, a mother and a corpse before her eighteenth year is complete. And I know, as I watch him, that he loves her and I envy her that deep affection, even at such a price.

In 1791 I changed my name from Shackleton to that of my friend William Leadbeater. Can I say more than that?

We were content.

I wish I could say we were passionately in love. I wish I could say I felt for him as I had felt for James. I wish I could say he was the love of my life or that I waited for him like I'd wait for someone I needed to see. But we were content.

What do I most remember of that day? I remember the American woman with the deep, musical voice, who said her name was Matilda Brown. Some of our friends, on their way to our wedding, had met her at the inn in Kilcullen. She told them she was the only female survivor of the sinking of the *Charlemont*.

Everything I own, all my money and clothes were lost on the ship. If you could loan me some money to pay my hotel bill, if you could give me something to tide me over.

And they, in their kindness, pay her bill and invite her to travel with them to our wedding.

Bring me with you to Ballitore, to your friends' wedding? Why, how kind!

And she, in her celebrity, graces our reception.

How good of you, Mr and Mrs Leadbeater, to welcome me here and treat me as one of your own family, such kindness in the wake of my recent tragedy.

Only afterwards did we discover that she was not Matilda Brown, had never set foot on the sunken ship, nor had she lost her worldly goods. She was an impostor who had swindled her way into our home, our wedding, our purses and our affections.

William was angry but I had a sneaking regard and affection for Matilda, who fled the morning after our wedding. Each time her name was mentioned, William's brow would furrow and his eyes darken and I'd be overtaken with a fit of giggling that only added to his annoyance.

In a peculiar way, Matilda Brown was the guest of honour at our wedding and people remembered her long after they had forgotten the occasion for her visit.

I often wondered what happened to her and what other families she entertained and relieved of their money with her tale of near drowning. Secretly, I wished her well, but only secretly.

*

But this is a happy day and I stand at my mirror and the woman I see is smiling. I can honestly say that I look less plain than I have looked before. Often, I've wished for my sister's beauty, but I know it's something beyond my wildest dreams. I will never be beautiful. I have passed the age when beauty is a possibility, when I might grow into even the shadow of beauty.

But I was beautiful once, sitting in the shade of a chestnut tree, listening to James Skinner's voice as he sang. I was beautiful then.

Our marriage was solid and stable, much like that of my parents. After we moved to this house, William and I grew to have a reciprocal affection. Had I known I would never leave it, even after death, would I have been so happy at the prospect?

So many people lived in this house. William and I and our children, who were born under its roof; Mary and Anne Doyle, who shared its rooms with us. They had their shop downstairs and a sitting room and bedroom upstairs. We shared the same stairs and I could step into their chambers or they into mine in any time of trouble.

We weren't long here when my father died. He was away from home, attending to school business in the town of Mountmellick, when he was struck by a fever. My good friend, Dr Johnson, took me to him and I was with him to see out his last hours of torment. And when he died, I came home with his body, home to The Retreat, where Sally and my mother waited, my mother who was already losing her wits.

Shortly afterwards, she came to live with us.

There was always someone coming or going, always company inside these walls, always people to talk to.

Sometimes I wondered whether I would have needed such company and so much of it had my life been different, had James Skinner and I been different people and had our lives run more closely together. Would he have stayed here? Would I have gone to live in France where there is sun and good wine and a language that still speaks his name to me?

I sit in a red boat on a sea that's green, beneath a sky that's blue and a sun that's white and hot. Water laps the side of our wooden boat and James sets the sails and takes us out from the shore and we drift in the stillness of a world away from the world.

And James lifts my veil and kisses my face and smiles.

And I say, *C'est bonne ici.*

But I don't smile because I want him to know how much this means to me. I want him to kiss me again. And he does, his lips meet mine and he says, *Je t'aime.*

And our boat sails along the coast, until we come ashore in a tiny village. And the sun is setting as we tie up the boat and climb a hill to an inn and James asks, *Vous avez une chambre pour une nuit?* And the concierge nods and smiles and hands him the key.

We lie in bed together and the moon is rising over the sea. We can see our boat tied up at the quay and its colours have faded in the moonlight and our faces and skin are the colour of parchment, the colour of death, the colour of love that was allowed to die.

The colour mine is now.

But dreams are not life, and William before his death and I then and afterwards share a real life with my mother's delusions.

*

William, Mother's gone wandering again. Anne Doyle says she saw her walking to The Retreat.

I'll go and bring her back.

No, you stay here. It's better if I go.

And I do, through the night, through the bitter rain and the sweeping wind, to the house I once called home. The back door is open and the leaves have blown in across the floor, and by the light of my lantern I find my mother standing in the empty kitchen.

She looks at me as she would at a stranger.

Who art thou?

I don't know what to say.

Thou hast no right to come in here, thou hast no right in my home. Thou left the doors open for the rain and the wind to blow about the place.

She shuffles around the empty room, never moving far from the walls, her left hand dragging along the flaking paint.

Was it thee who stole my furniture?

Her voice is deep and hollow.

Was it thee who took my husband? Art thou the one who took him away to Mountmellick and sent him back dead?

I'm thy child, Mother.

She laughs, a bitter laugh.

I have no children. I have no one. I know what thou want. Thou wants to lock me up, thou wants to steal my house from me. Thou wants me away from here, but I won't let thee take me.

Hush, Mother. I'm Mary, thy Mary. I haven't come to harm thee. I've come to bring you home, to bring thee safely home.

*

As if safety were mine to give. How could I promise safety when the country was in turmoil and through that spring people were disappearing and I'd tell my children the Brownie had eaten them.

What was I to say?

That they had been murdered by their neighbours and buried in ditches and sunk in rivers, their bodies burned and the bones thrown into wells?

But if the spring was dark, the summer was darker still and Ballitore was a hell of death and killing.

Jane and I are sitting in her room, reading, when the window smashes. I throw my child's body to the floor and cover her with my own. And then I smell the burning smell of powder from a gun.

Keep thy head down.

What's happening, Mama?

It's all right, Jane, I'll look after thee, I won't let anyone harm thee.

And Anne Doyle is on the stairs, calling to us, asking if we're safe and I shout to her to stay where she is and I tell Jane to go to her.

I want thee to crawl across the floor.

And she does, but then she stands in the light, her head a silhouette in the window, and I scream.

Don't stand up, Jane, for God's sake don't stand up!

And Anne is at the door and Jane is creeping across the floor.

Good girl, slowly, slowly, to Anne.

Art thou coming, Mama?

Yes, I'll follow thee. Good girl, now run downstairs.

And I feel the dampness on my back and my dress is soaked in sweat.

Through the kitchen window I could see him. He was lying on his back, his arms stretched out like this, and there was a wound in the lower part of his face that disfigured him almost beyond recognition and the air around his face was a fall of flies.

This was the man who had been my good friend since childhood, my neighbour, my doctor. The man who had brought me to my dying father, the man who had tended to the sick on both sides of the conflict and here he was, his body thrown over a low wall on a morning that was balmy and beautiful and mild, a summer morning in 1798.

I wanted to take him in my arms; I wanted to wipe the blood from the mouth that was a gaping wound; I wanted to carry his body back to his wife and children, but I was afraid. We were all afraid to touch him, afraid to keep his body in our houses for fear we'd be shot ourselves. The best we could do was to keep the snuffling pigs away from it.

Night falls. My husband and some other men take the doctor's body and bury it in our sleeping-ground. Three days afterwards, when the soldiers have left the village, we dig the body back out of the earth and wash and shroud it and put it in a coffin and bury it again. When the grave has been filled a second time, I see my dear friend's bloody waistcoat on the grass. But I don't have the courage to touch it.

Instead, I walk between the stones that mark the sleeping dead. All friends of my youth, Owen Finn, Richard Yeates, Tom Duffy, Paddy Dempsey. All buried here.

And the houses in flames on the Burrow and the glass of my window hot from the burning houses in the square. And my mother's mind like a child's and a militiaman in our kitchen with a gun to my breast and the rebels taking my green tablecloth for a flag and young girls dressed in white with green ribbons in their hair and rumours from Naas and Kilcullen and Castledermot. And Gavin's house burning, the roof timbers cracking like breaking bones. And soldiers telling me the milk I give them is poisoned and calling me names I have never heard before. And an officer, with the handsome look of James Skinner, smashing my plates and cursing me. And a fat tobacconist from Carlow lolling in one of my kitchen chairs, laughing as he tells me how he saw the infantry burn a man in a barrel. And my food tasting of blood.

What kept me sane that summer of madness? Playing with Jane, who would fear and then forget to be afraid.

Mama. The trees are drunk, Mama, the trees are going to fall.

Thou'rt flying, Mama, thou'rt flying round my head.

Swing me again, Mama. Again.

And I do and she glides through the sunlight, the child I once was.

Thou'rt upside down, Mama.

And, after everything, the silence of a late and lovely summer.

*

Anne Doyle and I are leaning over the bridge. The slow summer sun is dipping behind the distant hills. We watch a couple watering their horses at the river. They have servants with them, fully armed, and though the pair are young and newly married, their dress is mourning habits. Their unease, the armed servants, the stillness of the evening air are unforgettable. Mourning is our language, mourning is the dress of our country.

And, after everything, what was there? Silence and ruined houses, followed by the sounds of trees being cut and half-hearted hammering in this valley as people went about rebuilding their homes. And those of us who had been spared watched them, feeling guilty that we hadn't been struck by the same misfortune.

I go up to my beehive at the back of the garden, in a corner between the wallflowers and the sweet rocket, in the shadow of a Ladyfingers of Offaly apple and an old plum. And the evening gathers a long breath and holds it.

Ballitore fair day. The streets are drenched with sun and the sounds of singing and music playing and children laughing draw all of us out of our sadness. Even Maria Johnson, the doctor's widow, walks with her children among the tents and musicians in the Mill Field. If ever a day was made for healing, it is this day.

I think Maria Johnson must have some sense of comfort. How stupid of me!

The summer is refusing to surrender and the days stretch in the sunlight, like cats. Late into September the fields are filled with fresh flowers and the trees are as leafy as they were in spring. I take little Jane on picnics to Seven Trees Hill and she swings from the same trees where I swung in childhood. Her happiness reminds me of my own and she is forever wanting me to push her higher and higher, forever laughing.

Stupid! Stupid! Stupid!

Jane's birth. The midwife at one side of my bed and Anne Doyle at the other. Her birth is easy; she comes into the world as though she wants to be here, as though she has a great curiosity about the place, as though she wants to get here as quickly as she can. And when they put her in my arms, she settles there, content.

One evening … one evening as Anne Doyle … one evening, in that winter of 1798, Mary and Anne Doyle and myself were sitting at the fireside in our sitting room. My mother and her nurse were in the upstairs bedroom and I asked Jane to take a taper up to light the candle in my mother's room.

A thought crossed my mind, *Is she safe?*

But she was a steady, trustworthy child, as cautious as she was beautiful, and I thought nothing more of it.

Another thought, one that lives with me night after night. The thought that I could climb the stairs myself and take the candle to my mother. Instead, I hand it, time and time again, to my young daughter and bid her go carefully. And, time and time again, I hear the quiet crease of her dress followed by the singing anger of the flame as it gulps the linen, swells the runnel of her hair, melts the moonlight of her skin.

*

Everyone tells me there is no danger.

Jane never complains, she kisses us all, but she is thirsty and cold and can't sleep through the night.

The following morning, a doctor comes from Athy.

He has no way of avoiding what he has to say.

I'm sorry, but there's nothing anyone can do.

Not knowing she is leaving us, Jane gets her book and lies in her bed, reciting her little verses.

If James and I had sailed on that boat along the warm coast of France, would we have had Jane? Would she have lived? Would I have been happy or would I have been trapped, as I am now, but in some other house, lamenting, waiting endlessly?

The worst thing of all is that I don't believe so.

When I sleep, I dream of happiness and in those dreams I find passion instead of contentment. And then I wake to the sound of children playing, and I wait again for Jane and James, but neither ever comes.

1978

The season has changed, but the field has not forgotten the season that is ended. This is a day when the summer sun still lives in the low stubble of the harvested field. The earth gives off a warm smell, a reminder of days when the wind came from the west, blowing in rumours of other places, better times, people who woke to the sight of blue skies and the certainty of warmth and light.

Today the field is golden. The dark browns and the wet rust of winter are still months away. The tractor will turn out colours that have lain hidden since spring – each clod like a kingfisher, flashing prismatic as the day goes on, holding the tints beyond the onset of darkness.

Haws will burn in the ditches, but for today there is no need of warmth or fire: for today the summer might still be here and the land is open to its promise.

October Morning

A few women, with children straggling behind, were crossing the road outside the school. Becca sat in her car, the engine idling, waiting for them to reach the path. On another day she might have revved the engine impatiently, but today she was happy to sit there, feeling a kind of pity for these overweight, overburdened, unsmiling women who might be ten years younger than her but looked twenty years older. They had lines of washing and screaming rooms of children to look forward to. She had hours of warmth and loving in a cool bed before she collected her husband off the late afternoon train and set off for a weekend with friends.

She savoured the prospect. Five weeks since she'd had this much time away. One meeting in between, a hurried, furtive coffee. But this morning, this bright October day, would be different. There would be time to savour each other, to sleep when lovemaking was over, to come down to the kitchen and make fresh coffee. Time to walk the lanes behind the house, time to stop and touch, time to kiss. Time.

And now she was on the open road, clear of the school, driving faster than she should. Easing herself back in her seat, she tried to relax. The last of the houses disappeared from her mirror. Across the hedge, a tractor moved in a painstaking line between the biscuit-coloured remnants of harvested wheat and the fire brown of turned clay. She thought again of the limp dahlias in a vase on the dining room table, clinging to their petals beyond the season's end. A bit like her other life with Michael, clinging to a pretence of normality that was their home, his work, their friends, the life that was supposed to keep her fulfilled, make her happy, satisfy that thing called spirit.

And then these snatched mornings and afternoons came around which made the rest of it bearable. She could laugh in the golf club, knowing that tomorrow or the day after she'd be driving to meet, rushing to touch, dying to make love to someone she truly cared about.

And yet she sometimes suspected these days were no more than adventures, an adult big day out. If she took her courage in her hands and left Michael, would this other existence become the mundane, predictable disappointment that married life had proved? Ideally, she'd like to get away once or twice a week, whereby the novelty would remain and frustration would be relieved. Life at home would be manageable, but there'd also be time to sort out the lovers' tiffs that sometimes flared into rows, then dragged through the times apart. Conflicts that couldn't be settled in furtive conversations or the letters that had to be hidden before Michael got home. Just in case.

It was something she'd finally have to face. Compromise was the killer in a love affair; a decision would have to be made, but not today. Today would be beautiful, peaceful, satisfying. In her mind's eye, she pictured the great trees that stood around the house. Five weeks ago they were green, but now they'd be spilling their reds and browns over the gravel in the front yard, glancing against the bedroom window as they fell, resting momentarily on the ledge before twisting away on the breeze. Inside the unused wicket gate the leaves would pile like old snow and in the afternoon, as they went walking, she'd kick the deep, lush piles like children do.

Would there ever be a time when she could come and live in this lean, white house? Today would make her wistful for the thing she wanted most, the love that made her whole, the promise of happiness. She'd have made love anywhere – in the car, in alleyways, in empty buildings – but Jenny insisted on the comfort of the house or hotel rooms.

'I'm past all that fumbling in cars stuff,' she'd said. 'That's for kids. We're not kids.'

Once it had been in a hotel, five times in the house. Ten meetings, making love half a dozen times in eight months, little but everything. Today would be another time, a better time, the best. Today would be real and it would leaves its traces for the evenings when she appeared to be reading or watching television or preparing dinner. Michael would say something and she'd snap back from the remnants of a remembered, interrupted kiss.

She needed to concentrate, for her mind was racing backwards, forwards. She needed to be here, now. Turning on the car radio, she heard a woman talking about climate change. Becca glanced at the passing trees, the golden hedges, the clear blue sky. An autumn day, a strong day, a day when it seemed right and true to be away from worry and world catastrophes and the life she pretended to lead. She wanted to take off her clothes and drive with the windows open. She wanted to feel October nudging against her skin; she wanted to be in this day and this season. And then she wanted night to come down like a soft, warm mist over Jenny and herself.

Michael would laugh if he knew what she was thinking, if he had any idea of these notions. So would Jenny. Her husband and her lover shared a common failing – staidness. It was something Becca didn't like to think about too much. She didn't want there to be any mutual thread between the man she had loved and the woman she loved now.

The voice from the radio had faded and been replaced by music. She pressed her foot on the accelerator and the car quickened between the brown blocks of field. She thought of herself sitting in her music box, wanting to be part of the world outside, the world of shadowy crows and rustling field mice.

But she reminded herself that the possibility of escape should be enough. Perfection was an impossibility and the thought of a life lived alone was terrifying. She would always need someone to be with her, climbing gates.

Michael had been that figure. Jenny was that figure now. And there had been others before them. She had never stepped out of one relationship without having another to step into and she never would. She admired those who lived alone, those like Jenny who were not frightened by a silence that remained indefinitely unbroken.

She knew if Michael ever found out about this affair, he would, after the hurt, sit her down and analyse things, tell her it was only an infantile need to rebel, to shock, to draw attention to herself. He'd forgive her, treating her like the child he thought she was. He'd remind her of the other crazy things she'd done. The tattoo, the frequent changes to her hair colour, the drunken nights in the golf club, all that shit that passed for rebellion in his head.

*

Turning right, she drove onto the first of three short, winding by-roads that would take her to the house. Then left, then right again, along the bank of the wedged field that still awaited the plough. Some day she would walk across that field, sit in the shelter of the oaks, see what was beyond the river and the hill on the opposite bank. Some day, before the year was out.

And then the house was there in the windscreen and she was slowing, stopping, getting out to open the heavy wooden gate that swung easily into the neat, well-kept garden. She allowed the car to roll across the gravel and got out to close the gate again, Jenny's warnings in her ear.

'Animals, passing cattle, strayed horses, anything might come in.'

She parked in the shadow of the lilac. The last exhausted leaf had fallen from it. The day was cooler than she'd expected. Leaves drizzled from the oaks.

The house key was under its usual stone in the flowerbed. Becca opened the door and stepped into the quiet, warm hall. Taking off her jacket, she went slowly up the steep stairs. Easing the bedroom door open, she stepped inside. As she did, a single leaf froze against the window glass and then disappeared into the yard below.

It was a room with which she had fallen in love, a room with wide, high windows that opened onto three different fields. She loved the tidiness, the fact there were places for everything, and everything was in its place. She loved the enormous print of *The Dancers at Bougival* which dominated the wall opposite the bed. And she loved the sleeping figure on the bed.

She crossed silently to the window that overlooked the back garden and the field with the oaks and the river beyond it, gulping in the sweetness of the still, late morning.

'Hi.' The hoarse voice startled her.

She turned. Jenny was watching.

'I didn't hear you come in. Are you here long?'

'No, a minute or two. I'm sorry I woke you.'

'It's fine. I was out late. Dinner. Some old school friends.'

'Snap,' Becca said. 'We're going down to spend the weekend with a friend of mine from art college.'

'Come and sit beside me,' Jenny said, tapping the duvet with her palm. 'It's great to see you.'

Becca sat on the bed and they kissed.

'God, I'm tired,' Jenny said. 'Don't know when I've been so tired. What time is it?'

'Just after ten. It's a lovely day.'

Jenny kissed her again. 'And how are you, my love?'

'Fine, yeah, good.'

'Did you miss me?'

'Yes, I missed you. You know that.'

'What did you miss?'

Becca smiled and rolled over, kissing her each time she spoke.

'I missed your eyes. And your mouth. And your neck. And your breasts. And your flat little belly.'

Jenny laughed. 'And I missed you,' she said. 'I'm sorry I'm not up. I meant to have coffee ready and stuff. It's the bloody drive from Dublin, it was after three when I got back here.'

'And it was a good night?'

'Yes, it was. Better than I expected. We're going to meet again in a couple of weeks.'

Becca nodded.

'Why don't you get into bed?'

'OK.'

She hurried out of her clothes and dived under the duvet.

'Fuck, you're cold,' Jenny said.

'Am I?'

'You are.'

She put her arm around Jenny's shoulder and held her close. 'So what have you been doing?' she asked.

'The usual. Working, looking after the garden, went to see my parents on Tuesday night.'

'How are they?'

'They're well, fine, yes, fine. And you're away for the weekend?'

'Yes. I'm picking Michael up from the half-four train and then driving down to stay with this woman who was in college with me. Beth Harrison, I've probably mentioned her.'

'The half-four train?'

'Yes.'

'So you'll be going at, what? Two?'

Jenny's tone was aggravated, aggravating.

'No, not two. Three, quarter past.'

'I thought you could stay late. If I'd known, I'd have made arrangements to do something tonight.'

'I'm sorry. I'm sure I mentioned this on the phone. You could still get wherever in lots of time. If you leave here at three.'

'Why did you choose today to come down when you knew you'd have to leave early?'

'Because I wanted to see you, because Michael was away, because college is closed today. I said I was sorry.'

Jenny turned away, staring through the window into the empty sky.

'We'd better get up,' she said at last.

'Stay,' Becca said. 'Just for a while. Please.'

'I don't feel like making love.'

'I didn't ask you to,' Becca said.

I wish I could go out and come back in again, she thought. I wish I could open the front door again and come up the stairs and get quietly into bed and kiss her awake.

They lay in silence, the sunlight skewing through the orange trees.

'I'll make some coffee,' Becca said finally, getting out of bed and dressing quickly.

Downstairs, she filled the kettle and took mugs from the shelf. She could hear the shower running above her head. Hating herself for it, she looked over the papers thrown on the kitchen table, thinking – as she always did when they argued – that she might find a letter or photograph that proved there was someone else in Jenny's life. She found nothing.

Which proves nothing, she thought.

For Jenny, the sentimentalities of a relationship, the keepsakes and mementoes, weren't just an irrelevance, they were an annoyance. For Becca, the reminders of tenderness – letters, photographs, an earring – were an essential part of intimacy.

Once she had taken a pen from Jenny's desk and used it whenever she wrote to her. Had Jenny known she'd have been angry, seeing it not as an act of devotion but as an invasion of her privacy.

She spooned coffee into the mugs, poured the water and stirred it. Then she took the two mugs and went back upstairs. Jenny was still in the bathroom.

'Coffee's ready.'

Jenny came into the room, already dressed. Taking her coffee from the bedside locker, she walked to the window.

'Looks cold.'

'It's not bad when you're out.'

'How's Michael?'

'He's fine.'

'Good,' Jenny said. 'I think I'll have some breakfast.' She turned and crossed the room. 'Let's go down.'

Jenny sat at the kitchen table, buttering her toast as Becca watched.

'One of the women at dinner last night has just had twins,' she announced brightly. 'Three kids under five.'

'Sometimes I thought of getting pregnant,' Becca said. 'I thought it would be nice for us, for you and I, to have a baby.'

Jenny laughed out loud. 'That's quite an assumption!'

'I know that. Now.'

She was quiet for a time and when she did speak, her voice was low, almost as if she didn't want to be heard by anyone but herself.

'When I was eighteen or nineteen, I was babysitting for my sister. It was an early December afternoon and I was in her kitchen and I had the baby on my knee. I was watching some workmen in a house across the garden and they turned the lights on in one of the rooms and I started thinking how wonderful Christmas is for children, not the presents and toys and stuff, just the lights, the atmosphere. This feeling ran through me, I don't know how to describe it. I thought of the prospect of some day having my own child. Sometimes that feeling comes back. Or the memory of it.'

She fell silent then, as if she had run out of words.

'If you felt that way, why didn't you have a child with Michael?'

'That's an unkind question,' Becca said.

Jenny shrugged. 'It's an honest question.'

'And mine was an honest answer.'

'The honesty I need is your commitment,' Jenny said. 'Not talk of the past and the future. The present is where I live my life. And you're rarely in it. In spite of everything, after everything, you still have Michael. He's a companion, a constant in your life. I don't have that. All I have is the promise of something, sometime, somewhere. Vagueness. That's the sum total of it. And then you talk about babies and families and expect me to be all soft and pleased.'

'I'm sorry.'

For a moment, Becca thought Jenny was going to laugh, but instead she began to cry. Becca had never seen her cry before and she didn't know what to do. Eventually she put her arms around her and hugged her, stroking her hair as she did. She could think of nothing to say. Jenny pulled away.

'I'm just tired,' she said.

'No. You're right. It's time I did something. Give me a month.'

'You're not going to get a divorce in a month.'

'The divorce isn't everything.'

'That's typical,' Jenny sighed. 'You think things happen

overnight. All I want is to see you more often. To go out together without your being afraid we'll meet someone you know.'

'I could leave and move in here.'

'Oh, Becca.' Jenny was exasperated. 'You've got to sort out your life. Your life. Yours. You've got to sit down and work things out for yourself. I know you love me. And I love you, but this whole thing won't solve itself. Things don't just happen. We make them happen. Or we don't.'

Jenny looked old, Becca thought. Sometimes she considered propositioning younger women, the wives of her husband's friends. Not because she wanted someone younger, but simply to see how they'd react. Simply to have someone closer, someone in her position, to whom she could make love. She wondered if any of them, behind their endless flirting with each other's men, was like her, waiting to be asked or touched.

Sometimes, when a drunken party was ending and she found herself alone with one of the women in a hallway, collecting a coat or a bag, she was tempted to kiss her, just to see her reaction.

'Penny for them?' Jenny asked. She was standing at the sink watching Becca.

'I was just thinking how peaceful it is here,' she offered instead.

'Why did you marry?'

'Loneliness, I suppose.'

'It's not a good reason. Not for anything.'

'No.'

'It's not a good enough reason for us.'

'No.'

'No.'

'You think I'm running to you. For shelter.'

'I think I'm here to give shelter when you need it. You have done it with men. You told me.'

'It must be wonderful to be self-contained, self-certain, smug.'

Jenny laughed. 'If that's what you think.'

'Yes, sometimes that is what I think.' Becca walked to the sink and swirled her coffee down the plughole. 'Could we ever be happy?' she asked.

'That depends.'

'On?' She sensed Jenny shrugging. 'If I promise to be here with you for Christmas?'

'Let's see how things go. I can't be sure I'll be here for Christmas. I might go abroad.'

Becca picked a piece of fluff from her jumper. She felt foolish. She wanted to be away from here. She wanted to be that woman she'd been an hour before, that woman driving in her glass and metal box, a woman cocooned from the world.

'I think I should go,' she said.

'Why?'

'Because I need to.'

'We were going to walk.'

'No, I need to go, Jenny.'

'If that's what you want.'

I could cry, Becca thought. I could make her feel sorry for me. I could get her to take me back to bed. I could get her to make love to me. I could get her to do all the things I dreamed of doing. But I won't.

'I'll ring you next week.'

'You don't have to go,' Jenny said. 'This is silly.'

Becca said nothing. Jenny followed her through the hall and into the yard, stopping to put the latch on the hall door.

Typical, Becca thought, bloody typical. Being locked out would be worse than losing a lover.

She sat into her car and opened the window.

'You don't have to go,' Jenny said again.

'I do.'

'I'll get the gate.'

Becca turned on the engine and waited for the gate to swing clear before easing the car out. Jenny stepped forward.

'You'll ring?'

'Yes.'

'I'm sorry, things are catching up on me.'

'I loved you,' Becca said.

A woman passed, pushing a pram, walking fast, head bent into the low sun. As soon as she'd gone, Becca drove out into the lane and sped away, leaves swirling in her wake. Only when she was well clear of the house did she glance in her mirror, but all she saw was the distant figure of the woman with the pram, melting into the October light.

And then, quite suddenly, she burst out laughing, the peals coming hard and sharp.

1984

All summer, in one corner of the field, sheltered from the road and the knowledge of those who pass without looking, a bed of poppies scorches the headland and the ditch beneath the sloes.

To the children who elbow through the ditch on their way to the river, the blaze of colour is no more than they expect, no more than a glimpse in the corner of the eye. The poppies have always been there, will always be there, forever shining to light their way home, even when the moon is climbing through the eastern sky.

Moths

The man is cutting the grass and it's late in the evening and the mower is running smoothly, the engine purring so steadily he forgets all about it. The low noise is drawn back into the ground and he hears instead the faraway summer sounds of the children, three fields off. The sun has already slid out of the sky, but the air is still bright. He turns at the end of the long lawn and sets off once more. He walks slowly in the wake of the machine, the left-hand wheels overlapping the last line of cutting, the grass spewing neatly out, making another line, more or less parallel with all the other lines that stripe the grass into the shadows of the willow.

He turns again, manhandling the mower into place, and starts back down the garden, away from the house, towards the distant apple trees. The longer grass is damping now, clotting on the wheels, spitting out in wads, forcing the engine to run harder. A light wind carries across the lawn, rippling the dipped branches of the willow, and a moth flies up from the grass. For an instant the insect hesitates, its flight halted by the warm draw of the mower's engine. Its wings work hard, but the engine is sucking it sidewards, pulling it towards the heat. The man tries to turn the mower, but it jams in the heavy grass and still the moth is fluttering like a falling leaf, spiralling towards the hot engine. And then the breeze rises again, for an instant, and lifts the moth clear of the machine as it climbs, flapping, and sweeps towards the shelter of the trees.

The man pulls the mower sharply backwards, out of the long grass, and bends to release the throttle. The engine dies.

The voices of the children are louder now, two fields away. He hears them as he wheels the silent machine towards the tool-shed, the grass gobbing and falling from the rubber tyres, imagines them fording the low river, pulling themselves up the bank, their small hands grasping the low branches of one or other of the oaks.

And he thinks of another summer day, a long time ago.

It was morning. Throwing back the single sheet that covered him, he filled the small kettle and flicked the switch. Outside, he could see the heavy shadow of the house on the sun-dried lawn. The garden was empty. Weeds lay on the parapet of the stone wall, their petals blistered by the early sun. A dead towel hung, rigor-mortised, from the clothesline.

He remembered how the previous night had come down slowly, unnoticed almost, outside this same window, as they sat together, talking about the months she'd been away. Later, he had walked her to the bus stop and then returned to sit in the unlit room, listening to the empty buses returning along the coast road, beguiled by the lingering, musky scent of her hair.

Stepping out of the shower, he moved into the raw light of the hot morning and dressed. Across the road, the huge, empty strand stretched to a distant mirage that was the sea.

At the corner, where the avenue left the coast road, he turned into the shadow of the trees that marked another country, removed from the ocean and the smell of salt. There, the day tasted of the bunched and heavy lilac that dripped across the walls of hidden houses. The remnants of the previous night's fog were tattered rags caught on the branches of giant chestnuts and sycamores. Yellow laburnum powdered the black tar. He glimpsed three children at the other end of the avenue, playing in a garden. Glimpsed and gone again.

He was almost past the biggest of the sycamores when he saw Liz.

'Hello, Paul,' she said in that way she had, putting the emphasis on the first syllable.

'What are you doing here? I thought you were in college.'

'I was, but I met Stephen and got the books from him, so I thought I'd walk over and see you. I don't have to be home till lunchtime. You don't mind, do you?'

'No, no, of course not.'

'Where are you headed?'

'I was walking down to get a bus into town, going to see my sister at the hospital.'

She nodded.

'Do you want to walk with me? You can catch a bus home.'

'All right.'

They turned and, as they did, the railway crossing gates swung closed. He could hear the shuffling racket of a train coming from the coast and then it passed and the gates swung open again.

'I was going to ring you last night.'

'Why didn't you?'

'I thought Isabel might be there.'

'So?' he asked, as though the question deserved an answer.

'I didn't think you'd like to be disturbed. Was she there?'

'Yes, she was.'

'I see.'

'Don't say it like that, Liz. You don't see. You think I asked her over to get her into bed. I didn't. She called to see me, to catch up on the time she's been away. I arrived home and she was sitting on the steps, waiting. Nothing happened.'

He wanted to sound indignant but knew he didn't.

'Would it ever?' she asked sarcastically.

They walked slowly. He took her books and put them under his arm.

Passing a garden, he saw the children he had glimpsed earlier. One of them was red faced, sad eyed.

They turned left, onto a lane that would take them to the main road.

'Are you going out with her?' The question was blunt.

'No, I'm not. She just called to catch up, that's all. Anyway, if I did, would it make any difference? You're the one who wanted to let things go until after the summer. It was your idea to take a break. And there's nothing serious in this. She's a friend. Full stop.'

'Will you go out with her?'

He stopped and sighed. 'I don't know, Liz. Maybe we'll go to the pictures or something. Does it make any difference to you?'

'Of course it does.'

'But it was your idea.'

'Don't keep saying that. I don't like her. She's a bitch. She knew I was going out with you.'

'She thought it was over.'

'I wonder who gave her that idea?'

They walked on in silence. The air was sticky with flowering currant.

'I still love you, Paul.'

'I know,' he said. 'I love you.'

'Then why don't you let her go?'

'I can't just dump her; she's a friend. I owe her that much.'

'You told me she made all the running. You owe me something, too.'

'Why don't we just leave things till the end of the summer?'

'I want it on again. Now.'

'You're just saying that.'

They reached the main road. Taking her hand, he led her through the traffic and crossed to the other path. He kept her hand in his, working his fingers into the familiar space between hers.

'Liz, I love you. I really love you, but we have to leave things till October, for both our sakes. You were right about that.'

'I don't trust her,' Liz said.

'You don't have to,' he said and he kissed her face.

A man stepped from the shadows. He was middle aged, well dressed but unshaven.

'If you were a gentleman you'd walk on the outside of this young lady,' he said. His breath smelled of alcohol and his speech was slurred.

'Maybe I'm not,' Paul laughed.

The man ignored him. 'Young people forget the finer points in life. But they're important. Does he treat you well?' he asked Liz.

'He does,' she said quietly.

'He should. You're a beautiful girl. He should be proud to be seen with you.'

'He is.'

'If I was young again, I'd know how to treat you.'

'He loves me,' Liz said.

'You probably think I'm talking nonsense. My daughters laugh at me, but I had a few girls in my time. I could show you a thing or two. The older the fiddle, the sweeter the tune. Would you like to try a tune on me? Satisfaction guaranteed.'

'Come on,' Paul said, stepping away.

Liz followed, but the drunk blocked her way, staring at her breasts.

'Fuck off,' Paul said, the words exploding into the man's face. 'Fuck off and leave us alone.'

He braced himself to parry the man's blow, but instead the drunk stepped onto the road and wove his way between the passing cars.

'Dirty old bastard,' Paul said.

Liz smiled and took his hand again. 'Thank you,' she said.

They passed the entrance to a building site. A cement lorry backed through the open gate and sluiced its load into the foundation trenches.

'This must be the warmest summer ever.'

'I think last summer was hotter. I remember days when we were emptying wagons of sand. We had to get them done between trains. It was murder. Do you remember, I used to drive up every Wednesday to see the dentist and call out to you afterwards.'

'It's a pity you don't have the car this year.'

'I might be able to get it some weekend. We could go up the mountains.'

'Like the night we went up the Head. That was one of the best nights.'

She put her arm around him and pulled him to her and they kissed again.

He knew that when she talked about the past she was really talking about the future. He thought of his two student days spent in a cold police cell with the broken windowpanes. He thought of her voice coming through the dusk from the street below. And he knew Isabel's voice would never find him in places like that.

They walked on, reaching the bus stop in silence. He flopped down on the warm, scutched grass, his back against the crumbling wall that surrounded the new development of houses. Liz sat beside him. The short shadow of the low wall offered a little shelter from the sun. Above them the sky was a fierce, burnt blue.

A bus trundled around the corner.

'What number is it?'

'Seven.'

'Will you wait for the next one?'

She nodded.

'I think we'll laugh about this in ten years' time,' he said. 'We'll probably be down at the sea with three or four kids and we'll remember it and laugh.'

'Do you really think so?'

'I don't believe we'll lose everything,' he said. 'We couldn't.'

'That's what I hope too,' she said quietly, 'but then I wonder if you just imagine you love me. Or maybe you really are in love with me but that may not be enough. It isn't always enough. I'm not sure it'll ever be right again. Not now.'

'What do you mean, not now?'

'Just that. Today, this morning. Something. I don't know. Just something.' Her voice faded.

'I'm waiting, Liz. I'm waiting for you.'

She shook her head. 'When I was in your flat, on Thursday night, the way you talked about her. I felt that was the end. I almost cried.'

'But you didn't.'

'I kept it for the bus.'

'Why didn't you tell me?'

'Pride, maybe. Would it have made any difference?'

'It does, now that you've told me.'

She shook her head and smiled. 'It's best we leave it, like we decided. Till the summer's end.'

'I didn't know,' he said. 'I'll tell her not to call again.'

'No, no, no, that won't work. Just leave things as they are.'

'But what'll happen?' he asked desperately.

'I don't know,' she said. 'We'll see.'

Another bus swung into sight.

'I'd better get this,' Liz said.

They stood up and she signalled.

'I'll ring you tonight,' he said, handing her the books.

'OK.'

The bus dusted to a halt. Liz stepped onto the platform.

'Will you be in on Sunday night?'

'I'll be in,' she nodded.

'I'll call over. We'll talk.'

The bus pulled away and Liz waved.

*

Inside the shed, he turns on the light and pushes the mower to its corner, damp grass trailing the concrete floor like snail paths. Gathering the scattered clumps, he steps outside again. After the electric light of the shed, the night has fallen suddenly. Even the burnished western sky is ashing into moonlight. His shadow lies before him on the gravel.

And then the children loom, like ghosts among the apple trees, their arms waving, laughing in whispers, drawn towards the lighted doorway of the shed, showing him the wild strawberries aproned in their T-shirts.

'We got them in the River Field, there's loads of them down there.'

Later, much later, he steps outside the back door of the house, into the cooling night. At the corner he stops and listens to the sound from the trees across the road, the methodical sound of old wood slowly creaking.

Ten years, less a few months and a few days. A lot of laughter and bad times to laugh at when they were over. He had always believed that even after ten years there would still be glances he had never seen before. And excitement. But there are none left any more. There's contentment and love for the children, but the fascination is gone. Has been, for a long time.

He walks the length of the drive and leans across the rough, wooden gate, looking out over the dark and silent fields. Long ago, he had theories about all this, but he forgot them, first in the frenzy of love and then in the building and gathering. What has gone from his life? Is it only the newness or is it something more essential? He can't be sure.

He stays at the gate for a long time, staring, not thinking, and then he looks back over his shoulder, at the outline of the house that is home to them. Is love bound up with house, with home, or is it something separate? More questions without answers.

Turning, he crosses the lawn. Tree shadows are sketched on the gable wall. Smoke rises noiseless and straight above the chimney. He rounds the corner and opens the back door.

'They're in bed,' his wife says.

He nods.

'Tea?'

'That'd be nice.'

He stands beside her while she fills the kettle.

'Do you love me?' he asks.

'Of course.'

'Just tell me, just say it.'

'I love you. As much as I've ever loved you. More even.'

He smiles and reaches out his hand, laying it against her cheek and leaving it there, hoping this is enough.

1865

First there were the violets and now there are cowslips and soft primroses which bunch and clump in the early spring grass, carpeting the winding bank that steps from the next field into this. A yellow banner that spreads and quivers down into the drying dykes.

And in the field, the cowslips raise themselves above the bladed grasses, looking out for deep, deep summer and the endless shining days that are just beyond the hill.

Deep Midwinter

I often talked to myself, saying my first name out loud, playing with it, hoping to lose it in other words that sound the same.

'Sarah, smiling, solid, sunshine, simple, sacred, silly, sacrament.'

I'd keep reciting what I used to call my litany while I was tramping the road from Castledermot to Mullaghcreelan Hill, and the closer I drew to home, the louder and harder and angrier the words would get.

'Sick, stupid, stubborn, sack, sorry, shaky, shiver, shite.'

I'd never tell my mother how much I hated my name because she'd have an answer. She'd remind me that I was fortunate to have my health and that the name had been in the family for four generations and that I should consider myself honoured to be carrying it. And hadn't I very little to be complaining about, if that was all that was worrying me? And wouldn't my father turn in his grave if he could hear me and wouldn't I be better employed going about some useful exercise rather than spending hours thinking about things that couldn't and wouldn't and shouldn't be changed and had I fed the hens?

I remember this one day, at Hallahoise, when a breeze brushed a finger of dry clay from the road and Mullaghcreelan Hill rose up clear out of the fields. The afternoon sun was sucking the reds and browns out of the leaves. And I thought to myself, somewhere in the trees was a baker's dozen of houses. I always liked the idea of that baker's dozen of us. The scattered homes. Dowling's and Shaughnessy's and Quigley's and Roche's and an assortment of cousins and aunts and uncles. Thirteen houses but only four families.

I was always a regular visitor to all the houses on the hill.

'She's a wanderer,' my father used to say. 'And a wanderer will never get lost.'

When I was seventeen, my father was killed in a quarry in Wicklow, drawing stone for a farmer, crushed when the cart he was loading collapsed and a ton of rocks came down on his back. The farmer sent a letter of condolence and a five-pound note and we never heard from him again. Not that we wanted his charity. Between my mother's dressmaking and my wages as a barmaid in Rice's of Castledermot, we were never short.

After my father died, I felt obliged, for a time, to be around my mother, but she wrapped herself in a coat of mousy prayer and I stopped trying to comfort her and went back to living my own life.

'He's seven years dead,' I reminded my mother one All Souls' Night. We were making our way to the graveyard. 'I think he's well into heaven by now.'

'Well, I only hope, when your time comes, that there's someone here to remember that you're dead and buried. I hope your soul isn't screaming and crying in pain and torment, waiting for someone to remember you. How would you like that? To be standing at the gates of Purgatory with your face pressed against the bars, needing only a dozen rosaries to get you out and no one here prepared to say them.

Prayer is never wasted. A prayer sent up is a soul released.'

Sometimes, when I was in the church and the choir was singing the Latin hymns, the words lifted me, the way kisses lifted me but higher.

'*Panis angelicus, dat panis coelibus*,' the choir would sing, the sopranos rising above the other voices, and my mind would rise with them.

'*Pater noster qui es in coelis*,' the priest would say and I'd feel a warm breath on my neck, lips on my breast, cold hands thrilling my shoulders.

And the choir sang, '*Tantum ergo sacramentum*,' and someone's mouth was crushing against my belly.

I remember being late getting to work that Christmas Eve. Anne Rice had asked me to collect two geese in Hallahoise and the dirty old bastard of a farmer spent more time chasing me than the geese. All that afternoon and evening Rice's was thronged. And then my mother was in the kitchen, back from seeing my brother in Carlow, urging me to hurry or we'd be late for Midnight Mass.

'Your brother's doing well,' my mother said. We were hurrying down Abbey Street.

I said nothing.

Inside the church, the candles skittered every time the doors opened. The choir gathered in the corner of the gallery. Well-shod women paraded slowly to the front seats, young men in suits by their sides. The organist played the opening bars of a carol and a procession of altar boys led the priest on to the altar. I closed my eyes and heard the voices and I drew breaths from the warmth of the crowded church.

'*Christus natus est nobis: Venite adoremus. Dominus dixit ad me: Filius meus es tu, ego hodie genui te.*'

It was good to cleanse your head, I was thinking, to rid yourself of everything and everyone. But three people wouldn't go away: one my father, the second my brother, the third was William Dunne.

'*Kyrie eleison. Christe eleison. Kyrie eleison.*'

The Lord have mercy on my father, give him rest in peace. The Lord take pity on my brother and forgive him what he did.

'*Gloria in excelsis Deo. Laudamus te. Benedicimus te. Adoramus te. Glorificamus te.*'

'It's Christmas week, Sarah Dowling. It's the best time of the year for telling people things, secrets to total strangers. Tell me everything. Hide nothing.'

All right, I thought, I'll tell you everything. But what do I tell you? That all day today, every time I had the chance, I looked at the chair you sat on the other morning and tried to spirit you back there. That I went over every word you said and tried to ignore the stupid words I said back. That, when you invited me to your party, I didn't even ask where you live.

'*Laetentur caeli, et exsultet terra ante faciem Domini: quoniam venit.*'

Isn't that stupid. You're twenty-four years old now, Sarah Dowling. And your name is Sarah. Not Susan, but Sarah.

'*Benedictus qui venit in nomine Domini.*'

And there's nothing you can do to bring back your father and there's nothing you can do to change what your brother did. So get that into your head. What's dead is dead and what's done is done.

'*Agnus Dei qui tollis peccata mundi: misere nobis.*'

And there's nothing you can do to get William Dunne back to Rice's. And all the screwing up of your eyes in the world won't change anything.

'*In splendoribus sanctorum, ex utero ante luciferum genui te.*'

When the Christmas dinner was over, my mother went to visit the Shaughnessys.

'I'll follow you on,' I told her. 'I'm just going for a walk first.'

I walked up the old road and across the side of Mullaghcreelan Hill. The day was mild and grey but there was no rain. I walked fast across the fields, over the Big Bog and out onto the road at Ballyvass. Smoke was rising from every chimney and candles kissed the early gloom in every window that I passed. When I turned onto the new road, I walked into a veil of drizzle, the soft rain pulling down the last of the light, so that by the time I reached home, my coat and boots were soaked.

That night, when I came back from Quigley's, I tried to remove everyone and everything from my head and take William Dunne into my bed, but I couldn't. I couldn't remember his face, but there were other faces on the bolster beside me. My brother's, the faces of young men I knew in girlhood, men who were dead or had emigrated or married or were still living in hopeless hope like myself.

When the snow came, it wrapped Mullaghcreelan in a gauze. The houses on the hill were protected from the worst of the fall by the trees, but the roads and fields around filled up with snow and then froze over. There were five-foot drifts on the Castledermot road and the bridge at Kilkea was blocked for three days. I couldn't even get the three miles to work.

The Quigley and Lohan and Roche children spent their time making slides at the Gallow's Hill. Sometimes, in the afternoons, I walked the few hundred yards to the sandpit and tobogganed with the children down the steep sides.

Once, in the dead of a night in the second week of January, I got up and dressed and stepped quietly into the freezing false daylight of the brimming moon. I had it in my head to walk some way towards William.

I travelled as quickly as I could. In the shelter of the trees the road was passable, but when I got down to the round bush, the snow was thicker on the ground and rougher and my progress slowed. Nonetheless, I was driven to make for the road down to Kilkea, lurching on the uneven, frosted snow, trying to pick my way between the jagged slabs of ice, cursing and crying every time I slithered and fell.

When I could see, I imagined William Dunne's face between the stripped branches of elder and alder and white thorn that split the edge of the road from the fields beyond.

At Kilkea church I had to stop. I was exhausted and knew I had to turn for home. I could hardly breathe, my energy was gone and I could barely move on the empty road. I wanted to sink down and rest, to curl up against the freezing coldness of the night. I wanted to be back in my own bed, away from the eyes of the open night. But then I fell again and blood came out the side of my hand and the pain of the broken flesh brought me to my senses.

I remember looking ahead, picking my way slowly, stopping to plot a course from one gateway to the next, from one tree to the next tree. I was truly angry. I swore out loud, was glad of the freedom to do it, damning everything and letting off a torrent of abuse into the silent night. And I set my eyes on a tall tree and kept it in view, moving towards it, covering the hundreds of yards painfully. Twice, when the coldness tempted me to move more quickly, I slipped and fell and found it hard to get back on my feet. But step by step I travelled on, and I reached home just after four.

I stumbled into bed and fell asleep shivering and dreamed I was at William's house. I saw the surprise on his face as he lifted his head from his work and recognised me. I saw us lying together under a summer chestnut, shielding our eyes from the sun that was trickling through the heavy leaves.

Another day, months later, I remember leaving the house early. It was half-past four on Holy Saturday morning as I slipped away to walk the seven miles to Athy to see William off on the Dublin train. A morning alive with birdsong and the low sun sprinkling a warm, fresh light over the farmland as I passed.

I got to the railway station half an hour before the train was due and I sat on the low wall outside the stationmaster's house. And then I saw William. He was in a trap, driven by an old man who'd been with him at the Christmas fair in Castledermot.

The minute he glimpsed me, he leapt onto the roadway and came running. He was laughing and his eyes were bright and warm like the sun.

'You've changed your mind, you're coming to the wedding?'

I shook my head and smiled.

The old man brought the trap to a halt beside us.

'Is everything all right?'

'Yes.'

'When did you get here?'

'Ten minutes ago.'

'How did you get here?'

'I walked.'

'From Mullaghcreelan, this morning?'

I nodded and smiled again, but I could feel my eyes filling with tears.

'What's wrong?'

'Nothing,' I said as I both laughed and cried.

The old man stepped away to the other side of the trap, pretending to examine a wheel.

'I don't have to go to this damn wedding,' William said quietly. 'I can stay here.'

'No, no, you go. I just came to see you off. To see you.'

'You walked six miles to see me off?'

'Is that all right?'

William hunkered down beside me and hugged me. 'Anything you do is all right.'

And I knew I couldn't tell him the things I have been carrying.

The old man, George Greene, and myself saw William onto the train and then George drove me home. He left me at the head of the lane and I watched him reversing the trap and setting off down the hill before I turned and prepared a story for my mother.

'Where were you?' she asked before I was in the door. Mrs Quigley was sitting at the table.

'I couldn't sleep this morning, so I went out for a walk. I just lost track of time.'

'Jesus, Mary and Joseph, you had the heart crossways in us,' Mrs Quigley said.

'Why?'

'Michael is out. He got out last night,' my mother said, her voice flat. 'The police was here about eight, and when there was no sign of you, I didn't know what to think.'

'I'll send one of the young lads to the barracks,' Mrs Quigley said. 'To let them know you're back safe and sound.'

My mother hugged me, suddenly, silently.

'I know what you think, girl, about me going to see him, but I was worried for you.'

'I know that.'

'The policeman said we should maybe go up and stay in Quigley's, till they locate him.'

'When did he get out?'

'Sometime in the night.'

I didn't want to sit in Quigley's, worrying. I wanted to go to work. I wanted something to take my mind off things. Eventually my mother agreed. I could stay in Rice's and she'd stay in Quigley's. The Quigley boys would walk me to Castledermot.

'Have you just the one brother?' the younger Quigley boy asked. He was too young to remember Michael.

The older boy hissed at him to shut up.

'It's all right,' I said. 'Just the one.'

'They'll get him and they'll lock him up and they'll throw away the key.'

I had to laugh at him, ten years old, chest puffed out.

Anne Rice told me to work in the kitchen. 'Just in case.'

Her husband was away from the public house for the week.

'You might be happier with a man about the place. I know Michael is a hardy fellow, but he'll have to get past me before he gets near you!'

On Easter Monday afternoon, Michael was arrested in Carlow, a mile from the asylum. He was found wandering on the banks of the river and he put up no fight. I got word at teatime and, when I finished work, I walked to Mullaghcreelan, glad to be free to go my own way again.

William's letter was waiting for me when I got home from work on the Thursday night. My mother left it sitting like a turkey on the table. I ate my supper.

'Are you not going to open that thing?'

'Plenty of time.'

'The souls in Purgatory might not agree.'

Only when my mother finally went to bed did I take the letter to my room.

I leafed through the first pages and smiled at William's descriptions of his cousins and their dresses and their goings-on. I laughed out loud at the things his aunt said about life. But then I turned the page and it seemed I was reading a different letter, about strangers, and the words frightened me.

*

He went away for a couple of days and he found himself at the sea, walking along a beach, and he thought of her. He could think of nothing else. She filled up his days. And, for the first time in a long time, he dreamed of her and then he woke and she was in his mind and he fell asleep, again, and the dream continued.

In the dream, she was leading him across a field, a deep, dry summer meadow where the grass was high and the flowers were wild. She held his hand but she was hurrying ahead, hurrying to be out of the open, urging him to follow her, laughing. She led him into the young trees at the edge of the wood, into the shade, away from prying eyes.

And when they had taken off their clothes, he lay on the ground and she mounted him, as she might a horse. And he lay there, while her legs tightened around him, pushing him up into her. He wanted to bite her breast, to leave a crimson crescent like the harvest moon on her skin, but he didn't. He was a part of the earth, an animal with clay on his back and twigs in his hair. And when he woke from the dream he could still feel the tightness of her legs around him.

For the rest of that day he wanted her. And nothing could ease that longing.

I knew this letter was meant to be a mark of closeness and desire, but all it did was dredge up memories of fear and shame. Memories of one who did bite my breast and belly and neck and face, left me marked for weeks, my skin blue, then green, then black. The crescents left by his mouth grew uglier as they faded. His teeth bit into me. The nails of his boots wore into the flesh of my shins.

*

The following day, another letter arrived from William. Again, it was on the table when I got home from work. I was nearly afraid to open it, but this time it was only news. He told me about a show he'd seen, the clothes people were wearing in Dublin, how little understanding city people had of the country. He told me he missed me and missed home. He told me he'd decided to come back early. He'd see me the following Saturday. He hoped I was well. I was always in his thoughts. He hadn't seen one woman in Dublin who could come close to my beauty. He loved me.

I reached the end of the letter with relief, glad it was ordinary.

I made my mind up. I was set on telling William the things I needed to tell him. I could only hope my courage wouldn't fail me.

It was early the following Saturday afternoon when William arrived at my house. He brought me a dress-length of material. I rolled it out across the table and told him I thought it was beautiful. My mother said she thought it passable.

Afterwards, we drove across by Levitstown and back in a round towards Castledermot. And there, a mile from the village, we stopped and William let the horse graze the long acre while we walked in a field that ran down to the Lerr. It was a sharp field, pointed in its three corners but softened by two big trees that were planted on the bank above the water.

He told me about the wedding. It was only as we turned to walk back to the horse and cart that I broached the subject of Michael's existence and his escape from the asylum.

William asked me how long he'd been in Carlow.

'Seven years.'

'Will he ever come out again, come home?'

'No.'

'I'm sorry to hear it.'

I smiled when he said that, a weak, pale smile.

'You should have told me this before. You can tell me whatever you want to tell me, it won't change anything.'

I stopped dead. 'Sit down,' I said.

We sat on a bank that was thick with primroses, the river trickling away to our right. I took a deep breath and said what I had to say as quickly as I could.

'Your first letter from Dublin frightened me, William. I tore up the last two pages. I could not keep them. It's not that I was shocked. I was afraid.'

'Of what?'

'Of what you expect from me.'

'I don't expect anything.'

'Of course you do, and you have the right to, but I won't be able to be the woman you think I am.'

'What kind of woman is that?'

'The one that takes charge. The one that'll lead you and lie down with you in the fields, the one you talked about in the letter.'

'It was just a letter.'

'Are you saying it wasn't what you'd like, then?'

'Of course it's what I'd like. Isn't it what you'd like, sometimes?'

I looked away, along the length of the empty field. 'I've no idea what I'd like.'

William turned to me, his eyes on a level with my own.

'Tell me what's on your mind,' he said quietly. 'Are you in love with someone else? If that's what you have to say, I'd rather you said it. It won't end our friendship.'

I laughed. A short, spiky laugh.

'I have friends to burn. Everybody is my friend. I'm drowning in friends.'

'Do you want me to go then? I'd leave you alone if that's what you wanted,' William said, his voice like a little whisper. 'Or I'd marry you if you'd agree. Whatever it is, you only have to tell me.'

I could hear someone whistling and then a young man appeared on the bank above, surprised to see us sitting there. As he passed he touched his hat and looked back across his shoulder at us. I remember slumping onto the bank, my head bowed, my body numb and my face, I knew, was the colour of death.

'How could I marry you when I can't even keep your letter?'

'Tell me what's wrong. There'll never be a better time.'

I took a deep breath. 'I used to be all right,' I said. 'I used to knock around with fellows. I loved kissing them. I used to bring them to my secret place in the woods and I loved it. That's all I ever did or let them do, kiss me.'

'If you're going to tell me—'

'You have no notion what I'm going to tell you.'

I stopped. I wished he hadn't interrupted me. I wanted him to keep quiet, just to listen. How was I to make something merciless into something bearable?

'One evening, July of seven years ago, I was up in the woods with a fellow. I walked him to the end of the wood and, when I was coming back, I knew someone was following me but thought nothing of it, and I was halfway home when I heard running. I hadn't even the time to turn before someone grabbed me and put their hand over my mouth, lifted me off my feet and dragged me down through the trees and back to the secret place I had. He ripped my clothes and battered me. He bit me all over my face and neck and body. He kept telling me he used to watch me there with fellows. He said I was a whore. He said I'd go with anyone, do anything for anyone. He called me a cunt and said I deserved anything I got. He raped me. I thought he was going to kill me. I started screaming because I thought I was going to die and he ran off and left me.'

William sat perfectly still. The only sound I could hear was his breathing. The birds, the water, the entirety of the countryside seemed to have gone silent.

'That was my brother, Michael,' I said. 'He was sitting in the kitchen when I got home, like nothing had happened. They took him away. He was committed to Carlow. For good, they said.'

'And it will be.'

'Does it matter?'

I leaned down and picked a primrose from the bank, for no reason beyond having something to do.

'If I was a different woman, if this was seven years ago, I'd have loved your letter. Now it frightens me.'

'I'm sorry.'

I squeezed his hand. 'Is there any hope for me, William? I can't bear my name, my life, my past, nothing.'

'You've told me what happened.'

'Only because I had to.'

'Well, isn't that a start, that you felt you could? Isn't that a change for the better?'

'But I'm always changing. I saw you and I fell for you and then I started wondering if that was right. I walked to Athy to tell you what I've told you now and I said nothing. When you were away, I thought life might be easier without you.'

We were quiet for a while.

'Very few people know what happened to me. My mother, Mrs Quigley, the police, the judge, Michael. And now you.'

'I'm in good company,' he said and his voice was warm.

'Mrs Quigley's all right,' I smiled.

'You don't have to make your mind up now, you know. I can go away, not see you for a month, three months, a year. Whatever you decide.'

We stood up and walked on. He held my hand.

'There's one more thing, one more thing I have to tell.'

'Tell me.'

'I was carrying a child, after he attacked me. I never told my mother. I thought she'd suffered enough. I went to a woman in Maganey.'

William put his arms around me, like a ring around the moon, circling me but hardly touching me.

'Now you know more about me nor any other living soul.'

One by one the evening birds stopped singing as the late sunshine faded across the valley, its shadows creeping along the highest branches.

William asked if he could come and see me again.

'Of course.'

'The things I said, in that letter, I meant them for the best. I meant them to tell you I love you.'

We were standing at the gable of my house. I kissed him. I tried to forget everything, tried to be, for that minute, a woman kissing because I wanted to be kissed. I kissed him until I couldn't breathe any more, until my tongue was sore and my throat was dry.

Letters came.

Once there was a man who was full of words and once there was a woman who was full of beauty. And the man watched her but he couldn't form the words to tell her how beautiful she really was.

And, sometimes, I wondered what it would be like to be born again.

For me, the hot weather meant work. Drinkers packed the long forms outside Rice's like stickybacks. Children played around the pump on the square, dousing their sweaty heads in buckets.

I tried not to think about William. I knew he'd willingly have settled for the kind of marriage where companionship stood in for desire. To have us together in his home, to see me every day, to walk and talk and eat and sleep with me might seem enough, but I knew it couldn't be and that love could turn to hate. The summer was passing and I was surviving. But survival isn't a life and being in love is not the same as being at peace.

One summer day, Constable Mannion arrived at the back door of Rice's public house and asked for me. Anne brought him into the kitchen where I was working.

'You might stay yourself,' he said to her. 'I have bad news.'

I sat at the table. Anne drew the kettle onto the range.

'I just got word from Carlow. Your brother, Michael, was found hanged in the asylum. He took his own life sometime in the night. I'm sorry to be the one to tell you, but I thought you might want to break the news to your mother.'

'Yes,' I said. 'I will.'

'I knew someday it'd come to this,' my mother said. 'It all goes back.'

'Back to what?'

'My father's brother and my own sister, back to that. I only heard them whispering about my uncle. I was a child of seven or eight. But I was the one that found my sister.'

'I never knew you had a sister.'

'She was hanging there, like a doll. Her face was that white, like it'd crack if you put a finger on it.'

My mother was sitting perfectly still, as if her sister's ghost were swinging gently in front of her. And then she roused herself and came and stood behind me and put her hands on my shoulders.

'I never told you because I lived in hope.'

They brought Michael's coffin to the church door. Jimmy Rice persuaded the parish priest to allow the body into the church grounds while Mass was celebrated. Afterwards, they took it to the graveyard, down Keenan's lane in the sunlight. I stood beside my mother and watched while the simple wooden coffin was manoeuvred into the narrow grave. I saw Anne Rice's face across the open hollow and, behind her, in the crowd, was William. And I closed my eyes, listening to the shovels shidding into the clay, listening to the sudden sound of earth on timber and then the softer sound of earth on earth and, finally, the whispering of mourners telling my mother they were sorry for her troubles. Only when my brother was buried and his grave filled in did I open my eyes again.

A week after my brother's burial, William arrived at the house. My mother was in the garden.

She said, 'Sarah's not here,' before he had a chance to speak.

'Is she in Castledermot?'

'She left this for you,' she said, taking my letter from her apron and handing it to him. 'And I'd rather you didn't call here again.'

And then she turned on her heel and went inside, closing the door behind her.

She told me she watched William through the window. He walked back to the mare and led her away.

Dear William,

You have been kind, but my life is in a terrible state. I wish I could talk to you, but where is the point because I cannot find words. If you know a thing about me then you know I would not wish for you to be hurted. I think it's best for us not to see one another for a long time. I would like you to not contact me. If things change I will contact you, but I can't see they will. What you get will be better nor what you lose.

Sarah

*

Sometimes I imagined lines of people, down the generations, swinging gently on the ends of ropes, myself among them. And I saw William standing at a distance, watching. In my imagination there were children about his feet. And I knew he was regretting our marriage and wondering which of the children would step into the noose.

I couldn't sleep. I lost weight, my skin faded. Anne Rice and my mother were forever at me about not eating right.

'I eat enough.'

In November I got sick and was out of work for a week. My mother fussed.

'It's only a cold,' I told her.

'It's not only a cold.'

We were sitting in the kitchen, a roaring fire burning in the grate.

'Now, you listen to me, girl. There's a lot of things I don't see eye to eye with you about, but there's not one of them that's worth your health. I don't know what's going on between you and this fellow from Ballyadams.'

'William is his name,' I told her and I was sharp about it.

'I know his name.'

'Why don't you say it then?'

'Is that your concern, me and him? Is that what has you wasted to skin and bone? Is that why you're sick, you that was never sick a day in your life?'

I shook my head.

'I have nothing again him, any more nor anyone. I just don't like his cut. He reminds me of the man your father worked for, a snoss of learning and no heart behind it. Wait till he finds things out and you won't see his heels for dust.'

*

But he couldn't keep away from me and, deep down, I didn't want him to keep away. He persuaded me that we could find some way of being together. He persuaded me to come to his Christmas party. He tried hard to persuade me that life might work out for us.

My mother made a dress from the length of cloth he'd brought from Dublin. She laid it out on the table and cut it to a pattern and sewed it and bought buttons in Cope and Torry's.

But on the morning of the party, I woke with aches in my arms and hands. I'd hardly slept at all and, when I did, there were dreams.

'I'm not going to the party tonight,' I told my mother.

'Why in God's name not?'

'I don't want to.'

'But the dress is made. And isn't someone collecting you?'

William had arranged for a friend of his from Baltinglass to call for me on his way to Ballyadams.

'He's coming this way anyway. It's not putting him out.'

'It'll put William out.'

It was the first time my mother ever spoke his name.

'I know.'

'Is it something to do with me, because I wouldn't go?' she asked. 'I have no seem on things like that but I'd go if you really wanted me to.'

'I know you would. I just can't myself.'

William's friend from Baltinglass arrived at seven. I opened the door to him. His trap sat on the lane, the lanterns bright in the night.

'You must be Sarah, you fit the picture. I'm Liam Keaveney.'

'I can't go,' I said. 'I'm real sorry I took you out of your way.'

'Am I too early? I can wait.'

'No, it's nothing like that. I just can't go. I have a note here for William, you might give it to him. And I'm sorry.'

I woke to the sound of a horse's hooves on the lane outside. Day was breaking. I drew back the shutter and saw William, his back to the window, shoulders bent, head close to the mare's head. I watched him patting the animal's nose, steam rising from its back, smoking into the half-light between the trees. I pulled on a dress and boots and threw a coat over my shoulders and went to meet him.

The door scraped behind me and the horse snorted and William turned. He was still in his good clothes.

'I'm sorry,' I said and my voice was hoarse. 'I'm lost. I'm sorry if I hurted you.'

William said nothing. A bird sang shyly from the wood. I listened to William's breathing and watched the riderless horse nosing its way along the wet bank and the sight nearly broke my heart. I wanted things to be right. I wanted to be happy, to make William happy. I wanted happiness to come down on all of us, but I wasn't God and I couldn't work miracles.

'Why didn't you come last night?'

'I couldn't.'

'Why not?'

'Because I'm tortured. Tortured by my brother and my grand-uncle and my aunt. If they don't do me wrong, I do them wrong. I feel like I'm the one that's mad. My head is bursting with other people. You want me to marry you and, Jesus knows, I want that, too. I looked out and saw you on the road this morning and I felt such an emptiness. You did all that arranging for me.'

'You have to let some things go or they'll weigh you down and you'll never get up again.'

'I thought I was free. But then I could hardly drag myself out of the bed for work. How could I go to your party?'

'It was only a party. It's not important.'

'How could I marry you? We'd all be locked up before the year was out, we'd drown one another.'

'We wouldn't.'

'Yes, we would. You should go away, save yourself from more pain.'

'Do you think I wouldn't turn and walk away if I could? Do you imagine I got any pleasure out of riding over here this morning? I have no choice. As much as you're confused, I'm confused even more. I love you. I'm not laying down any laws for you. If you want a separate room and a separate bed, you can have them. I'll trade that for the happiness of being with you. That's all I can do.'

'If I could tell you what you want to hear, wouldn't I tell you?'

My mother and myself walked to Midnight Mass in Castledermot, the same way the family had done every Christmas Eve for as long as I could recall. I half remembered my father carrying me to and from the church when I was a happy little girl.

We sat, as we always sat, on the front pew of the organ gallery. The choir sang, the priest spoke, incense drifted up from the nave and finally we were standing for the last carol and the crowds were pushing down the stairs and out into the night.

My mother stopped to talk with some women from the town. I heard the voices floating in the night…must be very lonely for you, with poor Michael…still, aren't you fortunate to have Sarah…lonely old time…God never closes one door…well, have a happy…

On Christmas evening, we went to Quigley's and played cards. When we got back home, the fire was still blazing and we sat up talking.

'You're your father's daughter,' my mother said.

'Why?'

'You have his eyes. You're a Dowling.'

She paused, choosing her words. 'What'll happen between you and William Dunne? Is it settled one way or the other?'

I shook my head.

'I'll say only one thing to you. Don't saddle yourself with other people's cares and don't saddle him with the blame for what Michael done.'

'I never thought I'd see the day you'd be standing by him.'

'And I'm not. For all you know, when he finds out the whole story, he'll up and go.'

'He knows. I told him.'

My mother said nothing for a very long time and when she spoke her voice was low.

'If that's the case, what I think doesn't matter a two-penny damn.'

'William wants me to marry him.'

'Do you love him?'

'Yes.'

'But you have your doubts.'

'It's not that. I'm terrified.'

'Because of what Michael done?'

'That. And what you told me, about your uncle and your sister.'

'I have no answer for what happened with Michael. Some women I seen that were mistreated like that and it never seemed to make a differ afterwards, and with others it changed everything. All you can do is try to put it somewhere that doesn't get disturbed too often. When it comes to my uncle and sister, that was them, it doesn't have to be you.'

'But what if it is?'

'If was never a good fellow.'

Later, my mother came into my room and sat on my bed.

'I faced the same question when it came to marrying your father. My uncle was only twelve year dead and my sister was hardly cold in the ground. I had to take that chance. And I know you're going to say, look at Michael. But I'm going to say, look at yourself. There's not a one in the country wouldn't be proud of having you for a child. Madness comes to an end. Michael is gone and let all bad luck go with him.'

I stood at the gate of Rice's yard for a long time after William left. I was angry. I'd written him a letter that morning, before I came to work. It was in my coat pocket, hanging on the back of Rice's kitchen door. I would have given it to him, if he'd given me the chance. I was damned if things were going to finish like this.

In the end, I went back inside and then, a while afterwards, I saw him stepping in through the kitchen doorway.

When I finished work that night, William got the mare from McDonald's yard and brought it to the square.

'Do you want to sit side-saddle?'

'I do not,' I said and I was laughing. 'Do you think I never sat on a horse before?'

He lifted me onto the saddle and then got up behind me.

'Can I take the reins?' I said.

'Is this a sign of things to come?'

'It might be.'

The mare walked on, away from the lights of the public house, into the black darkness of the Athy Road.

'You're sure, about all this?'

'I'm sure,' I said.

'And are you happy?'

'I'm happy.' I paused. 'We'll make it all work out, won't we?'

'We will, whatever it takes.'

As we got used to the night, a light frost settled on our shoulders. We were two new ghosts on the road to paradise. For this slow, cold night in the Christmas season, everything was right in our lives.

When we reached my mother's house, William slid from the horse and lifted me down and I let him.

'You'll come in, we should tell my mother.'

'I suppose I'd better face the music.'

'I think she'll be happy.'

I started walking towards the door. William stood his ground, searching through the pockets of his great coat.

'What are you foostering for?'

'This.' He put a small box in the palm of my hand.

In the half-light from the kitchen window, I opened the box and saw a locket.

'Happy Christmas,' he said.

I kissed him. 'I didn't…I...'

'You didn't buy me anything.'

'I was going to, but…'

'You thought it might be a waste of money!' he laughed.

'Don't laugh at me, not now.'

'It's just as well I bought two presents then, isn't it?'

He took a ring from his pocket and slid it onto my finger.

I started to giggle and I couldn't stop. The giggling got louder until I was convulsed with laughter. William just stood there, watching, as the door behind me scraped open and the light of the kitchen fell over me, followed by my mother's shadow.

'Jesus, Mary and Joseph, girl, what's after coming over you?'

I looked at my mother's face, solemn as Benediction, and then at the disbelief on William's face and I doubled over, laughter splashing around me.

'Did you get this girl drunk?' my mother said.

I laughed even louder and gripped the door-post for support.

'No,' William said and he was stammering. 'I just brought her home from work.'

Mrs Quigley's face peered over my mother's shoulder.

'I didn't, honest to God,' William said, trying to reassure them both.

'Get in here, you.' My mother was hissing. 'Before the whole hill thinks you've drink on you.'

We struggled into the kitchen and my mother banged the door behind us. I sat at the table, breathing deeply, trying not to look at anyone, knowing the sight of my mother's frown or William's frightened eyes would only set me off again.

'Do you want a cup of water?'

'No, I'm grand. I'm grand. I'm sorry, it was just when William gave me the...'

'Don't start again,' he said.

'Right.'

I breathed as slow and as deep as I could.

'It was just when William gave me this.'

I held the ring up for them to see. It was the first time I'd seen it myself. My mother gasped and Mrs Quigley hurried around the table to examine it.

'Are you giving us a day out?' she asked William.

'I hope so,' he said, looking at me.

Mrs Quigley threw her arms around him.

'I'm delighted for ye. Delighted.'

My mother hugged me.

'I hope ye'll be happy as people that are always glad to come home.'

I saw William watching the two of us, mother and daughter, bent together over the table.

'Give your son-in-law a hug, for God's sake,' Mrs Quigley laughed.

My mother went to him and he put his arms around her.

'You'll be good to her.'

'I will.'

'That's all that matters then.'

*

'Do you know this is my first time on this side of the river? I was never in the Queen's County before.'

We were travelling out of Athy.

'You can make a wish then.'

'I'm dying to see your house.'

William started to sing, softly. 'Mid pleasures and palaces we may roam, be it ever so humble there's no place like home!'

I was surprised at the sweetness of his singing. 'You have a lovely voice.'

The mare turned off the main road.

'She knows the way herself,' William said. 'But then, I suppose she ought to by now.'

My heart was thumping while we were driving down the narrow by-road. We must be close to the house. I wanted to be there and I didn't. What if the place was derelict and overgrown? What if I hated it on sight?

And then the mare swung off the road and onto an avenue lined with beeches and limes and oaks. The trap moved over the level ground and I saw snowdrops and crocuses showered in the rich grass. At the top of the avenue, there was a trellis of overhanging branches and I caught sight of the gable of the house and the low sheds that made a courtyard outside. When we got closer, I could see that the yard was cobbled and clean, the shed doors freshly painted. Smoke was shivering above the slated roof of the house and I could smell the smell of wood in the air. And then I saw George standing in the doorway of the house, beaming. William brought the trap to a stop and George came to meet us.

'You're most welcome to Monascreeban, Ma'am, and I hope we'll see a power of you here from now on.'

'I hope so,' I said. I was smiling, but I thought the old man was very formal.

'I have the kettle boiling inside, you could be doing with tea.'

'Does he live with you?' I whispered as we followed George inside.

William laughed. 'No, he just came down to chaperone you!'

The kitchen table was an exhibition of sandwiches, pastries, cakes, tarts and jams. George lifted a steaming pot of tea from the range and began to pour.

'This is gorgeous,' I said. 'Did you do all this?'

'I did,' George said. And then he left us to the meal.

'I thought he lived here,' I said.

'He lives across the hill. He came to work here when my father was a young man.'

'And did he bake all these?'

'No, he didn't,' William said, laughing. 'He took the cakes out of the tins and sliced them and carried the tarts in from the larder and heated them. But he did wet the tea.'

'But he looked so serious when I asked.'

'You need to look at the corner of his mouth, that gives him away.'

I was upstairs, standing at a window, and I saw William and George crossing the yard immediately below me. A third, much younger man, with a short, limping leg, came from one of the sheds. I watched William hand the two men their wages and the three of them stood chatting.

Turning, I looked around the room again before going back along the landing, opening each door as I went, stepping in, enjoying the quietness about me. I felt welcome in the old house. The roof seemed to bend with a kindly age. The wooden floors were warm and comfortable and the banister of the stairs was smooth from use. I imagined the gentle ghosts of all the years, gliding up and down the steps and through these rooms they knew so well, smiling their welcome to another anxious bride. I knew I could happily live here.

William's footsteps sounded in the hall below. I waited for him at the top of the stairs.

'Well, have you found your bearings?'

'Yes,' I said and I retraced my steps along the landing and stepped into William's room.

'I'd like this to be my room, too. I've decided.'

Through the window, I could see George and the younger man on the brow of a hill field.

'Would you like to see the garden and the orchard?'

'In a minute.'

I turned from the window and kissed William.

'I love you.'

He lifted me off the ground and I buried my face in his shoulder. I felt like I was away from everything that had ever threatened me. I wished William would make love to me there and then, while the world, and every damage it had done me, was far away.

In July, I came to Ballyadams to stay for a weekend.

The sitting-room windows were open onto a burning day and bees were blundering around the room, pounding against a lampshade, battering against a mirror. William and myself worked our way through the long list of wedding invitations to relatives and friends, laughing about how we might pair them at the tables. We had arranged the reception for Rice's. Anne was positive that by using the bar, her dining room and sitting room, she could cater for the numbers we expected. She said she'd lay a board in the yard and, if the weather stayed fine, the dancing could be done outside.

When we had the invitations written, William took me out to the vegetable garden and there, along the picket fence that divided the garden from the field beyond, was a long line of sturdy sunflowers.

'I thought they'd be nice for the wedding, over the church door.'

They were beautiful. I'd never seen their like before.

That evening, we went to Ballintubbert to meet the Merediths for supper.

'I've known them all my life. They're like family to me.'

'Well, you do the talking.'

'I will, for a while. You'll be fine, once you meet them.'

Louise Meredith went out of her way to be friendly and told several stories against William.

'If he ever gets too big for his boots, you come down here and I'll give you lots of ammunition. I know things about him that even he doesn't know I know!'

'And there's nothing you'd like better than to hang me.'

'Correct.'

Later, we sat in the orchard at Monascreeban. Moths were fluttering around the lighted windows of the kitchen and sitting room.

'I love this place,' I told William. 'I hope we always have such peace and quiet.'

A full moon was sliding up from the Blue Field and its glow was lighting the small fruits hanging above us.

'Can I sleep in your bed, with you?' I asked.

'I'd like that.'

I took his hand and led him inside, up the silent stairs and into his bedroom that was washed by the moon.

We undressed slowly, too fierce to acknowledge our nervousness.

I wished he'd say the things he'd said in the Easter letter from Dublin. While the moon was growing in the window, we touched. Our first, hurried touches, uncertain but alive. He tasted my tongue in his mouth, the softness of my breasts against his face. He watched the way my hair fell down around him when I bent to kiss him. I wrapped myself around him. My breast was in his mouth, my teeth stung his skin.

And later the moon was smothered in apple branches, but it was bright enough for him to see my face, to watch my eyes and the shine of my lips. And the thirsty, rusted leaves were whispering and the sky was white and I imagined clay on his back and the smell of grass. The dark bones of the trees were over my shoulder, every branch as sharp as a stone and as soft as my body. I was kissing him, telling him I loved him. And he wanted it to be that way forever. He could wait for as long as I needed, it wouldn't matter how long, once he was sure I loved him.

*

'How will we ever get used to a house or a room or a bed?' I said.

We were lying against a bank on the headland of a meadow that was shimmering with wildflowers. Creamy yellow buttercups; heart-shaped shepherd's-purse, now blue, now white; blazing crimson poppies; clustered purple gentians; giant hogweeds on the headlands; cuckoo flowers; columbine; thistles; Queen Anne's lace all rushing together in a bolt of colour.

'We could let the quarter meadow at home run wild,' William said. 'For days like this.'

'Is it well away from the road?'

'Well away.'

I kissed him.

'Sometimes,' I said, 'I think I'd like another baby, that maybe it'd be some part of forgetting. Do you understand?'

'I think so.'

'I never thought of it as mine, not then. And I'm not sorry for what I did.'

'You don't have to be.'

'Do you mean that?'

'Yes, I mean it.'

'We never talked about this.'

'We can talk, when you're ready to talk.'

'I never went to see Michael in Carlow, in all the time he was there.'

'Why should you?'

'And I never asked after him, when my mother'd come from visiting him. Was that cruel?'

'If it happened to me, I'd want to kill him. I'd want to put him out of my head. I did that with my mother, after she and my father died.'

'Tell me about her,' I said, rolling onto my stomach. I was that close to him that I could see myself in his eyes.

'I was sixteen. My mother had been sick for a long time, with tuberculosis. She was on the mend; at least I thought she was. It was a hot summer, like this, fifty-two. Then one day my father dropped dead in the field. George found him. I begged my mother to get better, not to leave me. But she just gave up. She died three weeks after my father. I put her out of my head, never visited her grave, never prayed for her, nothing. As far as I was concerned, she deserted me. But for George, I'd have had no one. The minute my father died, she surrendered. She had no thought for anyone but him.'

'I have no thought for anyone but you.'

'If we had a child, and if anything happened to me, I'd want you to think of them, to live for them, wouldn't you?'

'This is fierce sad talk.'

'But isn't it good to be able to talk?'

'It is,' I said. 'I think we'll talk an awful lot.'

The night before my wedding, my mother and myself were sitting at the kitchen table, the door still open on the warm night. Daddy long-legs were skittering across the ceiling, moths bobbing about the lamp.

'Will you be lonely here?' I said.

My mother shook her head and smiled. 'Could I ever be lonely with the Quigleys about?'

'You could come and live with us, there's plenty of room.'

'I was born here and I'll die here, with the help of God. This is my place. I wouldn't survive anywhere else. Some people you can uproot and some people only grow in the one spot. This is my spot.'

I nodded.

'And you,' my mother asked, 'will you be happy?'

'I've never been happier.'

'That's everything.'

She walked to the door and looked out on the night and up into the blue sky that was spattered with stars.

'You'll have a beautiful day tomorrow.'

I went and stood with her. The air was full of the liquorice smell of furze.

'I know it's hard for you, Mam, with Michael gone and all. You've been very good to me.'

'And he doesn't haunt you no more?'

'No.'

'Good,' she said and she put her arm around me and drew me to her.

That August morning was everything I ever hoped for. The sun was high and hot in a crystal sky. Mrs Quigley and her daughter Joanna, my bridesmaid, arrived down just after eight and Mrs Quigley set to work on my hair, pinning it up and plaiting it with wildflowers. My mother made tea and then more tea and talked about how times had changed and how her own wedding day had been over and done with before she had time to enjoy it.

'It was just another day.'

'These are different times,' Mrs Quigley said over her shoulder, hairpins gritted between her teeth. 'Today's young ones wouldn't settle for what we settled for and they're right.'

At half past nine, the Shaughnessy, Dowling, Lohan, Roche and Quigley children set off walking for Castledermot. At ten o'clock Paddy Quigley drove his cart down to collect his wife and my mother. As they were leaving, Jimmy Rice was arriving to take Joanna and myself to the church. His trap was garlanded with ribbons and flowers.

'We've plenty of time,' he told me. 'Let the parish priest hold his water.'

As Jimmy turned the trap into the church yard, the first things I saw were the sunflowers, arched over the doorway, their full faces catching the light of the morning sun.

'God, they're beautiful,' Joanna said.

'Aren't they?'

Through the open door of the church, I could see the shadows that were the guests.

Jimmy Rice jumped down and tethered the pony. Then he helped the pair of us from the trap.

'Now,' he said and his face was serious. 'Are you happy enough to face the music?'

'I am.'

'I just wanted to say…to you…to tell you,' he was stammering, 'that there's nothing I'd like better nor for your father to be here this morning, walking you down the aisle. He was a fine man and a good friend to me and I'm honoured that you asked me to take his place. He'd be proud of you. We all are.'

We went to Dublin on our honeymoon. I loved it, but all the time I was dying to get back to Monascreeban for the first time as Mrs Dunne. And when we got there I was dying to get out and help with the first harvest of my married life. And when the harvest was in I was dying for my first Christmas in the house to arrive. Everything was new to me, everything was a celebration, everything was a happiness.

The days leading up to that Christmas party were a mad rush. Louise Meredith was in the house from morning till night. Young Peter Clarke was in constant demand.

We garlanded the whole stairway in ivy; hung twice as many lanterns on the drive, making it bright as day; made candle holders for the branches of the Christmas tree and lit it with three dozen small, red candles. We hung bunches of mistletoe in all the darkest corners and we cleared the kitchen for dancing.

'It's the biggest room, it'll be the best,' I said and I was right.

There were even more people than we expected. William's aunt and three of his cousins travelled from Dublin. Two carts came from Castledermot, loaded down with revellers. Liam Keaveney brought a crowd from Baltinglass.

'I'm glad I didn't have to call for you this year,' he said and he winked at me.

The house sang with laughter and music. The guests danced in the kitchen and some of the hardier souls danced on the avenue outside, the strains of the music carrying through the night, their steps lit by the lanterns hanging above them.

'You'll be careful of the candles on that,' my mother said when she saw the Christmas tree in the hall.

'We will. Are you enjoying yourself?'

'I am.'

When the band broke to eat, one of William's cousins played the piano and there were songs for an hour. William sang 'Black-eyed Susie'. Louise and myself were persuaded to sing a duet and William's aunt had to be encouraged not to sing a third song.

The dancing went on until dawn and it was eight o'clock before the last of the guests disappeared down the frosty avenue.

I remember an afternoon, early in the following autumn.

I saw William before he saw me. He was bent over, a spade in his hand, digging deep into the earth. Then he straightened himself and laid the spade against the ditch. I stood in the shadow of the hawthorns and watched. He put his arms around a six-foot length of granite and hugged it to him, walking it slowly to the edge of the hole he had dug. Then he stopped and I saw his shoulders rise as he breathed deeply before lifting the granite again and easing it down into the hole. The sunlight glimmered off the sweat on his face. Once the pillar was settled, he knelt and packed some stones around its base, straightening it as he did. That done, he collected larger stones from a pile that was lying nearby, then tamped them into place with the head of a lump hammer. I watched all this, saw the gatepost straightened and the base stones beaten into place and then the larger, sharper rocks that would steady it even further. I saw him test it for steadiness, saw him lift the lump hammer and drive it, time and again, against the stones, wedging them into place, strengthening the pillar.

Afterwards, he took the spade and filled the last ten inches of the hole with clay. When he'd finished, he lifted two iron hinges from a bag and screwed them through the holes in the pillar. Only then did he step back to eye the work.

I hesitated, not wanting to break the moment. I could see his pride in a job well done and I was proud for him. And yet I wanted him, wanted to be wrapped around his sweating body, to taste the wetness that was sweltering off his neck on my tongue. And then, as though he sensed someone watching, he turned and saw me, and his eyes brightened and his face was a broad, boyish grin. Rubbing his hands against the sides of his working trousers, he ran along the stubbled headland to meet me, brushing me up into his arms and kissing my face and neck.

'Black-eyed Susie, where did you come from? You look beautiful.'

'You look handsome yourself, Mr Dunne.'

One harvest night, we made love in an open field on the Sycamore Hill. Afterwards, lying awake in bed, William's arm across my belly, I saw the moon again, passing the window, slivered by the trees, and I felt the trickle of seed inside me.

I waited until the end of October, until I was certain, before I told him.

It was a morning when the fog swept up the fields in waves.

'That'll be a good day when it lifts,' William said.

He was standing at the kitchen window.

'Sit down for a second.'

He sighed, came back and sat opposite me at the table.

'I'm pregnant,' I said quietly.

William said nothing.

I went and stood beside him and hugged him to me, burying his face in my apron.

'I wanted to be sure before I told you.'

Still he was silent.

'Two months.' I answered the unasked question. 'I'd put money on the night you brought me up the Sycamore Hill.'

'And are you all right?'

I nodded and a tear dropped off my nose and I laughed, self-consciously.

'We must do things,' William said. 'Can I tell George? We'll drive over and tell your mother. Rices, they'll want to know. And Merediths, I'd like to tell them. And Bridie, I'll send her a telegram.'

He was like a child, the words tumbling out, his face radiant, excitement in his eyes.

'Are you up to that? Are you up to travelling? What would you like to do?'

'We'll do all those things,' I laughed.

'We'll take the day off, and once the fog gets up, we'll go to see your mother.'

Some things you know because you're there when they happen, but being there is not the only way of knowing. Some things you know from what other people say. A lot of the rest of this story comes from the things I heard from others, information I dragged out of George and my mother. Some of it comes from things I read in the newspaper and kept. But it comes, too, from things I know to be true because I either saw them or felt them in my heart.

*

At five o'clock, on the morning of December 20th, 1867, James Lawlor left his house at Hallahoise, walking with a horse and cart towards Athy. There had been rain in the night but the morning was overcast and dry. A few hundred yards from his house he met Michael Kinsella, with his mule and cart. The pair of them were travelling to the collieries at Rossmore.

They walked together, each man leading his animal, past the back lane to Bushfield farm and into the shade where the new road ran beside Mullaghcreelan wood. They had reached the main entrance to Bushfield when Kinsella's mule reared and bucked, turning before he could control him, and galloping thirty yards back the road he had come. Kinsella ran after the animal and, at the same time, James Lawlor's mare frightened and snorted. James caught her by the head collar and pulled her across the road, away from the narrow footpath that runs under the shelter of the trees. When he turned, he saw Kinsella leading the mule back towards him.

'Easy, girl, easy,' Lawlor said quietly. 'You're all right. Easy there.'

Then, as he turned to lead her from the other side, he saw a black lump lying in the ditch. It was still dark and for a minute he thought a boulder had fallen from a cart, but when he crossed the road, he saw the body of a man.

When I woke it was still dark. William wasn't in bed. I decided he'd fallen asleep in the kitchen, so I pulled on my coat and went downstairs. The lamp was still burning in the hallway and the kitchen was warm, but there was no sign of William.

I raked the fire and put the kettle on the range. I glanced at the clock. It was twenty past five. I thought he'd probably got held up and stayed in Rice's. The night had been wet in Ballyadams, so God alone knew what the weather had been like in Castledermot. I took the lamp and went through to look at the work Louise and myself had done in the sitting room.

Enormous red and white bows, sprigged with holly and ivy, were hanging high on the walls of the room. This morning, when young Peter arrived, we'd bring the Christmas tree from the hay-shed and put it in the hall.

I was wandering back into the kitchen when I heard the clop of a horse's hooves on the cobbles outside. William was home. I hurried through the back hall and opened the door onto the yard. The mare came towards me, shaking her head and snorting.

'William,' I shouted, and then louder. 'William.'

The mare backed away from me, clopped across the yard and stood at the stable wall. Taking a lamp from the kitchen, I crossed the cold, damp yard. The stable door was locked from the outside, so I pulled back the heavy bolt and stepped inside. The mare lifted and dropped her hooves on the cobbles.

Coming back out, I tied the mare's reins to a ring on the wall and ran down the avenue. I wanted to shout William's name, but I was afraid. At the gate, I stopped and looked up and down the road, but it was too dark to see more than a few yards. Turning, I hurried back up the avenue. I heard the mare's hooves on the stones and then a voice.

'Eaaasy there, girl, eaaasy. Eaaasy. It's all right.'

Lifting the lamp, I saw George's smiling face.

*

James Lawlor and Michael Kinsella drove back to Castledermot barracks. They called Constable Mannion and the three sub-constables that were on duty and, together, they travelled back to Mullaghcreelan. The body was exactly as they'd left it. Mannion examined the scene, writing the details in his notebook.

Body of man. Lying on back. Dead. Body touching curb-stone. Pilot coat thrown over him. Body stripped but for socks, shirt and bloody kerchief on neck.

His examination done, he walked slowly along the path and found a pair of brown woollen gloves and a pair of boots nearby and, three yards further on, a blackthorn stick. Retracing his steps, he made a note that the soles of the socks were dry.

Day was breaking by then and Mannion bent to look, again, at the dead man's face. He didn't recognise him. He called the other men to him.

'Does any of you know this fellow?'

No one did.

Standing, he tapped one of his men on the shoulder.

'You stay here with the body. And you,' he pointed to a second man, 'get on into Athy and get Sub-Inspector Webb out here. I'll go back to the barracks, see if we can find out who he is. I'll send Dr Clayton to certify the death.'

At first light, George Greene rounded up the neighbours and they searched the road, back from Ballyadams, for two miles without finding anything. When Louise Meredith arrived she and I sat in the kitchen. The women who had come to cook for the party worked around us. Every so often, I'd spring up from the table and walk into the yard and stand, staring down the avenue, fully expecting to see William walking up from the road with George, laughing, waving to me, hurrying to explain how the mare had thrown him and bolted, how he'd had to walk from Athy. But then Louise would come and put her arm around me and walk me back inside again.

By the time Sub-Inspector Webb arrived at Bushfield, Mannion had made extensive enquiries about the identity of the dead man.

'There's no one from the district reported missing.'

'It's early in the day,' Webb said. 'Most people are still sleeping off the effects of the fair. I suggest we get the body out of here. Is there anywhere nearby we can take it?'

'There's an empty cottage just down the road,' Mannion said.

'Right, have him taken there.'

'Yes, Sir.'

'Good.'

'Lord Kildare has some of his men out searching the hill and the fields.'

'A lot of good that'll do, but if it keeps him happy...'

Just before midday, Sub-Inspector Gibbons arrived at Monascreeban and talked to George and myself. He assured us that his men would organise a proper search and that there probably wasn't anything to worry about. I could see him thinking that William was another carouser, lying in some ditch somewhere, too drunk to get home, that the horse had more sense.

*

Sub-Inspector Webb had just escorted the body to the deserted cottage when one of the constables came looking for him.

'You're wanted up the wood, sir. The search party found something.'

He followed the man through the forest and came to a group standing around a tree near the gravel pit. Kneeling down, he saw blood-soaked corduroy trousers. The bottoms of the legs were still wet with mud. Searching about, he discovered a tweed coat stuffed under a gorse bush. The breast and sleeves of the coat were blood stained. Webb lifted the jacket from the ground and searched the pockets. There were several pieces of paper in them. One was a bill from Peppard and Sons, made out to William Dunne of Monascreeban. It was dated December 11th, 1867. The bill was marked paid.

Webb took the clothes back down to the cabin where the body lay.

'Right, I think we know our man,' he said. 'William Dunne of Monascreeban, Ballyadams. Now we need identification.'

'His mother-in-law lives on the hill,' Mannion said.

Webb nodded.

'I don't think this is a sight she'd like to see. Anyway, the less she knows, the better. Maybe she knows it all. Find someone else. And get one of your men to go into Athy, tell him to make contact with Ballylinan barracks, Monascreeban is their area.'

'He's not coming home, is he?'

George and I were standing in the sitting room. Darkness was falling.

'I don't know,' the old man said.

The fading light caught a tear on his face.

'I'm sorry, George.'

Tom Dunne, a cart-driver from Athy, stopped at Bushfield, where a crowd had gathered outside an old cottage. It was half past four in the afternoon and darkness had fallen.

'What's going on?' Dunne asked

'Someone murdered.'

'Who?'

'Jasus knows!'

At that moment, Webb stepped out of the cottage and saw Dunne in the light of a lantern. He knew him from Athy.

'Dunne, a minute,' he called.

Dunne pushed his way through the crowd.

'You live out the Ballylinan end of the town?'

'I do.'

'Would you, by any chance, be related to a William Dunne, from Monascreeban?'

'No relation,' Dunne said. 'But I know him, as I often draw stuff from the railway for him.'

'You'd know him to see then?'

'Of course.'

'Come with me.'

Webb led Dunne into the cottage, where a body was laid out on an old table, a coat thrown over it.

Webb took a candle from the windowsill. Pulling back the coat, he held it close to the dead man's face.

'Do you know this person?' he asked.

Dunne looked at the face. The hair was matted and blood stained, blue and green bruises colouring the ashy skin. The candlelight glimmered on the dead man's top teeth, which were driven into his lower lip. One side of his head was a raw red.

'That's William Dunne.'

'You're sure?'

'Sorry to say, I am.'

Webb turned to Mannion.

'Put two men on duty here for the night, with the body. Then when you get back to Castledermot, telegraph the coroner and get a jury together for an inquest, tomorrow.'

I knew the instant George stepped into the kitchen. The old man, always so detached and upright, put his arms around me and held me to him, his body melting against my own.

'Where did they find him?'

'Mullaghcreelan.'

'And Peter?'

'No word on him, Ma'am.'

A constable from Ballylinan called on George early on the Saturday morning. He was needed for the inquest, he told him.

'Do you think, would his wife want to be there?' the young constable asked.

George shook his head.

'Right.'

'Where will I find young Clarke's family?'

'The house below the church.'

'Right.'

'There's no word on him either?'

'No word at all.'

*

George walked over to Monascreeban. The house was quiet. My mother was in the kitchen.

'I have to go to Mullaghcreelan, for the inquest,' George told her. 'I just wanted to let the missus know.'

'She's asleep. I'll tell her, when she wakes.'

'The policeman was asking if she'd want to go. I said no.'

'You were right.'

'I'll take the trap. We'll have to make arrangements. I thought we should bring him back home, back here.'

In Athy, he stopped at Maher's, the undertakers, and arranged for a coffin and hearse to be sent to Mullaghcreelan.

At the cottage, George went to look at William's body. He barely recognised the man he had known since childhood. His skin was white and loose. His fingers and toes black with blood. His clear eyes were two pennies.

The coroner, Dr Carter, swore in a jury of twelve local men on the Saturday afternoon, December 21st. They sat on forms against one wall of the derelict cottage. William's body lay by the other. The afternoon was cold but the crowded room was warm.

George sat with Richard Beahan, a neighbour from Ballyadams who had been at the fair in Castledermot and seen William there. They listened while James Lawlor described how himself and Michael Kinsella had found the body. And then George was called. He told of being at the fair with William and of selling the cattle and of leaving in the afternoon.

'And your master was carrying a great deal of money?'

'Yes, Sir.'

'Do you know exactly how much?'

'Hundreds of pounds.'

The coroner produced the clothes that had been found at the sandpit.

'Did you see anyone in Mr Dunne's company who wore clothes like these?'

'They look to be Mr Dunne's clothes, Sir.'

'And was Mr Dunne travelling alone?'

'No, Sir, Peter Clarke should've been with him.'

'Who is this Peter Clarke?'

'A young chap that works with us on the farm.'

The procession of witnesses went on.

Stephen Dowling, who was working in Rice's that day, said he had been talking to Peter Clarke.

'He was wearing a blazing red jacket, sir. You couldn't miss it.'

And then Richard Beahan was called.

Sub-Inspector Webb interrupted.

'A question may arise here. The question is this. There was a stick found, and I took down a written description of a stick seen by Beahan with a certain party, before Beahan saw the stick with me.'

'Go on,' the coroner said.

'I took down a description of the stick Mr Beahan saw with that certain party. He described it, and I quote, as: "A blackthorn stick, small knob at the head, rough to the end where the branches were cut off, bark peeled at about three inches from the end." Furthermore, Mr Beahan told me and, again, I quote: "That stick, to the best of my belief,

I saw with Peter Clarke in Castledermot on the fair day, Thursday last."'

'Well, Mr Beahan,' the coroner asked, 'is this the case?'

'It is.'

'You're sure?'

'Certain.'

'And the clothes worn by Clarke?'

'I remarked on his jacket. You couldn't miss it, not if you were blind.'

'If there are any other witnesses who should be called, we can adjourn the inquest to any other day that suits the jury,' the coroner said.

'I believe I've proved sufficient to enable the jury to agree their verdict,' Webb said sharply.

He wanted the case finished so he could get about the business of catching Peter Clarke. As far as he was concerned, any postponement would only give Clarke more time to make good his escape.

'Well?' the coroner turned to the jury foreman.

'The jury thinks there's evidence enough.'

'Very well,' he said and he paused and walked to the window. The winter light caught the side of his face. When he turned, he faced the twelve men seated along the wall.

'Gentlemen of the jury, although it is my pleasing duty to congratulate you on the generally peaceful, quiet and tranquil nature of the neighbourhood in which you have the happiness to reside, yet it is unfortunate to think that in the very best regulated society it is sometimes our duty to investigate cases like the present, where a stranger in the neighbourhood comes to his death in the most mysterious manner and, from the evidence before us, by the hands of lawless violence. The clear identification of the body as that of William Dunne of Ballyadams in the Queen's County is one of the most important steps to be taken by the coroner's jury. The next part of the evidence is that the man attended the fair at Castledermot on Thursday, the nineteenth of the present month. We have heard from witnesses who saw him there. We have heard of the discovery of the body by James Lawlor. You have had almost conclusive proof of Clarke having the stick at the fair. And the evidence of the medical gentlemen goes to show that death was caused by concussion to the brain brought on by external violence. Gentlemen, you have the substance of the evidence in the few remarks I felt it my duty to make to you. If, from the evidence, you are of the opinion, judging from the stick and other matters, I think you can have little difficulty in coming to the conclusion that the deceased was wilfully murdered – not, unfortunately, by some person or persons unknown, but, so far as the evidence has gone, it throws suspicion upon the aforementioned Peter Clarke. Provided this man is taken, you will send him before the Grand Jury, who will deal with him according to the evidence produced before them. This is only a preliminary enquiry and your minds should not be burdened by any qualms as you are perfectly justified in sending a person for trial who is strongly suspected, without that proof of guilt and identification which constitutes a murderer.'

While the coffin was placed in the hearse, Richard Beahan suggested that he would ride ahead and let us know the time at which the cortege would arrive.

'That'd be a great help,' George said. 'What time do you think we'll be there?'

The undertaker took his watch from his pocket and looked at it.

'Say, half-eight, there or thereabouts.'

It was almost nine o'clock when William's body came home. By the time the hearse turned onto the avenue of the house, there were hundreds of people behind it. I insisted that the lanterns be hung and lit on the avenue and they threw the shadows of the mourners like crooked apparitions among the tree trunks.

Just before nine, I heard the muffled voices praying on the road at the foot of the avenue. The lantern light fell on the horses' plumes and on the roof of the hearse. It glinted off the glass walls and whitened the faces of the mourners shuffling between the trees.

At half past four the following morning, I crept downstairs. The hall lamp was low and the candlelight from the sitting room, where William's coffin rested, tottered and faltered through the open doorway. From the kitchen, I could hear soft voices. I paused at the sitting room door and looked inside. George and Louise sat at either side of the coffin.

As soon as they saw me, they stood up.

'I have to see him, George. I'll never forgive myself if I don't.'

The tone of my voice told him there was no point in arguing.

'All right, Ma'am. Miss Meredith, maybe you should step outside.'

'I'd like to see him myself, George. If you don't mind, Sarah.'

'He'd want the three of us to be here.'

Stepping forward, George unscrewed the loose fasteners and quietly removed the coffin lid. For a second, I thought there had been a mistake. The man in the coffin looked nothing like William. The side of his face was raw and battered, the skin a gruesome rainbow of greens and blues and blacks, and his mouth was set in a crooked, silent howl. George took my arm and guided me to the other side of the coffin. From there, I could see some semblance of the face I'd loved and kissed, but it was only that, a vague likeness. I leaned in and brushed my lips against the skin that was cold and polished.

'It's not him, is it, George?'

'No, Ma'am, it's not. But he's about the place.'

Ballyadams church was thronged. The parish priest droned the opening prayers of the Mass. I could smell the wood from William's coffin, mixed with the smell of burning candles and incense. I counted the arches on the altar. Six. And then the small crosses cut from the marble on each side of the tabernacle spire. Eight on the left, eight on the right. I watched how the cold light washed the marble. I hate marble, hate its grimness.

I thought of a warm spring evening, in the middle of the previous April, when William and I were sitting on the back step of the house.

My eyes wandered to the half-timbered walls, counting the boards. I thought about the child inside me and I thought about Christmas. I thought of how different this morning might have been. And then, George was stepping out of the pew and helping other men to lift the coffin and I was following it down the aisle.

Outside, the day was cold and grey. The pallbearers set off walking, down the road from the church. There was a delay while the coffin was lifted over a stile that opened onto the old Mass path. I glanced down the road to a barn that sat on the edge of a field and remembered an afternoon when we'd sheltered there from rain.

And then we were moving again, following William between the Island Fields, along the Path Field. There'd be no hearse on this last journey. Instead, relays of local men took it in turns to carry the coffin.

Across another stile and into the Five Acres. The breeze was biting there, coming down off the hills. And then we were back on a steep, winding road that took us up to Clopook graveyard. The priest stepped forward, standing at the head of the grave. Men lifted the coffin onto straps and I watched them take the weight.

'*Anima ejus et animae omnium fidelium defunctorum per misericordiam Dei requiescant in pace*.'

'Amen.'

Afterwards, I could only remember facts and places and names. I had no recollection of feelings. There was an almost endless file of visitors to the house. Many I hardly knew. All I was glad to see.

In early February, a man said to fit Peter Clarke's description was arrested in Monasterevin.

'They think they have him,' George told me.

'I see,' I said, matter of factly.

'I thought I ought to tell you. In case.'

'How will you feel, George, if it's him?'

The old man shrugged and said nothing.

'Why would he kill William? Just for money?'

'That's not the chap I thought I knew.'

I was silent for a while. 'Have you been to see Peter's family?'

He nodded.

'I'm glad. I've thought of it myself.'

'In a while you can,' George said. 'Not yet.'

The man in Monasterevin barracks was a tramp. The constable from Ballylinan wondered how the police there could have mistaken him for Clarke; he looked nothing like him. He was smaller, older, almost bald. Missing two fingers on his left hand, he walked without a trace of a limp.

I gave birth to a baby girl on the fifth of May, 1868. Five days later, I wrapped her against the evening air and took her up the Sycamore Hill. The early summer night was settling slowly across the countryside.

I told her this was her place. I told her about her father and I wished her happiness.

1987

The passing cyclist has no idea what it is that makes him look into the field. Nor is he sure what it is that makes him notice the small child wandering through the summer grass. The cyclist passes this field four times a day, five days a week, and he seldom gives it a glance, particularly not at seven in the morning.

But something catches his attention and he sees the toddler, her pale face, the way she stumbles, the lost look that doesn't fit, that doesn't belong here.

The birds are singing their early songs, the sun has been in the sky for a couple of hours, but the man feels a sudden coldness and knows, instinctively, that everything is wrong.

Friends

I was a fat kid. Does that change the way you think about me? I'm not asking if it makes you more sympathetic; sympathy doesn't come into it, sympathy isn't at issue here, as you'll be the first to tell me. It doesn't raise its head inside these four walls. But while you're sitting there with your bellies hanging over your belts, do you secretly have just the tiniest inkling of regard for me? Do you admire me the way you admire winter swimmers, from a distance, as people who've done something you'd like to have done but never could? Do you secretly envy the way I got myself together, slimmed down through my adolescent years, kept my weight under control by eating sensibly? You assume it's easier for me to control the middle-age spread, don't you, just because I have twenty-five years of careful eating behind me? Secretly you do. It's all about secrets in here, isn't it? My little secrets and your little secrets, except, of course, that I may not have the secret you want me to have, the one that would make your job that much easier.

I'll bet you were surprised when you discovered I sell ice cream for a living. Surprised that I could walk that line between selling and eating without ever – and I mean ever – crossing over. That's not something that comes easily to you, is it? Walking the line between the things you wish for and the temptations that make you surrender.

Sorry, maybe I'm doing you a disservice. Perhaps, deep down, you're not making too many assumptions because you don't know me, don't really want to know me and couldn't care less about what makes me tick. Perhaps all this is surface stuff. I mean, why should you care? I sell ice cream to the people on the streets, all kinds of streets, your street, your cul-de-sacs.

There's a thing! Have you noticed how the phrase 'cul-de-sac' was once used to describe a place like the dive I grew up in. A dirty phrase that meant the bottom of an empty coal sack on a wet Saturday. Now it's pronounced with all the Frenchness people can muster. Now it's OK, it's chic, it's cool.

But I digress. You want me to talk about her.

She's not chic, she doesn't dress to please or tease. She dresses for herself, to feel good, to be comfortable. That's how she dresses. It'd be easy to get sucked into lumping her with the rest, just because she lives on the kind of street they live on. That's the danger, isn't it, lumping people together, making assumptions? At a guess, I'd say you've made assumptions about me. Now, I don't want to tell you your job, but I don't think that's a healthy approach. We need to keep our minds open.

I didn't make any assumptions about her. That's not something I do. I don't want to blow my own trumpet, but I pride myself on my openness to people. It's my belief that we can only live in the hope that people forgive us our trespasses as we forgive those who trespass against us.

That line always appealed to me. Give us this day our daily bread, I could take or leave, never rang any bells, maybe because of the food connotation. And lead us not into temptation, well that's crazy, as we need temptation to keep our lives vaguely interesting; temptation is where life is happening; temptation is what keeps you in a job. But the forgiveness and trespass bit, that bit I like.

If, on top of being a fat kid, I tell you I was a troubled soul in my younger days, how do you feel about that? It's my experience that people, ordinary people, split, more or less, sixty/forty against the fat kids, but when it comes to troubled youngsters, it's always trouble was means trouble is.

But if I throw in the fact that I come from a decent, upright, hardworking family, good-living brothers and a sister, does that help redress the balance? I'm talking siblings here, not parents. Parents are random. Think about it. Take two people who, for some obscure reason, believe they suit one another, throw them together in a steamy car or, if you want, in a marriage bed and you never know what you're going to get. And nor do they. But that's only the start of it. Throw in their ability, their need, even, to interfere in their kids' lives and you have a lethal cocktail. They'll give you all the usual excuses – it's for his own good, you can't put an old head on young shoulders, if I'd had someone to advise me when I was his age. What they really mean is – if I screwed up my own life for you, you can carry some of the load yourself. They'll never say it out straight, but you get to know it and, later on, you have to laugh about it, don't you?

But brothers and a sister are another matter, they're the leaven in the mixture. If the recipe comes out more or less OK across the family cake, then the chances are that the slightly wild one will come round. That's my belief. I know I did. I wasn't the fat and lonely only kid. I wasn't the spoilt, overfed brat. I was just a kid. That's all.

If I could tell you I had a happy marriage and a doting wife, you'd probably be a little more impressed. You might look again at your assumptions, at the evidence of your bias, at me. But I can't. Unfortunately, I can't. Can't produce a wife. I lived with a woman once, for three years, but we got tired of arguing; neither one of us had the stomach for it.

I can offer you the evidence of a nice house, no porn magazines stashed anywhere, no dubious stuff on my computer, a reasonable living in the ice cream business, self-education, hard work as proof, if it's proof you want, that I'm an ordinary, decent, upright, law-abiding citizen. But that's not what you want, is it?

And then there's the little matter of what you call my obsession with her. I prefer to call it a fascination. The word 'obsession' has all kinds of connotations. It gets us all off on the wrong foot, doesn't it? So, I'd like to call it my fascination.

It started quite unintentionally, but I realised, very quickly, that it had a consequence in my life. It was an important matter. Even you must understand that; there must have been a time when someone captivated you. Maybe you're still a captive, maybe you still find times and places for your fascinations. You have the ideal job for it, don't you – power, two-way mirrors, long hours, unpredictable situations – to help you pull the wool over your wives' eyes. I see your rings and I see your opportunities.

Isn't it interesting the way fat fingers grow over rings, swallow them the way fat mouths swallow big dollops of food? I've always found that fascinating.

Anyway, you don't want to hear about yourselves, do you? You know all about yourselves. You know yourselves better than most. You don't want an ice cream seller rooting around inside your minds. That wouldn't be fair. That's your business. You want to know about me and her and the matter in hand.

The problem is, it wasn't just me and her. It's never a question of just two people in any relationship. Look at us, four of us sitting here around a table. Coffee cups. Shooting the breeze. But that's just surface stuff, there's so much more going on. And it was the same with us. If it had been just the pair of us, things would've been different. Or even the three of us, her and me and the little girl; that would've been OK, too. I'd happily have settled for that. But children have fathers and men tend not to want someone else in their patch even when they've deserted the patch. What we want and what others think we should have is seldom the same thing.

Actually, the kid was with her the first day I saw her and I didn't mind. That didn't throw me, not one iota. It was one of those days, late spring, when I knew I wasn't going to make any money. It was pissing rain. I remember drinking a cup of coffee at the window, looking out across the garden, watching the trees dripping. The front ring had burned out on the cooker that morning. I'd put the kettle on and gone off to have a shower and come back to find the kettle still cold. Strange the way details blister themselves into your memory, like you have a sense for the things you believe you'll want or need to remember. A sense of occasion, I suppose, even before the occasion happens.

I thought about staying at home, but I'd already been working three weeks at that stage and one of the tricks of the ice cream van trade is that, once the season starts, you never miss a day, hail or rain. People get to know the routine and that's how you build your business. Miss a day and you confuse them. Exact opposite to the way you guys work. Anyway, I did all the usual stuff, mixed the mix, filled the machines, checked the cordial bottles, ran the jingles. I do all that in the garage, don't want to disturb the neighbours with yet another blast of 'London Bridge Is Falling Down'.

It was just an ordinary, miserable April day, the kind of day you survive in the hope of better times. Your job must be like that a lot of the time. You must survive the bad days in the hope that one day, some day, people will hit the straight and narrow and not feel the inclination to veer into the undergrowth.

But that's all in the future or the past, you don't want to hear all that. Or maybe you do, maybe you make it all add up.

Anyway, I did my route that morning, drove as slow as I always drive. No one buying, hardly anyone on the streets, a bit of sun, and then the rain coming down like nails, and then another twenty minutes of an excuse for sunshine. It was sunny when I saw her. She was pushing the buggy across the open ground at the end of her road and then the skies opened and she was drenched before she could get under a tree. I drove beside her and she smiled at me and turned her eyes to heaven. I opened the window. Will I play a song to cheer you up, I said.

Do that, she said, and then she started running along the path, pushing the buggy in front of her and the rain was bucketing down and she was soaked. I stuck the 'Raindrops keep falling' jingle in the tape deck. She turned in at her gate and I saw her fumbling in her purse for a key and then she was opening the door. I stopped at the gate.

Would you like an ice cream? I said.

She started laughing.

No, she said, but thanks for the song, it's very appropriate.

And then she was lifting the kid out of the buggy, into the hall, and her shirt was stretched wet across her back and I could see her skin through it.

That was the start of it. If you want me to put a finger on a time and a place, that was it, the minute I saw her lifting the child into the hall, the colour of her skin through the wet shirt, the arch of her back, the curve of her shoulders, her hair plastered against her face.

I fell in love with her, there and then. Something about the way she moved. The way she said appropriate. There was something warm about it, something refined and yet friendly, inviting.

The problem is, it's a waste of my time telling you all this because you just want the sordid bits. The things you'd like to believe happened. You imagine there's a who, what, where and when that I can give you. Reasons don't really interest you. And do you know why that is? It's because you lack imagination. You have a limited view and a limited understanding. That's why you miss the things you might otherwise see. That's why you can only react, because you have an underdeveloped imaginative capability. You have it down there, for plodding, but you don't have it up here. Your biggest mistake is in assuming that people are stupid when the opposite is so often the case.

It's all this us and them stuff with you and that's real enough. But you're the ones who've made it that way. Your presumption has put us on the other side of the fence and we'll always be there, out of reach, beyond your comprehension. You think, by bringing me in here, that you're reaching some kind of conclusion.

Not so, my friends.

You're the ones who said that, about being my friends, that you want to help me, that you're here to listen. Trying to make a virtue of your weakness. If you're good listeners it's only because you have nothing to say, no perception of what you're dealing with or if you're dealing with anything at all. That's the sad and pitiable part of all this.

Anyway.

Do you remember that Joni Mitchell song, 'The Hissing of Summer Lawns'? Unlikely. Probably not your kind of music. Not that it matters. I mention it only to bring the summer weather to mind. Nor do we ever truly get that kind of thing here. The odd hose attached to one of those water-driven revolving sprays, but nothing like you get in the States. Have you been to the States? Actually, don't answer that because I don't really need to know and this is all about need to know, isn't it? I'm not boring you, am I? I certainly hope not.

You did ask me to tell you everything, but that's a tall order. What I believe to be important may not seem so to you. And the things you imagine to be important may be of little or no consequence to me. It's a question of perspective and that is not something we share, believe you me. I recognised that fact the moment we sat down together.

And do you know why? Because you want to clear things up, nail things down, tidy your desks, close the file. All those action words. But then that's what you are, isn't it? Action men. And yet, you think there's nothing you can do without me, isn't that right? No action you can take, no response, no operation? Nothing. You're stuck here drinking crap coffee, tapping your feet under the table, wishing you could beat whatever it is you mistakenly believe I know out of me.

A scenario. Your scenario, mind, not mine. Mad bastard becomes besotted with young, single mother. She rejects him. He becomes crazy with lust and anger. He kidnaps her and her child. He leaves the child in a field by a river and drives away. He kills the woman and dumps her body somewhere just out of your reach. You know he did it but you can't pin it on him without a body. If he'll just give you that much, you'll do the rest yourself. Semen stains, skin samples from under the woman's nails. Home and dry. The child's too young to tell you anything, too young to know her mother is gone. You need a body or, at least, co-operation.

Another scenario. This one is mine. Man drives an ice cream van for a living. Wet day, sees this woman. Watches her as she's caught in the rain. He remembers the way her skin shone through her wet shirt. But we're not talking wet T-shirt nonsense here. We're talking about a moment of beauty, a moment that lives in the memory. We're talking about a woman at ease with herself and her body. She's not embarrassed by how she looks or what he sees. She smiles at him and, yes, he offers her an ice cream cone and another to her kid and he chats to her and he looks forward to seeing her and, he believes, she looks forward to seeing him and, yes, he sees her again. Just because our ice cream man fantasises about taking off her wet shirt and kissing her shoulder doesn't mean he's driven by a need to hurt her. Where would be the point? Not everything is as crude as you believe it to be and not everyone is as destructive as you imagine.

I appreciate physical beauty and I appreciate sex but I appreciate other things, too. Things like, say, a summer night when the air is absolutely still. You take a night like that and you go and stand in your eight-by-ten garden and you squint up at the stars through the light from the street lamps and you think you're communing with nature.

Me, I'd prepare for an occasion like that. I'd finish work early and leave home before dark. I like driving into the tail end of a summer evening, into the mist and the shimmer. That gives me pleasure. I drive and drive until I find somewhere quiet and deserted, somewhere that doesn't have crying children or radios blaring or foul-mouthed teenagers kicking footballs or drinking. Say, a forest that's miles from anywhere. And, sometimes, I go there alone and sometimes I bring a friend.

Correction, not a friend. You tell me you're my friends, but I wouldn't bring you. I bring an intimate, someone who'll respect the silence and the beauty of the place. And we walk a little distance into the forest, just to be away from car lights and traffic and interruption. And we lie on the mossy floor of the wood or sit against a tree and listen to the sound of the night falling.

Did you know night has a sound that it makes when it falls? I can't describe it. Nobody can. But if you wait long enough and listen closely enough and have patience enough, you'll recognise it. The fall of night. It makes you one with nature, it sucks you into the soil and swallows you among the leaves and you do, actually, become one with the cosmos. I suspect Wordsworth experienced it. And Blake. If they were living now you'd probably have them outside, waiting to follow me in here.

But even the warmest night grows cold and, if you're prepared to allow yourself, you begin to detect the way the woodland shivers as the night goes on. It's a bit like that thing doctors say about the body reaching its low point around three or four in the morning. The earth is the same; it has a low point, a time when it comes close to death. A time when the moonlight is like dead skin. Inanimate. It just seems to lie there, like a corpse, still beautiful but lifeless. Extraordinary, really.

So you see, sometimes we get sucked in by the beauty of the moment and we need to reflect on the things we've seen and the places we've been and the people who've received those moments with us.

You're privileged. I hope you appreciate that fact. This is not something I've shared with many of my friends – ever. And I'm not sure why I'm sharing it with you. It's not something you can understand or even begin to appreciate without undergoing it. And sitting all night in a forest doesn't necessarily mean you'll appreciate it either. The grace of experience is what it's about and even best friends cannot share their experiences through words. You know that.

You could tell me now about the most dangerous times you've lived through. You could talk to me about the greatest risks you've taken. You could give me every detail of your greatest triumphs, the times when things fell into place for you, when circumstance and evidence and that sixth sense you told me about all tumbled together into that something that's compensation and gratification in one. But I wouldn't understand it because I haven't experienced it.

And you can't understand the beauty of the moment I'm describing because you weren't there. You didn't hear the wind whisper, you didn't feel the forest shudder, you didn't see the light of death come down from the moon, you didn't smell the smell of coldness and you didn't taste that particular taste that's like a mortal kiss on the mouth, like an inert tongue on your tongue.

You see, sometimes friendship is not enough, and some things are too personal for sharing, even with friends.

1978

If someone were to walk the headland of this field, down past the burrowed bank, down between the mighty oaks, down onto the riverside, they would catch the scent of death, the stench of an animal returning to the earth. And if they looked between the twisted grasses and the rotting spears of water irises they would find the collapsed, decaying carcass of a fox, its red coat turning slowly inside out, its grace and beauty gnawed by the water rats.

October Afternoon

Beth sat at the window, watching the cock strut and pick and strut again. Every so often he stopped and raised his head, crowing, and then he strutted again, eyeing the ground, choosing a morsel, pecking and swaggering across the garden. The baby stirred in the buggy and she got up from the window seat, pulled on her jacket and opened the kitchen door.

October rushed in to meet her, all sunlight and bluster, scattering crimson yellow leaves in its wake. She was glad to see it.

'Afternoon,' she said out loud.

She hated mornings. The daylight curtains were an immutable blade that sliced her eyelids. And mornings lasted up to lunchtime. There was always too much to be done. Even now with the baby toddling, she still hated mornings. Robert was constantly late rising and he never had time for breakfast. The principal at his school was not the kind of man to suffer latecomers gladly. Sometimes she wished Robert would stand up for himself, tell the principal what to do with his watch, miss the first bell for once. Instead, he raced around the house, cursing, slamming doors, stumbling into clothes, leaving mayhem in his wake.

In the early days of their marriage she'd urged him to adopt her attitude, to come and go as he pleased, not to be dictated to by a man who was ten years his junior, a man who lacked the imagination to know that time was made for people and not people for time.

'That's not how schools work,' Robert had told her.

'Well, maybe it's how they should work,' she'd said. 'You'll never find me working in one of them; they kill all art.'

'Thanks,' Robert had said sadly. 'I'll remember that.'

In those days she'd painted when she felt like painting. When she didn't feel like it, she'd done all the work on the house. Replacing windows, rebuilding the kitchen, restoring most of the stairs, fixing and undoing, arranging and rearranging. And, bit by bit, the painting had become a pastime rather than a passion. The children were born, their lives closed in around her, demand replaced ambition.

These days she didn't argue with Robert about his fixation with being on time. He was long enough in the tooth to fight his own corner. Instead, she got the older two out with him and cleared up after them and put some shape on things and then took the baby for his walk.

Closing the door behind her, she pushed the buggy onto the gravel drive. The cock crowed in the hen-run.

'Piss off,' she said sourly, and then she was away, out onto the road and away from the house, into the mouth of the breeze, over the hill and down the lane that led to the leaf-snowing woods.

She thought about change, about the almost imperceptible alterations that had crept into her life in the past few years. How Robert was settling into middle age, becoming more entrenched month by month, and she was the one being left behind. And week after week the children battled against him, against her, against everything. And day into day she survived at the centre of it all, compromising, bargaining, reconciling.

Only that morning, loading the washing machine in the garage, she had glanced up at her easel and boards and paint boxes, neatly stored on the highest shelf. And had been overcome, not by a desire to take them down, but rather by a melancholy that she might never use them again, might never seriously consider painting another picture. She who had plotted a lifetime of finding a studio space, painting and exhibiting without fear.

Was it possible, she wondered, to forget a dream, to relinquish it without regret? Was it possible to isolate yourself from everything you ever visualised without even realising it?

Stopping, she looked back across the fields, up the incline to where their house stood, white and clean against the dark clouds piling up across the sky. So different from the first time they'd seen it, dilapidated against the turquoise air. It had had a New England look, gaunt and full of character against the fathomless blue of a summer sky. An ideal spot for painting, Robert had said when they first looked at it. And that first autumn had convinced her that he was right, even if the canvases and the paints and the easel were now stacked neatly in the garage.

She pushed onwards, around another bend and down the path that slid into the woods. From the corner she could see the church roofline a mile away. She hated that roof, hated the way it protruded into her life, peering like a self-righteous busybody over a ditch. She wished lightning would strike it, but it had been there forever, since 1863 or thereabouts, and she knew it would watch her to her grave. Even with the lilac hedge they'd planted the summer after they'd moved into the house, the church was still visible from their bedroom window. It would take another five years for it to be hidden, and even then it would be lodged there in her mind forever, like a troubling sermon.

When her friends had come down from art college that first summer after she and Robert had moved in, they'd told her how fortunate she was, young and happy and living in a beautiful house. They'd said it with all the confidence of certainty, a confidence that never wavered. When Clare and her husband came this evening, to spend the weekend, they'd marvel at how fortunate and content she was. And perhaps they were right. Perhaps she'd never, in her heart of hearts, really wanted to paint, not deep down, not when it came to it. If she'd been meant to, she'd have kept at it all along. It wasn't as if it were some great gift left unopened after her wedding day, nothing like that.

She looked at the baby who was sleeping, then slowed and picked a handful of blackberries from the hedge, tasting the ripeness of the fruit juice, bitter and warm. Not over-ripe. She hated over-ripe fruit.

When she was small, her brother had squashed an over-ripe pear into her face and she had screamed. Her father had come in and beaten her brother and then sent him to bed. Later, she'd snuck up to her brother's room, to see if he was all right, but he'd refused to talk to her. Instead, he'd lain there sobbing, the red welts on his leg still stinging in the fading light. She'd stayed with him until he'd fallen asleep and then she'd crept in beside him and fallen asleep herself. Later, her father found them and beat them both, telling them they were disgusting, telling them they'd rot in hell. She was eleven then, her brother twelve.

The following summer her father had died of a heart attack. She remembered how no one had cried at his funeral. Two years later, her mother remarried. Beth had hated her stepfather, for no better reason than that he was replacing a father she'd despised. Her brother was more inclined to wait and see. In the end, fishing trips won him over and she began to hate him, too.

At fourteen, in boarding school, it had suddenly struck her that she was being pathetic. Her stepfather was a decent man. He didn't deserve this treatment.

That Christmas she'd got home to find her mother pregnant. She was shocked but determined not to let anything stop her turning over a new leaf. That holiday had been the happiest time of her life, a childhood crammed into two idyllic weeks.

In January her mother had lost the baby. Beth had written to her from school, woman to woman, a confession of things past and an invocation for the future. Her mother still had the letter in her jewellery box, with the other bits and pieces that were precious to her.

When Beth told her about Robert, her mother had said very little, beyond pointing out that he was closer in age to her than he was to Beth. Did it matter that when Beth was forty-four, Robert would be sixty? she wondered.

No, Beth had told her, it didn't.

'And you love him?'

'Yes, I love him.'

'Well then,' her mother said.

*

She came to a gateway, its rusted sunrise of metal unhinged, sloping back against the ditch. Through the opening, a stubbled field stretched along the boundary of the rabbit warren before dipping out of sight towards the river. A single shaft of sunlight caught the sides of the granite pillars that had once held the gate in place. Beth pulled back an overhanging branch and examined the blackberries in the sheltered ditch. They were soft and sludgy. One disintegrated in her hand. Wiping her fingers on a tissue, she moved on, away from the sight of the church roof, away from the outline of the house, away through the woods, towards where the sea would be, if there were a sea.

Robert had told her once, years before, that you could smell the sea from the woods.

'All you need is imagination,' he said.

She feared the sea.

When she was eight, she'd seen a woman's body taken from the water in Kerry. She'd gone down to the harbour with her aunt and her cousin. They were wandering, reading the names of the boats, when a crowd gathered and they walked on, to see what the excitement was about. She had seen, between the adult legs, a pale, bloated face on the steps that led down to the water. The rest of the body was still in the sea.

Afterwards, she'd wondered why her aunt hadn't hurried them away from the sight. Instead, they'd stayed to watch the jellied flesh lifted onto a dry tarpaulin. The canvas had gradually darkened as the seawater ran from the corpse. Somebody named the barely recognisable woman as the local schoolteacher's wife. Beth had fled up the pier, terrified.

Later, her aunt had chided her for running away.

'You could have been lost, you could have been hurt, the ambulance might have come around the corner and killed you!'

Beth had said nothing, but ever since she had feared the rotting power of the sea. She liked being inland. She felt safe. Safer. In college she had turned down the offer of a flat overlooking Sandymount Strand. She didn't want to open her door to the possibility of a sodden, rotting body on the sand across the street.

When she was sixteen and on holiday in Courtown, she had gone, after a dance, with a boy to the dunes. They had lain together on his anorak, kissing and petting, but the constant thunder of the waves a hundred yards away had terrified her. She had imagined a silent corpse washing methodically up the beach towards them. Finally, she'd pretended offence at the boy's hand on her breast and asked him to take her home. For the rest of that holiday she'd tried, unsuccessfully, to win him back.

Stopping, Beth breathed deeply, sucking in the smells of the autumn woodland. Exhaling the sea and its horrors. She thought of other holidays, other boys, the first boy who had driven her home from a dance. She was seventeen and they'd stopped on the lane that led to her uncle's house, in the shadow of a chestnut that arced above the gateway. They'd sat there talking, each willing the other the courage to touch. And then her uncle had stepped out onto the back porch of his house, clear in the yard light, and pissed onto the small lawn. She had been mortified. Did the boy know this was her uncle? Could he possibly think the man was her father? Either way, she had been too embarrassed to explain.

Robert said fate had seen to it that no one got close to her heart before he came along. And maybe he was right.

He'd begun as another holiday romance. And then he came to visit the flat in Dublin. More embarrassment. What would the other girls say about this ancient mariner who hardly had a word to throw to a dog?

Her flatmate, Clare, had done her best to entertain him. The others had given up and drifted away.

'I think he's lovely,' Clare told her later.

'He's older.'

'Everyone's older than someone,' she laughed. 'Except for whoever's the oldest person in the world.'

It was the kind of thing Clare did, qualifying things, being precise.

There had been a month when it seemed things were coming to an end, but during the holidays Robert had asked her to marry him. They'd been going out together for four months. He'd come down to her mother's house for the weekend and they'd gone walking on a clear, frosty, big-moon night. Even the air smelled of Christmas, the kind of night she'd dreamed of in childhood. Well wrapped up, boots, scarves, hats, duffle coats. He hadn't even stopped walking as he'd asked her, just kept on going, pointing out the reasons why she might refuse him, playing devil's advocate. They'd walked three hundred yards before he'd given her a chance to answer.

And then they were searching for a house. And then she was pregnant. Looking back, she saw there had been romance, but there had been a kind of inevitability, too.

*

This forest smelled nothing like Christmas. It was autumn to its roots, berried red and rusted ochre. Johnnyma'gories, rosehips, sloes and blackberries that suddenly resembled the flesh of a dead woman on a Kerry pier. Crows gathering overhead, drawn in by the rising wind. And then a glimpse of a tractor three fields away, the reassurance of the actual.

'You need to cop yourself on,' Beth said aloud.

The baby stirred, opened his eyes, smiled and slept again.

She turned the buggy and walked back the way she had come. There was reality to face, visitors to prepare for. Things to do. Real things.

What would someone soaring away from the earth see if they looked down on me, she wondered. A woman, pushing a buggy with a sleeping child. Three autumnal fields away, a tractor going its mechanical way, ploughing and turning. That's what someone would see. As they got higher, their line of sight would widen to include a tall house on a hill and a small town with a church. And they'd see the woman making her way along a country lane; passing the gateway of a house where a woman stood in the garden while another drove onto the roadway without waving. They'd see her walking up a gravelled driveway to the door of her own house. They'd see her standing, a frightened child, fearing a decomposing body at the foot of the hall stairs, frightened by hauntings of her own making, petrified in broad daylight.

'Shit,' Beth said. 'I am cracking. Fuck off, spaceman.'

She forced herself to open the front door and to step inside without thinking. Checking the sleeping child in the buggy, she opened the garage door and turned on the light. Taking down her easel, she propped it against the wall. Some of the paint tubes were hard. She threw them into an empty box. The others she piled in a dish, beside her brushes.

After the weekend, after the visitors had gone, she'd try to begin again. The laneway. The gate at the forest. The River Field. The granite posts. Systematically, she would paint all there was to paint.

She hoped Robert and the children would be delayed in coming home from school. She hoped the baby would go on sleeping. She hoped that when she cried, as cry she would, she might find a way to stop the tears that fell.

1939

In the moonlight the field is haunted by shadows. From the open gateway, down between the angled sides, past the rabbit burrows to the riverbank, everything is brilliance and darkness. The gateposts lengthen, their silhouettes stretching slowly like cats, while the shadows of the oaks umbrella half the field and the moon drifts over the hill and up into the empty sky.

The darkened ivy takes on a lighter gloss, the summer flowers on the headland are a single colour, the hayricks stand scattered guard, and the river is a road of golden eddies that burns forever.

The Berrigan Sisters

The Berrigan sisters had only just arrived in this country when I met them. Their mother, with characteristic accuracy, had foreseen the coming war and taken the girls, plus the two big old Morris lorries and a Ford car, across to Ireland. Once here, she gathered an assortment of either variously talented performers or hard workers and put a show on the road. I wasn't sure to which category I was meant to belong. Certainly I could play the piano, but just as certainly I was not a talented pianist. Nor was I a shirker, but equally I was not overly enamoured of hard work. Still, I seemed to slip in somewhere between the wheels and cogs of the travelling company's machinations, as I would otherwise have been fired. That was how it was with Mrs Berrigan, who was forthright to a fault – usually someone else's fault.

Her daughters, however, were different propositions. Joan, the eldest, was a tall, calm redhead. Shortly before I joined the show, she had married Jim Whelan, an Irishman who had been with the company in England. Jim was a big, gentle, quiet man who worked hard, yet played the violin with a subtlety that belied his strength. To watch him hammering tent pegs into the ground was to wonder at how one man could possibly harness so much power. To sit on a summer evening and hear him play 'Le Cygne' was to believe in God. At the same time, I often wondered how he had found the words and courage to ask Joan to marry him. All the more so given that he was a staunch Catholic and the Berrigan family were given neither to belief nor practice when it came to matters spiritual.

The other sisters, Edwina and Georgie, gave Jim an awful time about his faith, their particular target being a statue of Blesséd Martin de Porres that Jim carried about in his bag. It was a small figure whose cracked and lined face gave it a cross-eyed leer. Sometimes Joan would join in the routine, but Jim always smiled and took the ribbing in good part.

Once or twice Mrs Berrigan had overheard the girls and delivered a stiff lecture. She might not share her son-in-law's beliefs, but she respected his right to hold them. Yet on those occasions, Jim was always first to come to the girls' defence.

It was all good fun, he'd say. They meant no harm. He didn't mind.

I was party to most of this because I was very keen on Georgie, the youngest of the three. Wherever she went, I followed, like a dog at her heels. I suppose I thought I was in love with her. At nineteen, love is a constant in the air.

Edwina, the middle sister, had been the original object of my affections, until I discovered she had someone in London to whom she frequently wrote, and whom, she told me, she would one day marry.

How could she be so sure, I wondered.

Because you knew these things, intuitively, she told me. When you met the love of your life, you knew. When you saw them, you recognised them – that was all there was to it.

At that point, I thought it best to redirect my attention to Georgie.

*

When I first landed the job with the Berrigans, I could hardly believe my luck. I was young, I was free, I was in the company of three gorgeous women who, in fairness to their mother, were given the latitude to live their own lives. As long as the work was done and the show went on, the girls were free agents.

Altogether there were twelve of us in the company. The Berrigans and Jim Whelan; an English couple, the Crossthwaites, and their son and daughter; a mime artist who claimed to be French and his wife, plus myself.

Our show – a variety of music, comedy, mime, melodrama and acrobatics – was popular wherever we performed, whether in our tent in a village field or in the halls of provincial towns. Crowds flocked to see us night after night.

The routine was to work a town for two or three nights, depending on its size, and then move on, always taking two days rest in a week. In this regard we were very fortunate. Mrs Berrigan believed that the labourer who worked hard, and was worthy of his hire, was also deserving of his rest.

Our favourite places were the towns with good halls where we could set up quickly, take in the local sights in the afternoon, enjoy a meal in the comfort of our digs and relax after the show in the local hotel.

It was on a road near the town of Carlow, in the late autumn of 1939, that the first of the trucks struck the rabbit. I remember the day clearly. Obviously, I couldn't have known the chain of events that would ensue, but the incident made an indelible impression on my mind.

Jim was driving the first truck and Joan was travelling with him. He immediately pulled over to the roadside, and thinking something serious had happened, I immediately pulled the second truck in behind him. By the time I got down from the cab, he had gathered the injured animal into his hands.

Believing the rabbit's back was broken, I suggested putting it out of its misery, but Joan wouldn't hear of such a thing and insisted it would recover with time and care.

'Dunno,' Jim said. 'Hard to make good a hurt animal, specially a wild one. They fret.'

'We'll try,' Joan said and that was that.

Jim wrapped the animal in a cloth and I carried it back to the lorry, feeling its tiny heart drumming against my hand. I was sure the noisy jolting of the cab would frighten it to death, but to my surprise the rabbit was still alive when we reached the town where we were to play the following evening.

Jim promptly made a cage for it by wiring the sides on an old orange crate, which he left in the weak sun on the grass outside the hall while we unloaded our set. By the time we'd finished it was dusk, and by the time we'd settled into our digs it was dark.

The boarding house was less than palatial, the rooms rank with stale air and the beds, as Mrs Berrigan remarked, like plots of damp turf on legs. Not for the first time, we mended and made do.

After dinner I went upstairs and knocked on Jim and Joan's bedroom door. Georgie opened it.

'Come to see Arthur, have you?'

'Who?'

'Arthur, the rabbit. Come to see him?'

'Yes, I suppose so.'

She stood back and I stepped in.

Joan and Edwina were on their knees, cooing over the animal, which lay on a bed of straw beside its cage.

'I've been telling them he needs rest and quiet,' Jim said, his tone suggesting a resigned hopelessness.

'Fussy,' Georgie said. 'We'll leave him be in a moment.'

'I think he's going to be all right,' Joan said.

'Bit early to know,' Jim said. 'Could drop off in the night.'

'Cheerful.'

'He's right,' I said. 'Sometimes they die of shock, when all the excitement is over.'

Georgie glared at me.

'I mean, I hope he doesn't, of course. He may not.'

'What'll we do with him if he gets better?' she asked.

'Set him free,' Jim said.

'We can't just drop him somewhere strange, where he'd never get his bearings.'

Jim and I laughed out loud.

'He'd get by,' Jim said. 'He'd adapt. He's a wild animal.'

'Anyway, I don't think that's a question we need concern ourselves with for the moment,' Joan said as she lifted the animal back into his cage.

'Will you take me to the pictures?' Georgie asked. '*Follow the Fleet* is on. I'm dying to see it.'

'Of course,' I said.

Never mind that I couldn't stand Fred Astaire or Ginger Rogers.

When the picture was over, we walked the length of the town. It was one of those nights I will remember all my life. Not because anything earth-shattering happened, but simply because it took on an idyllic tranquillity that I've often dreamed since of recapturing, but never have.

A mile or so beyond the edge of the town, in the white light of a huge moon, ricks loomed in a hayfield. We climbed the metal gate and walked slowly across the stubble, our shadows leading the way down a gentle hill to a small river that shone electric in the moonlight. There, we sat on a small pile of granite fence posts that someone had dug out of the ground and left beneath two oak trees.

The moon settled in the gaps between the branches, marking the pillars with its milky light.

'You'd never think there was a war on over there,' Georgie said.

'No.'

'I think war is the most stupid thing in the world.'

I agreed, though I wasn't thinking of war or death or freedom or ideals. Rather, I was thinking what a fool I was not to tell her how much I loved her, what hopes I had for us, how much she meant to me. It was something I'd thought about for months, but, in my own cowardly way, I reckoned it better not to speak. If she rebuffed me, I'd feel obliged to stop going out with her and I didn't dare believe she might offer me hope. It was after midnight when we got back to the boarding house. The others were playing cards.

'Enjoy the picture?' Mrs Berrigan asked.

'Seen better,' Georgie said.

Mrs Berrigan nodded, drawing the pack of playing cards to her and standing up.

'I'd like everyone to be in the hall at ten in the morning,' she said. 'I have one or two new things I want to try.'

We nodded and she left the room.

'How's Arthur?' Georgie asked.

'Still there,' her sister said. 'Still panting, still staring, but still there.'

The rabbit lived, but its recovery was painfully slow. It took weeks before it was at ease with its surroundings, and only then did it begin to regain its strength, moving around its cage, grazing the lawns of the various boarding houses we lodged in, or looking up inquisitively when someone came into the room.

Jim built it a bigger cage with a run that could be put outside when we stayed in towns for three or four days. Joan cared for the animal like she would for a child, but as it regained its strength, hobbling about in the winter sunshine, she herself grew less well. At first it was just a cold. We often got colds from the wet weather, from the freezing lorry cabs, from damp beds and draughty halls. Indeed, I hardly noticed that Joan's cold continued over the Christmas. It wasn't until Georgie remarked on it that I took any notice of the fact that her sister's skin was suddenly transparent. Georgie told me that she'd come on Joan in the cab of the lorry one night, coughing blood. All the same, she'd refused to see a doctor and sworn her sister to secrecy. I was more flattered at being the exception to this oath than truly aware of the possible implications of Joan's illness. Finally, in the second week of a bitter January, Georgie broke her silence and told Jim and her mother.

That afternoon they took Joan to see a local doctor.

The following day she was in a sanatorium outside Dublin, and by the end of the week we knew she had tuberculosis.

*

We worked in Midland towns all that spring. Jim and Mrs Berrigan and one of the girls visited Joan every weekend. The rest of us made the visits in turns. It was early April before I got to see her, and by then she was dying. It was impossible not to recognise the imminence of death and I believed each of us in our way accepted it.

Jim for his part continued to talk about what they'd do when Joan recovered, and how different life would be when she came out of the sanatorium, and where he would take her when she'd be back travelling with us. I believed he was trying to keep our spirits up, trying to break the fall for her mother and her sisters, being as he always was the strong one.

I was wrong.

One Sunday evening, in mid-May, I heard the lorry stopping outside our lodgings and went to hear the news from the sanatorium. Jim passed me on the pathway without a word. Mrs Berrigan followed him inside, nodding silently.

I found Georgie in the yard, locking the lorry.

'What happened?' I asked.

'Joan told him,' Georgie said. 'He was talking about the summer and she told him. Said it straight out. Told him to stop gabbling, that she's dying. He reacted as though the possibility had never crossed his mind, like he'd thought she had a headache or something, like she had the remedy in her own hands. And then she got cross with him and that made her weaker. So he started blaming himself for upsetting her. They both cried then, so that the nurse asked us to leave for a time. When we went back in, he kept apologising and she just smiled at him and rubbed his head.

In a way I felt sorry for him, but, Christ, he must have known. You can see her fading away like blotting paper. It's so bloody obvious, isn't it?'

'Yes,' I said. 'It is.'

'I don't know,' Georgie said, shaking her head. 'I just don't know.'

We walked down the long lawn that stretched to the side of the boarding house. At the foot of the lawn, where a gate opened onto the early summer fields, was the rabbit run that Jim had set up. As we approached, the animal stopped its nibbling and hopped to the wire, waiting for one of us to take it out.

'He's coming on well,' Georgie said.

'Yes. We should let him go soon. He's ready.'

The following Wednesday a telegram arrived for Jim. It wasn't unexpected and there were no tears this time. He simply gathered us in the dining room and told us Joan was dead.

'We'll have to go up and make arrangements,' he said.

'We'll go now,' Mrs Berrigan said. 'Who'll drive?'

I said I would.

The journey to the sanatorium was a silent one. When we got there, I sat outside on the running board of the truck and waited. The sun was hot and the sky clear, while all around me patients sat on the verandas of the green, wooden chalets that were home to them.

That night, as Georgie and myself sat in the dining room, not saying much, there was a crash from the room above. Running upstairs, we found Jim seated white and silent on his bed, with the statue of Blesséd Martin lying shattered on the floor. Mrs Berrigan was already in the room and in full flight.

'I hold no belief whatsoever in your religion,' she was saying, 'but if I did, I wouldn't desecrate those things I hold in esteem. Do you believe this statue was to blame for what's happened? Or whoever it represents? Because if you do, you're a fool. Joan has been dying for months. She knew it and you knew it. We all did. Do you imagine she'd have wanted you to do what you've done here? Do you believe this in some way makes something up to her?'

Jim was silent.

Mrs Berrigan shook his shoulders, her fingers digging deep into his flesh.

'Well, do you?' she shouted.

The landlady came to the top of the stairs but said nothing.

'No,' Jim whispered.

'Of course not,' Mrs Berrigan went on. 'She respected you and your beliefs and then you turn around and do this childish, self-centred thing. I think it's shameful that you should try to blame some manifestation for something that was unavoidable.'

'I didn't, I had to, I...'

The landlady turned and went quietly down the stairs.

'I had to do something,' Jim finally managed.

'Well, pray for her, then,' Mrs Berrigan said. 'You say you believe in God.'

'I have this feeling, of things opening up, pulling everything from under my feet, taking everything away. God won't fill that hole and prayer won't cure it.'

I didn't think I had ever heard Jim say so many words at one time, but as suddenly as they'd begun, the words dried up. I picked the broken pieces of Blesséd Martin from the floor while Georgie sat on the bed with Jim.

'I know when all this started,' he said. 'That damp kip near Carlow, last autumn. I know it.'

'It could have started anywhere,' Georgie said. 'There's nothing you can do, nothing any of us can do. It gets people.'

'It's time everybody went to bed,' Mrs Berrigan said. 'We have an early start tomorrow, it'll be a draining day.'

Georgie hugged Jim and left the room. I said goodnight and followed her. From the landing, I could hear Mrs Berrigan's voice.

'You've got to accept this. Get on with living. Otherwise you're no good to anyone. You do your job or you go. That's a difficult thing for me to say, particularly on this night, but it's the truth. And the night is as dark for me as it is for you.'

Georgie took my hand and led me downstairs.

'She's got to be like that,' she said. 'We lost Dad and the two boys to TB in eighteen months in England. She kept things going because she had to, so that we could eat. That's the way things are.'

I slept very badly that night and awoke to see the first light dawdling under the flowered curtains. I heard someone stirring along the corridor and then steps on the stairs and the sound of the back door opening. I got out of bed and went to the window, holding the curtain a finger from the wall.

Jim was in the grey garden, opening the door of the rabbit run. I considered pulling back the curtain and opening the window latch, but I didn't. Instead I saw him lift the rabbit, twist its neck, jerking it back as he did so, then drop it, dead, on the lawn. And then I saw him cross the wet grass again and heard the back door close quietly.

Once his footsteps died along the landing, I pulled on my trousers and shirt. But as I turned to slip into my shoes, something made me glance again through the gap in the curtains. Below me, Georgie was crossing the garden in her dressing gown. I watched her kneel beside the dead animal, lifting it gently and stroking its fur, as though it were still alive, before she carried it around by the side of the house. I stood at the window, waiting. She was gone for a long time, and when she returned, she paused for a moment at the back door step, looking out across the dawning garden and the fields beyond. Only then did she step inside.

Undressing, I got back into bed and lay in the rising light, thinking about Jim, wondering how life would be without him and Joan, as I was certain that Mrs Berrigan would prove as uncompromising as she had promised to be. His wife had died, but she had lost a daughter.

We were eating breakfast when one of the Crossthwaite children came in from the garden and said the rabbit was missing. As Jim's mouth opened to form a word, I closed my eyes to hear what he would say, but the voice I heard was Georgie's, sounding already like a voice from the past.

'I let it go this morning,' she said. 'It's recovered and I thought it best. We won't be around to look after it today or tomorrow. It needs to be free again. It was time we let it go.'

1987

When the wind blows from the east, in the valley between the furze-covered hill and the walls of the small town, rain chases along the surface of the water. You can see it where the river straightens in that stretch between the last houses and the oaks.

You can stand and watch the stampede of drops charging along, ploughing up the shallows where the children paddle in summer, leaping the bar that bridges the river for some long-forgotten reason. The rain is gunning the wide pool that mirrors the trees, so that the branches break up and re-form and split and come together again, shivering and dancing away, uneasy, uncertain. And then the shower passes and the leaves find their branches and the branches find their tree and the water reflects the oaks above the clearing sky.

End of Season

The five days of rain came to an end on the last day of August. By midday the clouds had peeled and the full heat of the sun poured over the roofs and oozed onto the narrow seaside streets. The tinsel music of an ice cream van monotonously washed the pier, inflicting 'Raindrops Keep Fallin' On My Head' over and over again. Caravans and chalets emptied their frustration onto the beach so that the waves were suddenly alive with swimmers, diving and thrashing into the early afternoon. On the promenade the little shops bloomed again, putting out their parasols of beach balls and buckets and swimming rings. Tufts of candy floss floated across the crowded counters.

On the beach the boy rested on his towel, a straw hat shading his pale face from the sun, a rug wrapped around his legs. He lay on his side, watching the distant swimmers, and timing the fall of the waves on the sandy shoreline. Passing bathers glanced at him and nodded to his parents before moving farther down the beach.

While his father went swimming, his mother sat and read her book, smiling at him, occasionally asking if everything was all right. The boy remembered the first week of May, when his parents had taken him to the river at the end of a long field near the town in which they lived. They'd had a picnic on the bank, in the shelter of two oak trees. He had been able to walk a little then.

Later, when his father came dripping from the water, his mother marked her page, folded her glasses and walked slowly into the sea. The boy watched her, saw how brown her legs were against the yellow of her swimsuit. He knew he would never see this again, knew with a certainty that comes from wherever it is that we call soul.

A tiny child stepped into the boy's eye line and swayed on unsteady feet before venturing inquisitively closer. Suddenly a tall man swooped, whisking the child away, tossing him playfully into the air as they crossed the sand.

The boy's gaze returned to his mother. She was swimming parallel to the shore, her arms lifting rhythmically, strongly, the yellow strap of her swimsuit rising and dipping with each stroke. Blue sky, yellow strap, golden sand, until he felt his eyes begin to close.

It was late afternoon when the boy awoke. The day was still hot but the sky was raven with clouds. His mother was gathering the towels and books from the sand, packing them carefully into a beach bag. His father was lifting him, the rug still wrapped around his legs, and starting along the beach. And then the clouds burst and the rain came in sheets, lacerating the turreted sandcastles, cutting into the boy's face, bouncing off his father's sinewy arms. Behind him, his mother cursed softly and then his father began to run, his feet sinking into the wet sand. Above him, along the promenade, he saw the scurry of shopkeepers as they pulled the racks of newspapers and postcards from the dripping walls outside their doors.

His father was racing now, reassuring him, telling him they'd soon be at the car. The boy held his breath and said nothing. The raindrops bounced off his face. He felt their warmth on his skin and he opened his mouth to let them gather on his tongue. They were simply rain and rain would never kill him. His father stopped dead, hoisting the boy to get a firmer grip on his slight body, laying him across his shoulder, his back to the rain. He caught sight of his mother running behind them, the car keys in one hand, the beach bag in the other. As she smiled and waved, sprinting to catch them, the boy felt his energy drain, felt the dark cold fingers on his spine, and knew both the day and his life were ebbing much faster than anyone but he could imagine.

Driving back to the rented house, the boy watched the cowering, silent groups trapped beneath the flimsy awnings of shops, watched the men in white coats pulling down the shutters on the promenade kiosks for the last time.

And then, through the other window, far out on the edge of the shore, he glimpsed a man walking slowly, a deckchair carelessly folded beneath his arm. As he watched the man ambling through the rain, stopping now and again to watch the changing light above the sea, the boy was gradually swamped by a deep and desperate envy that rang like an anxious bell.

2005

Sunlight from the riverbank slips its feet into the warm water, easing down through the yellow flagged irises, swimming away in the blueness of sky.

Among the branches, it softens the lichen, melting the pale green into ancient wood.

In the meadow, it fills the early poppies and the dandelions with the energy of summer.

Along the headland, it nests between shadows of the may and the crab apple that sing like a bird.

Husband

When Liz got home from work her husband was sitting in the garden, in his favourite spot, on the bench beneath the big sycamore. He was sitting very straight and very still, staring out across the vegetable patch and the raspberry canes, focusing on some distant place beyond the end of the garden and the snowing whitethorn hedge.

At first she didn't see him. Having come into the kitchen and dropped the shopping bags heavily onto the breakfast counter, she flicked the switch of the kettle and turned the radio on. Later, she would think it ironic that Mozart's 'Piano Concerto No. 21 in C' was playing. *Elvira Madigan* was the first film they'd seen together and her husband had been enthralled by the music.

The groceries put away, she made herself a cup of coffee and went into the dining room to find the newspaper. And still she did not know he was there. She had left her crossword half-done and was determined to finish it before tea. She sat with her back to the window, labouring over the last three clues, determined not to resort to her thesaurus. The Mozart ended and the announcer introduced Bach's 'Sheep May Safely Graze'. She looked again at seventeen across, where 'elucidate' was suddenly obvious, and once that was apparent, 'ductile' and 'quaint' were equally so. She wrote the –int with a flourish and throwing the newspaper onto the table, sighed contentedly as she downed the last of her coffee. Only then did she turn to look across the garden, only then did she see him, his back set rigidly, his feet firmly planted on the ground, his face turned to the north, watching for that something that she could never see. She felt herself go cold.

Anne felt herself go cold. The moment she stepped into the kitchen and saw the open door, her heart tripped and her back turned to ice.

'Oh Christ,' she said out loud. 'Oh, Christ, Christ, Christ!'

She had left him sleeping in his armchair in the bay window, warm in the late afternoon sun. She had gone upstairs to vacuum and then the phone had rung and then rung again. How long had she been? Twenty minutes, half an hour, no more. She was sure the back door had been locked, as sure as she ever could be. She'd cleaned the grate and taken the ashes out in the morning, brought in the washing, collected the post from the box at the gate and then locked the door again. Hadn't she?

'Please Jesus, don't let him be gone far,' she said as she stepped into the yard, scanning the garden, hurrying past the empty shed with its open door, and down through the orchard to the gap they had used years before to escape into the fields beyond. But the gap was blocked now, overgrown with brambles and may bushes. The bile rising in her throat, she turned and ran between the trees, out onto the drive and down to the open wooden gate that swung aimlessly onto the road.

'Fuck.'

Running back to the house, she grabbed her keys and bag from the hall table and got into the car. Driving along the avenue, she glimpsed something moving between the birches, slowed, ground the gears into reverse, but what she had seen was nothing more than a shadow of the bay tree.

Out on the road, she couldn't decide which way to go. Left was open countryside, right was the road into town. If he were seen in town, someone would recognise him, someone would bring him home, someone. If he got to the woods there was no telling where or when he'd be found, or if. She put that thought out of her mind and turned the car for the open road, driving fast between fields that were hurrying to cover themselves in the flimsiest of barley dresses. Glancing continually left and right, she blessed the farmer who had levelled the ditches and converted the countless fields into open tracts that offered no hiding place to a man trying to lose himself when the things he had known were already lost to him.

Liz closed the patio door quietly, the handle clicking smoothly into place. The birds went on singing in the ditches around the garden. Her husband went on sitting as he had been, poker-straight, his sight line still snagged on a distant bush. She moved tentatively down the bark-mulched path, waiting for him to hear her, waiting to become the distraction that would catch his attention, but he remained unaware of her presence.

She stopped a half-dozen steps from his seat and watched the revenant of someone she used to know. What did she recognise? The ray lines darting from the side of his eye, the dark channeled furrow down his forehead. Lines and gouges and this vehement silence that refused to even acknowledge the birdsong or her presence.

She moved closer and sat beside him on the narrow wooden bench that sagged with their weight.

'You came back,' she said.

He looked vacantly at the place her words had come from, then looked away again.

'Does anyone know you're here?' she asked, and before he could speak, answered her own question. 'Of course not.'

They sat together in the early summer sun that dipped and danced between the frayed clouds. Around them the hawthorn choir built melodies, pointing and counterpointing, a soloist rising only to be drowned by the surge of other voices. She thought of Edward Thomas's blackbird and all his other birds of Oxfordshire and Gloucestershire.

'I used to think the birds sang for pleasure,' she said. 'You were the one who told me they sang for power.'

The sun disappeared, only to reappear almost at once, shadowing the freshly cut grass. He lifted his hand and wiped something from his jacket.

'Are you all right?' she asked.

'All right,' he said.

She nodded and sighed.

'All right,' he said again.

'Good.'

'The moon will be here in a short time now.'

'I suppose it will.'

'It'll be all right.'

She turned to him.

'Why did you come back?'

His brow furrowed in the light of the sun but he said nothing.

'You're all right there, aren't you?' she asked.

'All right.'

'I'm popping back inside. Do you want to come with me?'

He looked at her, then brushed his hand across his jacket again, but he made no move to follow her.

'Don't be late,' he said. 'Your mother never sleeps till you're in.'

Anne stopped the car on the roadside and got out. A sudden sweep of sunlight galloped across the empty fields, billowing the ground and blinding her. She shaded her eyes with the back of her hand and sat back against the wing of the car.

'Where the fuck are you?' she said out loud.

And then the sunlight was gone and she covered her face with her hands, breathing deeply, smelling the soap from her palms, allowing herself, for that instant, the remembered indulgence of her morning shower. Uncovering her face, she swept the landscape slowly, methodically trawling the emptiness for some sign, some stumbling figure coming out of the tide of early dandelions, some hand waving helplessly far out in a sea of grass. But there was no one, nothing to do, just the emptiness of a triangular field running down to the vast shadows of two trees on the bank of a river that was hardly deep enough to drown in.

And then her phone rang and she fumbled the passenger door open, pulling the mobile from her bag, spilling money, mints, plastic cards across the seat.

'Hello.'

'Anne?'

'Yes.'

'This is Liz.'

'Yes.'

'Paul is here, with me. Well, not with me. He's in the garden. I'm looking out at him now. He's sitting in the garden.'

'Thank God!'

'Where are you?'

'I'm out on the Barrack Road. Driving. Looking for him.'

'He's fine.'

'How long has he been there?'

'I don't know. Not long. I saw him five, six minutes ago. He was here when I got back.'

'I was working upstairs. Not for long.'

'I know. It's OK. He's OK. Don't worry.'

'Thanks, Liz. I'll be over – give me ten minutes.'

'Take your time. I'll look after him. He's very placid, very much in himself; there's no problem, seriously.'

'I'll be there.'

'OK. Drive carefully.'

Liz put the phone back on the table and stood at the door, watching her husband. But there was so little to see. A rigid figure, with a transfixed look that might have passed for determination had she not known better. The feet so resolutely firm on the same ground he had once dug with such fervour, clearing, weeding, composting, drilling and raking, sowing and tending. Morning and night in the late summer and early autumn, overseeing the harvest of his labours, sharing his excitement with the children. And then, one spring, she'd looked out into the garden and realised that he was gone, that their marriage was over, that he had left her. And year by year she'd returned more and more of the garden to low-growing grass, so that now the vegetable plot was a delicate patchwork that might comfortably fit on the large kitchen table.

The garden he'd known had grown away, the man she'd married was missing in action, every design they'd been familiar with was lost beyond recovery. All she saw, when she looked at the figure sitting beneath the tree, were haloes and auras, betrayals that might have been confusions, and bewilderments that might have been mistakes.

Anne sat in the car, checking her eyes in the mirror, wondering if the lines about them said enough, or possibly too much, about the past thirty months. Not that there was much she could do about any of it now.

Turning the key, she opened her window, pressed the CD button and looked again, across the suddenly vast and indifferent fields. Beth Nielsen Chapman's voice drifted into the warm air outside, something about years, how they take so long and they go so fast.

'Too fucking true,' she said ruefully, and sighing deeply, turned the key again till the engine crooned.

'He's asleep upstairs,' Liz said.

She led the way into the dining room. Through the window, Anne could see late shadows stretching across the garden.

'How did he get here?'

'I have no idea.'

'Whenever I take him out for a drive, whenever we come out this way, I always ask him if he remembers living here. I tell him this is where you still live.'

'It was the place,' Liz said. 'It was the place he came back to, not me. He has no idea who I am, that's patently obvious. But he found his old seat in the garden, and when he came in here, he came in of his own accord. And then he went upstairs and got into bed.'

'I'll go and wake him,' Anne said.

'You don't have to.'

'He could sleep for hours.'

'It really isn't any problem to me, unless you want to wake him. I've put some dinner on; you're more than welcome to stay and eat. I'd like that.'

'Are you sure? You don't have any other plans?'

'I'm sure.'

'Would you mind if I checked on him?'

'Not at all, follow me.'

Liz led the way up the wide stairs. 'He can't get out,' she said. 'There's a dead bolt on the front door; the only other way is through the dining room.'

Liz opened a door at the top of the stairs and Anne stepped into the big, bright room. Her husband was sleeping soundly, the lines and frowns washed from his forehead and eyes, his hands unclenched.

'He's fine,' Liz said and then, as if correcting herself, 'isn't he?'

Anne nodded as they stepped onto the landing, leaving the door open.

'I'm really sorry about this. It's only the second time he's done it in, what, two-and-a-half years?'

'Nothing to be sorry about. I really don't know how you deal with the constant pressure. Is he ever violent?'

'No, never,' Anne said quickly. 'Never, there's nothing like that. Mostly he doesn't even talk to me now. It's just silence and…unease, I suppose. No emotion, nothing like that.'

'I often wonder,' Liz said. 'The children tell me, of course, but I do sometimes wonder.'

'There's no reason for you not to call.'

'I don't think he'd want me calling, not if he knew.'

'But he wouldn't know,' Anne said quietly. 'Maybe his coming here today was a kind of invitation.'

Liz smiled. 'Perhaps it was. But I doubt it.'

The women ate on the patio. Evening trailed into a night that was calm and close, the light from the garden lamps falling in flat pools on the blossoms around them. They talked about flowers and gardens and work. Occasionally one or other of them went upstairs to check on the sleeping man. Liz opened a second bottle of wine as the moon rose above the sycamores and the talk turned to death and release.

'I think I'm almost ready for that,' Anne said. 'I told myself at Easter that if this summer was a good one, if he was well enough to go places with me, if we could get out and go for walks, if we could get to the sea, if we could go back…to places we'd...been together when…well, you know...'

'I know.'

'I thought if we could do those things, I'd be happy to let him go. But he may not want to go, he may not be ready to go for years. It's not as if he's capable of deciding that, or anything else, is it?'

Liz shook her head before she spoke. 'Perhaps he came back here subconsciously today, to see something he's getting ready to leave?'

Anne said nothing. She doubted that was why Paul had travelled the two miles between one house and the other, but she didn't feel it her place to say so. Instead she glanced at her watch.

'What time is it?' Liz asked.

'Just after one.'

'Will he wake now?'

Anne shook her head.

'Looks like we're here for the night, then,' Liz said. 'I have just the thing.'

She went inside and came back with fresh glasses and a bottle of liqueur.

'I brought this back from Greece last year,' she said. 'I was saving it for something. Why do we have this mania for saving things?'

'I don't know,' Anne smiled. 'For hope?'

Liz poured generous measures of the liqueur. 'I'm not so sure,' she said.

The two women drank in silence.

'If that's not to your liking, leave it,' Liz said.

'No, it's fine, I've never tasted it before. I'm sure it could do some damage to the grey matter.'

'So they say. Strange, isn't it?' Liz said, pointing to the upstairs bedroom. 'In all his life he never drank, and yet it's gone for him so soon. It must have been hard for you, in the early stages, when he knew what was happening.'

Anne nodded.

'I know, from experience, that he wasn't a patient patient.' She giggled at her own pun.

We fucked a lot, Anne said, but not out loud. We fucked to forget that he was forgetting. We fucked as if every time would be the last time until, finally, it was. And every time, I wanted to feel him inside me for as long as that was possible. Sometimes, I imagine I still do.

'I shouldn't really talk about him this way,' Liz said. 'It's unfair. It's better that we don't. It's your life and his, to whatever extent. It's a different time.'

'I don't mind talking about him,' Anne said. 'Really, I don't. It's good to talk to someone who knew him when he wasn't the way he is now. When he was whole. So many people never really knew him then. They look at his drawings and I tell them which buildings he designed and I know they can't believe me.'

Liz refilled their glasses. 'He's had so many lives,' she said. 'His time as a boy, his student days, his time married to me, his time married to you and now this twilight time when he's not anchored to anything.'

'I think he's very anchored,' Anne said quietly. 'He mentions the children sometimes, talks about them as though they're still young. Sometimes in the evening when we walk in the garden, he stands at the top of the lawn and asks me where they are and I explain to him that ours is a different garden from yours. I don't tell him they've grown up, as that wouldn't mean anything. But I think his coming back here was another chain to that anchor.'

Liz nodded, shrugging her shoulders. 'Are you warm enough?' she asked. 'I could get you a jumper.'

'No, I'm fine. Thanks.'

'What do you think of this liqueur?' Liz asked, the words stumbling slightly over one another.

'It's different.'

'It's disgusting. I have just the thing to bury it.'

She went back into the house and returned with brandy glasses and a bottle of Cognac.

'That should do the trick. The devil you know and all that. You pour.'

Going inside again, she put on some music. It streamed quietly through the open doors.

'That won't wake him?'

Anne shook her head.

'You talked about hope,' Liz said, taking a sip from her brandy glass. 'Do you still have hope for him, in spite of the emptiness? I don't have to live with the emptiness, and I don't think I could. There was an emptiness when we went our separate ways, but I imagine it was of a different kind. I could still see him, be angry with him, make him angry with me, until over the years it became less important, faded away. But you have to live with this hollowness, day in, day out.'

'I don't think about it. I do what has to be done. There are times when it's almost possible to forget, like when we're sitting together and I'm reading and he's watching the birds in the garden. Times like that have their own normality.'

'But then there must be other times, like this. When he escapes, when you have to search for him, when there's no normality in anything.'

'That rarely happens,' Anne said quickly, too quickly.

'I didn't mean it to sound accusatory. I meant there must be times when you wonder if there's any way out of this...'

The sentence went unfinished.

Anne looked away, across the shadowed garden, into the darkness that leeched the light from the open door.

'I suppose I try not to think that far ahead,' she said sadly. 'Maybe I haven't had to, or maybe I've chosen not to.'

The two women sat quietly, notes and phrases drifting up into the night sky like smoke.

'"How sour sweet music is when time is broke and no proportion kept."'

'It's beautiful,' Anne said. 'What is it?'

'Mascagni. The 'Intermezzo' from *Cavaleria Rusticana.*'

Silent again, they suddenly heard the music lift in an immense and passionate wave, swelling and trailing above the garden, where it hung for a moment, and then for a moment longer, until finally it washed back gently over them.

'That's the most beautiful thing I've ever heard.'

'It is beautiful, isn't it?'

It was sometime after five and light was fingering the sky. They were still sitting at the table, drinking large tumblers of water.

'I have to go to bed,' Liz said. 'My eyes are closing. You can have my bed, that's where Paul's sleeping. It's just the way it happened, where he went.'

Anne laughed. 'It doesn't need explaining.'

'Of course.'

'I'll probably just crash on the couch in the dining room, if you don't mind.'

'No, fine, absolutely. But you're welcome to sleep upstairs.'

'If he wakes early, he may want to go home, to our house. I won't wake you.'

'All right.'

'But thank you, again. It can't have been easy…you know. Thank you.'

Their bodies arched uneasily as the two women hugged, and then Liz was gone.

*

Anne woke to the sound of gentle, hesitant music. She lay on the couch listening. Sunlight lapped from the garden, through the open doorway, music following. The slow, uncertain, disconnected notes of 'Greensleeves'.

Walking barefoot across the room, she stepped into the lemony day. Her husband was sitting at the patio table, last night's accumulation of glasses lined up before him, tapping out each note with a teaspoon. Stopping, he poured a thimble of water into one of the glasses and sounded the note, listening closely, tapping again, listening, his head bent close to the table. He straightened then, and for a moment was very still, before the tune began again.

'Alas my love you do me wrong…' Anne softly sang to herself while her husband played on, a one-man band, making a bewildered, irregular and desolate music.

1939

In the fog the field forgets the river, forgets the trees and the road that passes its missing gate. In the fog it loses its shape and its identity. It might be any field or none. It has no dips and hollows, and springtime is hidden in the smoking roll of its coughing mist.

The light that seeps through the constant dullness is weak and grey, giving nothing back to the land. It might be the light of the sun or the light of the moon, as it hardly changes with the coming day and the falling night. The fog has settled as though it means to make a home of this field forever.

Deep Midwinter

The countryside had been swollen with fog for three days. The clothes on the washing-line at the end of the orchard were no more than suggestions, looming and fading in the numb morning light. John Hardy threw an armful of turf sods and two buckets of slack into the mouth of the kitchen range and opened the damper before banging a kettle onto the hot-plate and pulling his still-damp working trousers and coat from the rack above the range. It was a few minutes off seven on what should have been a clear, bright April morning. Instead, the small windows of Hardy's cottage were ashed with mist.

Twenty minutes later, when he opened the half-door, the fog swept in around him. Swinging onto his bicycle, he glanced quickly across the yard and up Barn Hill and knew the sky was set for another dreary, dreeping day. At the top of the lane, he turned for Prumplestown and work.

He was damned if weather was going to get him down. Weather was nothing. It might go on like this for days, and there might be more rain to follow, but it wouldn't dictate to him. And so he sang out loud, careering along the narrow roads and finally into the farmyard with his song echoing ahead of him.

His arrival drew a shout from one of the stables.

'Have you nothing better to be doing, Hardy, than annoying me with your singing on a miserable bastard of a morning like this?'

'The fog is like velvet to the skin,' Hardy laughed, freewheeling through the open door where Paddy Lawrence, the farm foreman, was brushing down a horse.

'Well, no sun, no wind, no drying today.'

Lawrence stepped away from the animal.

'I think you could take this fellow into Castledermot and have his shoes done. There's not much else to be at the morning.'

'Is there anything you want, while I'm in there?'

'Ten Woodbine.'

'Ten Woodbine it is.'

There were two horses in the forge yard.

'Not much doing this weather,' a waiting ploughman said as Hardy poked his head around the corner.

He knew the man to see but not well.

'What've you brought me?' the blacksmith asked.

'Dogger.'

'Fair enough, I could do with a quiet one. This whore'd kick you into kingdom come if you didn't watch her. And she's jink-backed.'

'Aye, but her drills are straight,' the ploughman said.

'I'll remember that when I'm prising her shoes out of my forehead.'

Hardy eased himself onto the worn wooden bench that ran the length of one wall of the forge. It was a good place to be on a cold day.

'Have youse got a start at all?' the ploughman asked.

'Not a sod. They brought the tractors down last week but this fellow ended up pulling them out of the field. It'll be a late one.'

'If it gets there at all.'

A figure passed on the lane, a woman bent low, the mist smoking around her and settling again after she'd gone.

The only sound was the hammering on the anvil and the *skuush* of a hot shoe plunged in water. And then the smothered noise of children's voices came from somewhere beyond the lane. Dogger snorted and Hardy walked out to pat his head and whisper a few sounds.

'Have you the word?' the ploughman asked.

Hardy shook his head.

'You?'

'No.'

The blacksmith looked up from his work, the firelight catching one side of his face.

'There's a lot that says they have, but devil the one I ever met in here that convinced me,' he grumbled.

Voices drifted from the schoolyard, dampened for a time, and then suddenly cleared again. Hardy had never been to the sea but he imagined this might be how it was, the waves breaking and creeping away, sound and then hardly any sound at all.

'Did you ever go to the sea?' he asked, walking back into the warmth of the forge.

'A few times,' the blacksmith said. 'Not a place to be of a day like this.'

Hardy wanted to ask him about the sound of the waves, what kind of noise it made when it fell on stones and rattled them, whether the water was loud when it turned to go back out, how it smelled. Things like that. But he didn't.

'I'm just going over to Kinsella's for fags,' Hardy said. 'The horse'll be all right there. I'll be back to hold him.'

The forge yard, the lane and Main Street were all soundless. The schoolyard had emptied of children and crows swooped quietly for crusts, scowling out at him from across the wall.

'And fuck you, too,' Hardy muttered.

He wished the fog would lift, wanted to catch sight of the sun, wanted to know there was a blue sky up there, to be reassured that life was going on and would go on.

Clattering in the door of Kinsella's shop, he said loudly, 'Ten Woodbine, Bill. And I want you to be the first to know that I'm going to go and look at the sea before the summer is out.'

'Good man yourself,' the shopkeeper said nonchalantly, already counting out the cigarettes. 'Give it my regards when you get there.'

'I will because I'm going to do it. I decided coming up the street. There's going to be sun and warm days and dry land and weather that'll make people want to get out and enjoy themselves and, when it comes, I'm going to be on the bus and going to the seaside. The summer of 1939 is the summer John Hardy goes to the sea.'

'Would you say this weather's getting you down?'

Hardy laughed. 'It might be, but I'm serious about the sea. It's something I'm going to do. It's madness living to forty-seven years of age and never catching sight of it, and we surrounded by it. So, it's done and decided, and there's the money for the fags.'

Cycling back to the farm, the horse trotting beside him, Hardy ignored the wet fog and imagined the sea. He allowed its resonance to build around him. Listened to the sound of water on the rocks. A sound, he imagined, like mugs swinging and clinking gently on a dresser. Inhaled the smell of the seaweed, something sharp like nettles. Tasted salt on the air. Considered how the little runner waves might quiver at his feet.

He would visit the sea, it was something he would definitely do. He had harboured notions, once, of singing with a dance-band, but they had faded. And there had been the possibility of marriage for some years, but that hope had sunk, too, and the woman was living in Birmingham. The last time she'd come home she'd had a boyfriend on her arm, and when he'd met her alone on the Church Lane, all she'd said was, 'You're a good man but I couldn't wait forever.'

But the sea would be his.

Lawrence roared at him from the doorway of a shed the farm labourers used as a canteen.

'You must've smelled the tae. It's a good man gets back for the tae. And, I bet you, you forgot the fags.'

'Clean forgot,' Hardy apologised, only his grin gave him away.

When the men came out of the shed twenty minutes later, the mist had thickened.

'For fuck's sake,' Lawrence said, 'it's enough to make a man go and stand in the canal.'

He looked up and down the yard.

'I'll tell you what, John; take the horse and cart, throw a crowbar in the back and go up the River Field and pull out the granite pillars along the primrose bank. The boss wants that fenced off with wood posts and wire, so we might as well get the pillars out of the ground; at least it'll be one thing done. Take it nice and handy. But sure, who am I telling?'

*

Climbing onto the seat, he jigged the horse out of the yard and onto the track that ran along the headlands of the fields. It was difficult to make out the gates until he was on them. He could see the outline of the hedges but not the wooden bars.

'If we get lost in this, horse, we won't be found for a week.'

The headland tracks were firm, despite the rain and snow of the previous months. Here and there the wheels gave him trouble but, all in all, it was an easy journey.

As they went up the last field, where the granite pillars staggered crookedly on the headland, Dogger slowed and pulled to the side. Muffling his coat around him, Hardy sang to the horse to calm him.

Two fields away, through a gap in the haze, he could see the back ditch of his own plot. Climbing down from the cart, he spoke to the horse.

'You stay here, now, fellow. Not a meg out of you till I run over and bank the fire.'

Pushing his way through the whitethorns, he was into the field that backed onto his garden. From there, it was only fifty yards to the orchard. On his way up the yard, he took two buckets from the coal shed and carried them into the house. Riddling down the ashes from the range, he threw in the slack and opened the damper slightly.

Turning, he caught sight of an envelope on the mat inside the door. What was seldom was wonderful. And the stamp was English. His name and address were carefully printed, the writing might be anyone's. Nine chances out of ten it was from his brother, but then again, you never knew. He put the envelope on the mantle. He'd save it, like a promise, and read it over his dinner. If it was from his brother there'd be plenty of news, enquiries about locals, the promise of a visit in the summer. But it might be from someone else, from Jenny O'Brien even. You never knew.

Taking the tools from the back of the cart, he set about his work. The granite posts, used as fence carriers, with the wire run through them, stood on the edges of fields all over the farm. Over the last two years, the boss had begun to replace them with wooden fencing. There was a shed in the low yard filled with granite posts that had been taken out of the ground, hundreds of them in neat stacks.

There was no doubting that the wooden fences were easier to wire, Hardy thought, but there was something about the pillars that was stout and reliable. They might be a hundred years in the ground, maybe longer, he had no real idea. But he did know local people had erected them, men like himself, farm labourers who worked in all kinds of weather. And there was a lot to be said for the fact that he was one in a line.

These pillars had been hacked out of the face of some granite cliff up in Wicklow, loaded onto sturdy carts and lugged down into Kildare. Slow days on the road before they were dropped off around the fields, buried feet deep in the sandy soil, chiselled and wired. That was work and sweat and history, something to be thinking about.

He spat on his palms, grabbed the pickaxe and started on the first pillar, peeling back the strips of sod and driving the head of the tool well into the sand, cutting around the stone. To look at it, you'd expect the pillar to keel over, but Hardy knew from experience that it was well buried, its root jammed hard with rocks and shale. He picked away at the ground, loosening the soil and the small stones. Then he took his shovel and cleared a dyke before picking deeper again.

Sweat bubbled on his face and he felt it dropping from his armpits.

'Summer weather, horse,' he laughed over his shoulder.

He was digging deeper now, lifting out fists of stone, the shovel catching on awkward corners of rock, levering them with the head of the pick, painstakingly rooting until finally the first pillar swayed slightly in the ground.

'Now, horse,' Hardy said. 'Your turn to do a bit.'

Putting one end of the chain around the pillar, he tied the other to the back of the cart and slowly urged the horse onward.

'Easy now, easy now, easy. Easy.' His tone was low but firm.

He kept his eye on the pillar, watching its progress. Inch by inch it grated out of the rocky ground before falling quietly among the wet primroses.

'Good, horse. Good,' he said, patting the animal's head before going to remove the chain.

The second of the pillars, resting between two boulders, was going to prove more difficult. Again Hardy dug a shallow trench, but he quickly saw that he'd have to move at least one of the boulders if he were to loosen enough earth to pull out the pillar. Nothing for it but to dig the clay and gravel from around the boulder and then try to shift it with a crowbar and chain.

Methodically he picked at the sods, the clay, the sand and loam, opening a wound around the squat, mossy boulder. As he dug, the horse stirred uneasily, his harness creaking and brasses jingling dully.

'Easy, horse, easy now, good horse,' Hardy said without looking up from his work.

But the horse didn't quieten. Instead he backed away further, pushing the cart behind him, the wheels catching and scraping on brambles. Hardy looked up and into the animal's startled eyes. If the horse kept backing like this, he'd end up with the cart in a dyke. Dropping his shovel, Hardy took the head collar, running his fingers inside it, soothing the animal, leading him away from the ditch and down the headland.

'Easy there, horse. Easy on.'

He walked the animal twenty yards down the field, calming him as he went.

'What's at you, hah? What's at you? Now, take it easy there.'

There was no point in rushing things, and anyway he still had an hour's work ahead of him before he could even think of trying to chain and shift the boulder.

'Now, you stay there. Good fellow.'

Returning to the work, Hardy began to dig again. There was no telling how deep or wide the base of the boulder might be. Better to clear away the shale and see the damage.

The spade sank cleanly into the ground, and he lifted the sand and threw it to one side. And down again, the face of the shovel shining after the wash of gravel. Each time he dug the shovel face came up cleaner, catching whatever light there was in the dull afternoon. And then the shovel jagged on something. Hardy propped it against the boulder and lifted the pickaxe, angling the sharp head under the obstruction, prising it out of the ground. It came away easily enough and he bent to lift what appeared to be a soft rock from the ground. But it wasn't a rock. Turning the light shell in his hand, he found himself staring into the empty eye sockets of a yellow skull.

By the time Hardy and Paddy Lawrence had uncovered the rest of the skeleton, it was dusk. The boss had gone to find Sergeant Kavanagh and Doctor Bates. In the meantime, the two men dug carefully around the remains of the body.

'How long do you reckon this fellow is here?' Hardy asked.

'Jasus knows. He has the look of a Carlow man about him though, the thin jaw and the sunk eyes.'

The pair laughed quietly.

'That's if it is a fellow.'

There were remnants of a coat of some kind, scraps of red woven cloth along the arms.

'It might be a woman,' Hardy said. 'The cloth might be a dress or a coat.'

'It might.'

That possibility subdued them and they worked on silently, brushing away the sand with their hands, the remains taking shape before their eyes.

Around and above them the birds sang in the early evening.

'The Lord have mercy on them,' Hardy said.

When finally the boss arrived with the sergeant and the doctor, the skeleton had been fully uncovered, and Hardy had put the skull back, more or less where it belonged.

'A while there,' the sergeant said.

The doctor knelt over the bones.

'Can't say for certain, but we'll find out.'

'Man or woman?'

'Male.' He ran his hands along the skeleton.

'One hip bone damaged, from birth; walked with a limp, I imagine,' he said to the sergeant, who was making notes. 'And the boots are still there, in bits and pieces. We'd better get him out of here. I'll get Carver to send out a hearse and a coffin, take him to Naas, try to put a date on him. Can we bring him somewhere, in the meantime?'

'Put him in the cart, bring it down to the yard,' the boss suggested.

'I don't think the horse'll take him. We can try, but I doubt he'll do it,' Hardy said, describing the animal's behaviour earlier in the afternoon.

'Right,' the doctor sighed. 'We'll just have to carry him. Put everything in, bones, whatever cloth there is, boot leather, the lot.'

'There's a tarpaulin in the cart,' Hardy said quietly. 'If you want, and I'm just saying, my house is only over the next field. We could take him there.'

While Paddy Lawrence and the boss took the horse and cart back to the farm and the doctor went to get his car, the sergeant and Hardy carried the skeleton carefully in the tarpaulin, manoeuvring it through the gaps in the ditches.

Reaching Hardy's cottage, they left the skeleton in the shed and went inside.

The fire was blazing in the range, the kettle humming softly.

'A cup of tea?'

'I wouldn't say no.'

It was almost eight o' clock when the hearse arrived and the skeleton was taken away. Hardy had gone out with the sergeant, the doctor and the undertaker and held a lamp for them while they lifted the tarpaulin into a plain coffin and slid it into the back of the hearse.

When he finally sat down to his evening meal sometime after nine, the sergeant's words came back to him.

'Mark my word, John, once someone sees the hearse coming out your lane, they'll have it all over Castledermot that you're dead.'

Smiling at the thought, he decided against going into Doyle's for a drink. If the word was out, he might as well give it legs.

It was only when his meal was over and the dishes washed that he sat at the fire and opened the letter that had come that afternoon.

It wasn't from Jenny O'Brien.

He mulled over the news his brother had sent from England, smiled at the comments about men they'd grown up with, read that his niece was getting married in August and they'd love him to come over. His brother's letters came every three months or so – Christmas, Easter, late summer and Hallowe'en, more or less – and they were always packed with bits and pieces of gossip and sharp comments about the locals.

Finishing the missive, he found a pen and a copybook and sat at the table to write a reply. He was glad to hear they were all well. It was great news about Eileen. Yes, of course he would come to the wedding, why wouldn't he, wasn't she his goddaughter?

He thought of the sea again. Of sailing across it, seeing both shores. And he thought of Jenny O'Brien. The Castledermot community in Birmingham was closely knit. There was every chance she'd be at the wedding. It'd be nice to see her again. But he didn't say as much in the letter, just that he'd love to be there to share Eileen's day, and it'd be great to see them all and to catch up with some of the old crowd.

Later, lying in bed, he pictured the scene in Doyle's, half the village assuming he was dead, and he laughed aloud.

And he thought of Jenny, ten years younger than himself, thirty-seven and still beautiful, still so like the young girl he'd fallen in love with. He remembered singing for her on evenings when they were walking back to her house.

Drifting off to sleep, he woke around midnight to hear the wind squalling outside his window, rising with every gust, and he knew the fog would be gone by morning. And thinking again of Jenny, he sang out loud in the dark, solid echo of his bedroom. Sang for her, for the first time in fifteen years, using the raging wind as a level, his voice rising above the gusts that roared. He sang, he imagined, like he had never sung before, his tenor coming back from the bare walls of the room, ringing around him, each line swallowed by the echo of the one that had gone before.

The weather finally took up the week after he found the skeleton at Barn Hill, the first week of May 1939, and John Hardy got to do the ploughing he should have started eight weeks earlier.

All the bushes along the ditches suddenly put out buds and the whitethorn snowed overnight. The headlands were littered with wildflowers, cowslips coming late and primroses spreading like yellow fire along the sides of banks. The bluebells, dormant for weeks, began to bloom, rinsing the grasses in the wooded, shady paths behind the barns. In the orchard, the trees were unexpectedly alive again, blossoming in one blue-skied week.

On the Saturday afternoon, the sergeant called, just after Hardy arrived home from work. He was beaming.

'Well,' he said, ducking in through the open door, 'you'll be glad to hear our bony friend is ready for burying.'

'Do you know who he was?'

The sergeant shrugged. 'No. There's a few possibilities, but nothing certain yet. Investigations are ongoing, as we say,' the sergeant laughed.

'How long was he buried above?'

'Sixty, eighty years. Something like that.'

'I should go to the funeral.'

'That'd be good. I'll be there myself.'

There were six people in the church. Hardy had taken two hours off work. He knelt near the front of the main aisle. The church was bright and hot, sunlight pouring through the stained-glass windows, soaking the plain coffin in runs of red, blue, green and yellow. The sergeant knelt in the pew behind him. The undertaker and the gravediggers sat across the aisle. The priest spoke some words about loss.

Afterwards, Hardy followed the hearse to the graveyard and when the burial was over, he folded his coat and snapped it onto the carrier of his bike. The sergeant was crossing the stile in the wall, leaving the gravediggers to their work.

'No word since on who he might be?' Hardy asked.

'No. Still nothing definite, dead and gone. What we don't know won't worry us.'

'I suppose.'

'That'll be another roaster,' the sergeant said, peering into the sunlight.

'It will.'

He pulled on his cap and buttoned his tunic.

'Now, back to the land of the living.'

2007

It's a twelve-acre field. Triangular.

A narrow country road still sidesteps along one ditch as it passes the wide opening framed by two cut stone pillars.

At the far end of the field, the headland still tumbles gently into the shadowed water and two oaks bend as they have bent, slightly towards each other, for over two hundred years.

The third side of the triangle is strung with a broken necklace of granite pillars on a rabbit-warrened mound.

And the meadow that draws these sides together is still deep and bountiful with the shining flowers of July.

Breathless

A light suddenly shatters, splintering down the side of Rice's Hill, between the few remaining furze bushes, tumbling into the mirror of the river, smashing that too, throwing beams in all directions. Morning has fractured and night is over.

Look carefully and there are five pairs of footwear scattered in the grass. Silver stillettos, white runners, brown walking shoes, black boots and a tiny pair of pink Wellingtons, with elephants on the side. Suddenly, as if spirited from nowhere, three women and a teenage girl come walking through the dewy field, as if unaware of each other, bent on finding their shoes.

'They used to crucify me,' the slight woman says, but to herself. 'Something about the arches, I don't know what it was.'

The young girl pushes past her and picks the runners from the ground.

'They weren't the best pair in the shop, but I got a staff discount and that…'

Her voice trails away as someone laughs from behind her, the voice of a red-haired woman.

'Surrounded by shoes. There must have been twenty pairs scattered all over the place, everywhere you looked, shoes, shoes, shoes.'

And near the ditch, the fourth woman, fair-haired, quietly spoken, takes the silver stillettos from the grass, wiping them dry.

'I got these for a wedding,' she says. 'My first cousin's

wedding. On my father's side – my father's brother's daughter.'

The red-haired woman is still laughing, speaking quickly, twirling as she does so, as if trying to include the others in her conversation.

'The right one of this and the left one of that and one of a pair in the wrong box and the sales assistant, as she liked to call herself, standing behind me going *tsst tsst tsst*, like I was taking the last place in the last lifeboat off the fucking *Titanic* and leaving her behind.'

'These fitted fine in the shop,' the slight woman says, as if ignoring the other three, 'but once I wore them for more than twenty minutes my feet felt like they were ready to fall off.'

The young girl – how old is she, fifteen or perhaps sixteen? – kneels on the grass and holds her runners close to her face. We need a name for her. Something plain, something ordinary, but there are no names to give. A name would be a certainty and there is no certainty here. We can't even be certain that we're hearing or seeing what we believe we hear and see.

'I bought these and then I bought a football shirt for my little brother,' she says, but no one listens because the red-haired woman is still laughing, still talking.

'And I wouldn't mind but half the shoes weren't mine. I'd only tried on eight or nine pairs. The rest belonged to someone else. She was just too fucking lazy to tidy the place, it was like she expected me to do it for her.'

The girl looks up, as if trying to find a face that's interested, and then continues.

'I just tried them on and they fitted, were comfortable,

really, really snug. It was like I'd been wearing them for months. I put the old ones in my locker in the canteen,' she says, but still no one is listening.

The slight woman sits on the damp bank and pulls on the black boots.

'I'll bet they still fit like a glove when I put them on. I can wear them for a while but then they cut the feet off me. A friend of mine one time bought a pair of shoes for a wedding and she had to take them off in the church, halfway through the Mass, they were that bad.'

The girl smiles, diving into the silence that follows.

'My father used to say every pair of shoes takes you on a journey. When we were kids, he'd tie up our laces and say: Let's hope today's is a long journey and a happy one.'

As silence closes again about the women, suddenly each is aware of the other three, and all of them wary. It's the red-haired woman who finally speaks, smiling again.

'The gas thing is that I was thinking about leaving anyway. Be careful what you wish for, you might get it. Of course, thinking about something and doing it are horses of a different colour. Plus, if I'm honest, I was probably thinking of leaving from about eighteen months into the marriage. But I think that's the way with a lot of people. The other gas thing is that this was only the second time in my life that I got my picture in the local paper. The first time was at a night out in one of the local pubs: there was four of us, scuttered, and we looked it. But to make things worse, we were all over the shop, like we had moved when the picture was being taken. But we hadn't, it was the way they printed it. Each of us with three eyebrows and our mouths up around our noses and our noses pushing up our eyes. Plus whatever way it happened it looked like I had no top on. He looked at it and went *tsst tsst*, like he was a fucking teacher or something, and says: You look like a whore, like you were gagging for a ride. I said nothing but I thought about it, all that night and all the next day when he was at work. And I thought, You fucking bastard. It's all right for you to call me a whore when we're in bed and you think it does something for me, and it's all right for you to laugh and call me a ride in front of your mates, but it's not all right when it doesn't suit you. But that's the way he is, just the way he is and I don't know why. Could never put my finger on what it was that changed him. Anyway, this is not about him. This is about me. Me and my body. Bodies are funny things. We're never satisfied with them; well, I wasn't anyway. I wanted to change these. Not that I want to be going around with a pair of Dolly Partons in front of me, like outriders in the President's cavalcade. But I'd like to have something…out there…you know. But that's another thing – it depends on how you're feeling, doesn't it? It depends on the way you see yourself. Even blind people must have days when they think they look great, and days where they feel like the sweepings off the hairdresser's floor. And that can't be down to looks, could it? I mean, a blind person saying How do I look? is talking through their hat, aren't they? It's all in the head. Same as the rest of us. Not that I'd want to be blind. Deaf before blind and dumb before deaf. That's the way I'd have it. And have it now: dumb, deaf and blind. Sort of. Not that it feels the way I imagined it'd feel, if I'd ever thought about it, which I didn't.'

She looks at the others but they seem not to know what to say. And then she laughs out loud.

'Just forget it. Forget it. If Alice was here she'd be laughing at me. There you go, she'd say, there you go complicating things again, making mountains out of molehills.'

'I often wondered about that,' the young girl says quietly.

'About what?'

'About how blind people know whether they look good or not, you know; whether their teeth are clean or their hair is straight or their shoelaces tied.'

'They wear slip-ons,' the slight woman says.

'Huh?'

'All blind people wear slip-on shoes.'

'Do they?'

'Yep, unless they have guide-dogs that are trained to tie laces. The problem with Labradors is that they can't do that, their paws are too big, too awkward. So most blind people have to wear slip-ons. Collies can do it, but you don't see too many collie guide dogs, collies aren't great in other respects. They tend to walk out in front of lorries, so it's swings and roundabouts. No good having your laces tied if you get pancaked by a juggernaut. Jesus, that bus made a terrible mess of him, didn't it? Where's the dog? Oh there he is, under the back wheels; still, they went together, didn't they. That's nice. And his laces are nicely tied and that's the main thing! I often thought it'd be a good idea to return the favour – you know, blind dogs for the Guides. Worn-out sanctuaries for the donkeys, that kind of thing.'

'Piano donor cards,' the red-haired woman adds quickly.

'Sorry?'

'Piano donor cards. Why is it just organs that get donated? Why not pianos?'

'Good one. Yeah, that's it.'

'Spawn shops for frogs.'

'Short grass for small sheep.'

The two women laugh uproariously.

'Primates in the Vatican.'

'Is that true?' the girl asks.

'Is what true?'

'About the guide dogs and the shoes?'

The red-haired woman looks at the young girl and realises she's serious.

'No, it's not true; don't mind her, she's taking the piss.'

'But it'd be a good idea.'

'Yeah, great,' the slight woman says, sneering. "Blind man seeks far-seeing woman. No ties."'

But any irony is lost on the girl.

'I'd hate to be blind,' she says.

The red-haired woman is laughing again. 'Are all Venetians blind?'

'It'd be curtains for the tourist trade if they were!' the slight woman says, standing up suddenly, her laughter competing with the rising birdsong from the ditches around them.

'There's a thing, seriously, that's puzzled me for years,' the red-haired woman says, trying to keep a straight face. 'If it's anal, why isn't it the Royal Canal?'

'Ask my arse!'

And the pair are off again, gasping with laughter.

The fair-haired woman walks away from the other three, skirting the side of the field, until she reaches the riverbank. There she squats in a length of early shadow from a whitethorn, watching the river flow, never lifting her eyes from the running water. Behind her, the laughter dies away and she can hear the voice of the red-haired woman.

'I have this friend, my best friend, Alice. We grew up together, started school together, left school the same day, got jobs in the same factory, all that stuff. Got poled the same month – how's that for getting the timing right? The difference was that I got married and she didn't. Wise fucking woman. Anyway, when things started going skew ways between him and me, when I started looking at other guys and thinking – yeah, well maybe or yeah, fucking too right, I'd ride him – Alice sits me down one night over a few jars and starts on at me about not throwing everything away. But I told her: "You can't wake the fucking dead, Alice; he's not Lazarus and I'm not Jesus. I can't resurrect him." She told me I was only saying that because I was pissed. She said I'd end up sad and sorry and trying to find someone on one of them computer sites. I hadn't the heart to tell her I'd already met someone that way. "Tall, single, handsome, self-employed, good talker." Bollocks. Married, no hair and a wart like a frog's arse over his left eye. Conversation! Hah! "You've lovely tits. Do you wanna fuck?"'

The fair-haired woman gets up and walks farther along the bank, away from the other three. The slight woman watches her and then says loudly, wanting to be heard, 'Be careful – you might offend someone.'

She then follows the fair-haired woman along the riverbank until she's standing beside her, so close they might touch, if touch were possible.

'Just go away, get out of my space, go!' The fair-haired woman's sharp voice rises above the birdsong and the sound of the river. The slight woman giggles and shimmies around her, forcing her backwards, back towards the other two, laughing and pretending to dance erotically as she follows.

'You're a good dancer,' the young girl says. 'I love dancing.'

The slight woman goes on with her performance, dancing about an invisible pole.

The girl smiles.

'Do you like dancing?' she asks.

'No,' the fair-haired woman says, not wanting to be a part of the conversation.

'Why not?'

'I just don't.'

'Her legs are stuck together, that's why,' the slight woman laughs.

'Why are you doing this?' the fair-haired woman asks, her face suddenly animated.

'Doing what?'

'Going out of your way to provoke me? Your attitude – your attempts to shock – your assumptions.'

The slight woman laughs in her face.

'Cop yourself on,' she says. 'The minute I saw you, I knew you were a dry, stuffy, self-opinionated, miserable fucker. I see people like you every day – Plan fucking V for very important in the VHI, house private, Off-Roader with bullbars to collect the milk from the shop, off-shore account, up your own arse. "I have an appointment with Professor Menyamenya – it's a personal matter." We all know, dearie, the whole clinic knows your tits are drooping and your arse is sagging and you think he can do something to help you recapture the youth you never had because your nose was in a book and your mind numbed with information. That's why, since you asked. Three years of frustration and bias and you're the lucky recipient. Next case!'

The young girl stares, mouth open, stunned.

'Are you a doctor?' she asks.

'Some chance, Angel-Arse. I'm Florence Nightingale, the smiling nurse in the nice, tight, white uniform. Sister of mercy and fantasy figure. Bedpans, blow jobs, colonic irrigations, whatever you're having yourself. D'you mind if I put your dick in my mouth? Which reminds me, have you ever noticed the stupid look men get when they're coming? The way their eyes roll up in their heads and their mouths drop open like the door of a dishwasher, you know that kind of Aaaaaah, I'm dying, no one's ever come like me before. Wankers.'

'I'd love to have been a nurse,' the girl's face lights up.

The slight woman sighs deeply. 'No, you wouldn't.'

'I would. I was sorry I left school early. I'd love to be a nurse, it's a nice job, nice doctors. It'd be lovely to marry a doctor.'

'Fuck!' the slight woman says, exasperated.

'Interesting how often education is more valued in its absence.' The fair-haired woman's voice is quiet, not sure the others will hear, or want to hear, her.

'Huh?'

'Think of all the people who say – I wish I'd worked harder or stayed in school.'

'Yeah,' the girl nods. 'I suppose.'

And then the slight woman is talking again. 'Oh, Jesus, spare me your shite talk.'

But this time the fair-haired woman doesn't back away.

Instead she stands her ground, face to face with her persecutor.

'What is your problem with allowing other people to have an opinion?'

'Sorry?'

'You have to dominate everything, don't you?'

'Yes, Miss. It's just that I hate hearing people talking bollocks.'

'No, it's more than that.'

'You'd know – of course. You'd know everything. I bet you've known everything all your life; I bet you came out of your mother's cunt knowing everything.'

The fair-haired woman is silent for a moment and when she speaks her voice is quiet, as if she has already withdrawn from the argument.

'There are things that are appropriate and things that aren't. That is inappropriate.'

'Inappropriate?' The slight woman laughs, a dry, humourless laugh. 'Do you think so? Do you think it really matters? We're all in the same hearse here, baby. Nothing's inappropriate here. Do you know how I got here? A pair of my own knickers pulled tight around my neck in a nice warm bed, in a nice detached house in its own grounds, with a nice respectable well-educated man, till my face turned blue and my eyes went pop. I went there for fun, for a shag with someone I knew, someone I thought I could trust, and I ended up dead – now if you were to ask me, that's what I'd call inappropriate. The rest of it is just fucking inconvenient.'

She steps quickly away. The other three women stand in silence, watching her go, absorbing the truth in what she has said, the truth that has hung, unspoken, between them since their arrival. And then she's turning, walking back towards them, her finger pointing, talking loudly.

'What would you call inappropriate now? Seriously, I'm asking you. Now that we're all dead and shoved into some hole in the middle of a fucking bog or thrown in the sea or buried under a field of thistles, what else might be inappropriate?'

'Nothing,' the fair-haired woman says and her voice is a whisper.

'I still think a nurse is a good job,' the girl says.

She and the slight woman are sitting on the bank at the side of the field. The sun is well up now, a vibrant blot on the open sky, its brightness diluting the blue around it.

'Don't you believe it, Angel-Arse. What did you do?'

'I was a cashier in a supermarket.'

'Like it?'

'It was all right.'

'Boyfriend?'

'Sort of.'

'Is that why you're here?'

'God, no,' the girl says, genuinely shocked. 'He's really quiet. I only just started going out with him – first he was a friend, just someone. I was working on it.'

'Good for you. What age are you?'

'Fifteen, but I'm nearly sixteen; my birthday's the end of next month.'

'Not any more,' the fair-haired woman says from the shadow of the whitethorn.

'Sorry?'

'No more birthdays – for any of us.'

'Well, we'll have birthdays anyway. Won't we? Being dead doesn't stop us having birthdays, does it? We went to my father's grave on his birthday.'

'Yeah,' the slight woman says, 'but you were alive – you were going there, he wasn't going there. It's the bloody living who keep remembering, not us. Is he long dead, your dad?'

'Eight months.'

'And you?'

'I don't know, six, seven weeks, something like that.'

'Have you got family?'

'My mam and my brother.'

'Right.'

'They must be sad,' the girl says, as though it's something that has just crossed her mind.

'That's one way of putting it,' the slight woman replies, unable to mask her sarcasm.

But the girl isn't listening, she's miles away.

'I loved my dad. He only worked in the sewerage plant, but when he'd start talking about it, it was like he was talking about something that was so important. The gravity feed and the greaser and the screens and separators and the aeration system. "Two-and-a-half million litres a day coming in there," he'd say, like it was money he'd won in the Lotto, something to be really proud of. And he was proud of it, proud of the treatment plant, proud of the fact that he worked there, proud like it was his. "The bacteria is the boy that does the work," he'd say, "that's the boy to make you hop."'

'Them,' fair-haired woman interjects. 'Bacteria are plural!'

'It was, it was like, like it was all working away there for him, because he told it to. And you'd always know when he was annoyed, really annoyed with someone. He'd say: "There's more than one kind of shite."'

'Man after my own heart,' the slight woman smiles.

'That was the thing about Colin, the guy I fancied. When we got talking, in the canteen in work, he asked me what my father used to do and I told him and he didn't laugh. Maybe because my father had just died, maybe because he thought I'd be upset, but I don't think so – I think it was because he's a nice guy. Kind. It's nice when people are kind, isn't it?'

She looks about her, expecting an answer, but the other three are silent. She's not sure if they're listening or if they've lost interest. But their silence forces her to continue.

'When my father died, my brother, Jeffrey, told me he wouldn't cry. He said my aunt had told him he was the man of the family now and that he wasn't to be crying at the funeral. She said it'd only upset my mother. Jeffrey is only thirteen years old and there he was, afraid to cry! He was a kid, still scared of the dark, of girls, of most things, and on top of that he was afraid to cry because he thought he'd be letting my mother down, letting himself down. I remember him carrying my father's coffin. He's tall but he's as thin as a rake and the coffin was digging into his shoulder, the weight of it pushing him down. That night, I went in to his room to see if he was OK and to say goodnight to him and I was sitting on his bed talking to him and I noticed this welt on his shoulder, where the edge of the coffin had cut into his skin, a big, ugly, red welt where the angle of the coffin had worn it away and it looked just so sore and cruel. I felt so sorry for him.'

Again she is silent. But again the silence of her companions compels her to go on.

'I'm glad he won't have to carry my coffin; I'd hate to think of him having to do that, I'd really, really hate it. I'm better off out here. Never liked graveyards anyway, everything in straight lines, like the way I used to have to stack the cornflakes when I started in the supermarket. I was a stacker then, before I was a cashier. I reckon I'm better off away from the town. I wouldn't want my mother seeing me go down into the same grave as my father. There's only room enough for two in the plot and it's only right that she'd be buried with him. It's funny, I kind of don't mind being dead for myself; just for them, for Mam and Jeffrey. But then, they don't know I'm dead. Not for sure.'

Only then does anyone speak. It's the fair-haired woman, still seated in the whitethorn shadow.

'I think they do. They all do. I think, deep down, they're as certain as we are.'

'Do you?'

'Yes, I do.'

'How did it happen?' the slight woman asks the girl.

'I was walking home from work, it was about half ten at night. Two guys in a van pulled up, they pulled me into the back. There was this dance music going, you know, with the heavy bass, *badum badum, badum*, going real loud in the van. Every time I asked them to let me go, they'd tell me to shut my mouth and turn the music up louder. They drove for a long time, out of the town, it got darker and darker and then we turned off the road and down a track and then they stopped the van. When they were taking me out of it, they pulled me by the hair. It really hurt.'

'And then they raped you,' she says, matter of factly.

'Yeah.'

The slight woman laughs again, the same dry, humourless laugh.

'The bastards are always the same. Let them fuck you and they want to show you who's the boss; don't let them fuck you and they're even more determined to show you.'

'They both did and then…again…and then I thought they were going to leave me there but one of them went to the back of the van and got a shovel and I knew. And then he hit me with it, across the face, with the back of it and the pain went right through me and I started praying that they'd do it fast. Then, when I was lying on the ground, he brought the side of it down on my skull.'

She touches the side of her head, tenderly, as though expecting to find blood.

'Do you believe in God?' she asks, turning to the fair-haired woman.

'I believe in something greater than me.'

'I wonder!' the slight woman mocks.

'Do you believe there's a heaven?'

'I believe heaven is a place – no, a state – of being, just being. It's peace and freedom and connection. There's no isolation, no aloneness, no separation, no needs, no desires; it's desire that causes human suffering.'

'I used to nick money from the till in work. I was always worried that if I died without confessing it, I wouldn't get to heaven.'

And then the slight woman is laughing again, standing over the young girl, bending to look into her face.

'If there was a heaven, Angel-Arse, do you think you'd have been taken off the roadside? Or do you think some

God, in his fluffy cloudy paradise, surrounded by little cherubs strumming harps, would have said: "Take her, she's fifteen and she'd been robbing the till in the supermarket; get that pair of bastards to pull her into their van and rape her and beat her head in with a shovel. That'll be a lesson to her and everyone else not to pilfer again."'

'You have no right to say that to her,' the fair-haired woman says, her eyes angry.

'This isn't about rights. She's dead, you're dead, we're all fucking dead. We have no rights. Rights are for the lucky ones. I'm sure you had rights, lots of rights, when you were alive, but not here, not any more. This is the democracy of the dead, Mrs Fucking Look-at-Me-I'm-Great.'

Even the birds have fallen silent in the midday heat. They sit like deeper shadows in the stumped shadows of the trees and bushes along the water's edge. Only a kingfisher flicks over the face of the river, a spurt of colour, there and gone, if it was there at all.

The three women are lying in the yellow grass at the foot of an oak, eyes closed, their palms open to the sky. The young girl is sitting, her back against the tree, staring into the blue above her.

'Will I get to dance in heaven?' she whispers, not sure that anyone is still awake.

'Fucking hell,' the slight woman says, without opening her eyes. 'How did I end up in the place where the crazies go? A dancing wanna-be nurse! At least you'd never be stuck for work in a club! Bring your own pole.'

'Are you a good dancer?' the fair-haired woman asks quietly.

'I think so,' the girl says.

'Go on, show us,' the red-haired woman says, opening her eyes and raising herself on one elbow. 'Go on, do, please.'

Seeing the older woman's smiling eyes, the young girl gets up and moves out of the shadow of the tree. She dances, uncertainly at first, but then with growing confidence, spiralling and pirouetting in the sunlight, closing her own eyes now, nodding to a melody from somewhere, some memory of a rhythm that was life.

'Pity you didn't dance away from the two bastards in the van,' the slight woman says, squinting into the sun.

The young girl stops dead and walks away, out into the middle of the field, away from the women and the shadows of the trees and the whisper of the river.

'What is it with you?' the red-haired woman barks, her rage plain to hear. 'Can you not let anything go? She's just a kid. Why are you so angry?'

'What a stupid fucking question.'

'Right then, why are you angrier than the rest of us? What gives you the right to be more hurt, more badly done by than anyone else?'

'Because I'm sick listening to this shit. Listening to Miss High-and-Mighty talking down to us.'

'Bollocks!' the red-haired woman laughs. 'You were angry before you met her.'

'And what if I was?'

'So why?'

'Is this a fucking inquisition? What are you, a Jesuit?'

'I'm just asking,' she says evenly.

For a moment the slight woman is silent, and then she launches into her reply.

'All right, I'll tell you. When I was growing up, there was a cross at the end of our lane, where it came out onto the main road, a little white cross with a girl's name on it. Margaret Murphy. She was four years old when she ran out in front of a car and her mother never got over the fact that she was dead. She used to wander around the farmyard or the garden or the house all day, talking to Margaret, and she'd shout at me when I was going to school in the morning, and she'd shout at me when I was coming home from school in the evening, and I was terrified of her. I was sorry for Margaret and I hated her at the same time, for getting all the attention and I hated my mother for always talking about her, for being so consumed by her, for keeping this dead little girl alive in her head, for forgetting that I was her fucking daughter too, for not seeing that I needed to be hugged and held and pampered and loved. And I despised my father for not standing up to her, for not telling her that I was important, just as important as the little dead girl in the flowery summer frock. Will that do for starters? And by the time my turn came, that mad woman was dead and buried herself, still raving about little Margaret this and little Margaret that. When I died, when I disappeared, there was no one to look for me, or to talk about the kind of kid I was, or say how well I'd done, or to meander up and down the garden talking aloud to me. Nobody and nothing. People forget the ones who disappear, forget we even lived. And they don't know we're here, still…existing…wandering, fucking wandering, bumping into one another like a game of blind man's bluff, just talking, then drifting away. Listening to little Miss Nijinsky singing and dancing around heaven all day.'

'Nijinsky was a man,' the fair-haired woman says, delighted. And then the slight woman in on her feet, screaming.

'Fuck off, you fucking fuck.'

'I thought Nijinsky was a horse,' the young girl says, from the middle of the field.

'He was one of the foremost ballet dancers of the twentieth century,' the fair-haired woman tells her.

'Thank you for that,' the slight woman says, her tone now controlled and bitter. 'You must have worked as a travelling encyclopaedia in your spare time, did you? I'll bet your husband couldn't wank without consulting your inner pages. Sorry, darling, don't come just yet, I'm on fourteen across, it's an anagram of my fanny. If you had a husband. If you didn't drive him away.'

The slight woman, the young girl and the red-haired woman are dawdling on the riverbank, their toes only inches above the blue water. The trees have begun to grow shadows again in the early afternoon. The red-haired woman is speaking.

'I was never sure…that life goes on… for us…here. I was never sure about that, about what would happen after it was over. I never expected life to go on here, too. I thought it'd be different. Better. Or worse. But different.'

'I thought there'd be choirs singing and that I'd be in one,' the girl says.

The slight woman laughs.

'And you'd have angel wings to match your angel arse!'

The red-haired woman frowns, waiting for her companion to add something else, something even more cynical, something hurtful, but there's only the near-silence of the river at the their feet.

'There must have been things in your life, before all this; things that were good.'

'Obviously,' the slight woman says.

'It'd be nice to hear about them.'

'I hate that word – nice – it means nothing.'

'Good, then. Good to hear about the good things.'

'Why?'

'Because maybe that's all we have – memories. Maybe they're the only things we have any control over. Sometimes I think about my husband, about the fact that most people probably believe he killed me. They're walking around the town, pointing him out to their kids, telling them to keep away from that man because he murdered his wife. I laugh about that because there's nothing else to laugh at and sometimes you have to laugh at something, or it just gets worse and worse and drags you down. I used to hate it when my mother said, You have to have a laugh, don't you? But I think she was right; I do now, anyway.'

'I don't see it that way.'

'One time, in the pub, I was talking to some of my friends about a course I was doing, telling them about how the instructor guy told us we had to think outside the box, when my husband pipes up with this pretend thick-o expression: Thinking outside the box, that's foreplay, isn't it? He was just trying to fuck up my story, trying to make me look stupid. But sometimes I think back and it makes me smile. It was funny. He was just acting the bollocks, but it was funny.'

The slight woman smiles and is quiet for a while. And then she starts talking, determined to have her say, afraid almost that she will lose faith in the story she is telling.

'We remember our lives, you know, and the things we remember are different from the things other people remember. Or they don't remember at all. I have cousins and an aunt, but what'll they remember of me? They remember things, but not the things I remember or the way I remember them. No one will remember me as I was. Or you. They'll remember the picture they had of you. My cousins will remember a wild woman that liked to drink and fuck and live life for today. But they won't know about the woman that went back to her home place three weeks before she died, back to the farmhouse, back to the orchard that's gone to hell and the sheds that are falling down. And they won't know anything about the woman that was saving her money to put a new roof on that house so she could move back there and watch the sparrows rising up out of the trees when she opened the back door in the mornings. And they won't know it was her that put the bunch of apple blossoms at Margaret Murphy's cross. No one will know I was coming home, that I wanted to live there again, to give that raving woman's ghost another chance to be my mother. All they ever saw was the me that couldn't stay; they know nothing about the me that couldn't stay away.'

It's late afternoon; the sun is sliding into the tops of the trees, spiking the highest branches, the listlessness of midday sliding along with it. The river has taken on another shade, a crimson that will lighten to golden red and later to melted flax.

The red-haired woman and the fair-haired woman are walking slowly around the perimeter of the field, stopping now and then to peer at flowers in a gap of the ditch.

'You don't say much about yourself,' the red-haired woman says.

'What is there to say?'

'I don't know – things. Are you married, do you have kids, stuff, things?'

'Yes, I am married. No, I don't have children.'

'Were you happy?'

The fair-haired woman stops and lifts her face to the falling sun. She smiles, a tight smile.

'Yes, I was.'

'Did you get on with your husband?'

'Yes, I did. Really well. He has a beautiful smile. He's quiet but in a reassuring way. I don't think I ever did anything that he didn't fully back me on. Not that he ever tried to confine me, as we actually lived our own lives. I think because he has a great sense of self-worth, nothing shakes him.'

'You were lucky.'

'Yes.'

'Did you have a job?'

'I was a teacher.'

'I'd never have guessed!' the red-haired woman laughs. 'Daughter of teachers?'

'No, my father was a doctor. Is a doctor.'

'I'd have taken odds you were a teacher's daughter.'

'Maybe it's much of a muchness.'

'Maybe. There was a girl in my school when I was in primary whose father was a doctor. I always wanted to be invited to her birthday parties. But I never was. I loved her house. I thought it was real posh. The only time I ever got to go into it was for injections. I loved the smell of it, that antiseptic smell.'

The fair-haired woman walks on, her companion following, only now her face is half-turned away.

'Wherever we lived, my father's surgery was always in the house. In a front room of our first house; then in a converted garage to the side of our second house and then in what had been a drawing room in our last house, the house my parents still live in. From the time I was six or seven, that always played on my mind, having the surgery and waiting room in the same building we lived in. I had some sense of an awful consequence around that fact. I even thought as a small girl that waiting room was spelled w-e-i-g-h-t-i-n-g room. A place where people sat with the weight of the world on their shoulders, a phrase I'd picked up from my parents' conversations. I'd see them coming and going though the hall, sad faces, sick faces, shoulders bent, doubled over. And as I grew up I realised that it wasn't just the elderly who were carrying that weight. I'd see a beautiful young woman and I'd know, from the code my parents used at the dinner table, that she was seriously ill or dying, even. Often I'd go and sit in the waiting room – at night when my parents were out – sit there and soak up that fear and uncertainty. It was an ominous feeling, and I wondered if I was the only one who felt it, wondered if it was telling me something, something waiting for me. When I was fifteen, I had this very close friend in school. We lived our lives like sisters. I'd stay in her house and she in mine. One weekend she came to stay and on that Saturday night when my parents were out, I brought her into the waiting room. We sat there, in the darkness, and I tried to explain to her that there was something there, waiting for Monday morning's patients. For some woman who thought everything was going just right for her. For a little boy that didn't even know why he was being brought there.

Something waiting for the next victim. Waiting for someone who thought they had only a cold or a cough or appendicitis. Something waiting to bring the bad news, waiting to write a last prescription. Always waiting for the door to open, to say: That's the one I'll throw my shadow over. But my friend just hushed me and then she kissed me. Perhaps she thought she could exorcise the place by kissing me. Perhaps she wanted to kiss me. Perhaps she was in love with me.'

'Love is a strange thing,' the red-haired woman says quietly.

The fair-haired woman nods. 'My father still sits up every night, waiting for me to come home. You'd think by now he'd know that's not going to happen, that there isn't going to be a tap on the window at three in the morning. That he won't open his eyes and see me at the door, that he won't struggle up out of his chair and hobble over to turn the key in the lock. It's not going to happen.'

For a long time the red-haired woman says nothing, and when finally she speaks, she might be speaking to herself. 'I beat cancer. Isn't that a joke?'

'Not a very funny one.'

'No, but I beat it. I'd just got the all-clear. I was out celebrating with my friend, Alice, who works in a travel agency. We went on the piss and then on to a nightclub, or what passes for a nightclub in our town. That's where I met him. I was out of it and I told him to shag off when he asked me to dance. I was so pissed I walked off and left Alice chatting up some guy, had it in my head that I'd go and get a taxi for the two of us, never even told Alice, started walking to the taxi rank. He must have followed me. He pulled up beside me, told me to get in, and I did. Don't know why, I knew who he was but I didn't expect...this. Who does? But I knew when he started talking, I knew I was in trouble. I asked him to stop, said I wanted to pee, but he just kept on driving. I said, If you don't stop I'll piss on the seat, but he just laughed. I asked him what he wanted from me. I want to teach you a lesson, he said, not to look down on people, not to be ignorant to people that ask you to dance. Just because you're tarted up, he said, that doesn't give you the right to treat someone like dirt. I'm sorry, I said. I'm sorry, I'm sorry, I'm sorry. I'm so fucking sorry. Not sorry enough, he said. Too late for sorry, he said. Time to learn a lesson, he said. And I knew there was no point crying, no point begging, just run for it when I got the chance. He drove into a field. It was October and the ground was hard and stubbled. He parked at the far end, in a dip, where no one could see the car. He knew the place, knew the car wouldn't get bogged down. And then I started laughing, I couldn't help it. What are you laughing at? he said. Everything, I said, the whole thing, everything, life. You're laughing at me, he said. No, I said, I'm just laughing at the whole thing. And I laughed so much I wet myself and I wet the seat of the car and I couldn't help it. You could smell the warm piss in the car and he grabbed my head and started punching me, hard, across the face, punching my nose until I heard it breaking and I didn't laugh any more. Not so funny now, he said. No laughing matter now. What do you want, I said. Do you want sex? You can if you want, whatever you want. I wouldn't touch you with a tongs, he said. I wouldn't dirty myself by stroking you. There was something in that word, stroking, something about the way he said it, softly, like he'd thought about it, like it meant something to him, that brought it home to me that this was it. This was the end. And I started laughing again, laughing at him. I knew there was no way out of there; I just wanted it to be over, just wanted him to finish it. So I thought I'd provoke him into finishing it, quickly. "You're not a hard man," I said, "but you know that, don't you? Real hard men take the chance that they'll be caught, that they'll swing for what they do. They take a risk. They're not afraid of what might happen. No, you're just a fucking gouger, you have no courage, no balls, you've nothing to lose. You're just a scumbag, a miserable, crawling, cowardly little bastard. Fucker, fucker, fucker." I don't know how long I went on. In the end, he opened the door and pushed me out. I was kneeling on the stubble and I could see the motorway lights across the field and it was the saddest thing I ever saw because they were just there. Just there like I could touch them, like I could run to them, across two fields, up the embankment, wave down a car, be safe, be looked after. I imagined it all in my head, the warmth in the car. A man driving, there'd be a woman with him. She'd sit into the back seat with me, put her arm around me, hug me, tell me I was all right, everything was all right. Yet all I could do was kneel there and listen to the cars whistling by. Warm, wrapped-up people looking out at where I was but not seeing me, not even knowing I was there. And I could feel the stubble cutting into my knees and I couldn't get up and I couldn't run. I just couldn't. When I got cancer, when the doctor told me I had it, I was so fucking angry. With myself for getting it, for being the one. I had to tell someone so I told my mother-in-law. I asked her not to tell anyone else. But she did, she told my husband. I didn't want him to know. But she told him anyway. And we talked about it and I tried to be matter-of-fact. And then one night, the end of that week, we were in bed together and we were having sex and he asked me to put my bra back on. I can't touch your tits, he said. I can't look at them, knowing what's in there. That's what he said. And I did, I put it on and he fucked me. And he never mentioned it again, never asked me how I was, nothing, just wiped it out of his mind because he couldn't deal with it. But I beat it. I fucking beat it. Didn't I? After that there was nothing anyone could do to hurt me.'

She pauses for a moment and a smile darts across her face.

'The guy that killed me, he has a family. He takes them out for lunch on a Sunday and then for a spin in the country. Is it a little lap of honour that he has in his own mind? Envisioning where he picked me up, where he killed me in the field, where he buried me in the bog and then back home for tea and a nice quiet night in front of the telly. Does he take me on holiday with him, in the back of his mind? Am I always there with him, like a prize he's proud of? All these questions that I'll never get the answers to. And everyone else thinking my own fella did it!'

The four women are at the gateway to the field. The young girl leans against one of the pillars, the other three loll against the bank, the rays of the sinking sun shining straight into their eyes, lighting up those eyes as if there were life inside them to light.

'I was in Tramore with my mates on holiday last year,' the young girl says, her brow furrowed. 'I nearly drowned there and it wasn't funny. And all your life doesn't flashbefore you either, when you're dying.'

'I think we all know that by now,' the slight woman says.

The girl is silent, a furrow still ploughing her forehead.

'So why did we end up here, now, today, together?'

'Maybe this is Purgatory – the halfway house.'

'Do you think so?'

'No, I don't.'

'Do you think we'll be together forever now?'

'Jesus, I hope not! I can't think of anything I ever did to deserve that.'

'So what do you think we're doing here? Why is it happening now?' The young girl turns to the fair-haired woman.

'I have no idea.'

'We're waiting for Godot,' the slight woman laughs. 'Or the Blessed Virgin-O. Or the Holy Ghost-O. Maybe this is the great Lost and Found in the sky. Where the dumped and dislocated all find their way in the end, limping in with their battered faces and broken necks and stabbed hearts. "The winner takes it all." Bet that's not one of your songs.'

The fair-haired woman shakes her head.

The young girl settles herself more comfortably on the gate.

'Do you believe in God?' she asks the slight woman.

'He hasn't come looking for me, not even a text message.'

'Do you?'

'Yes, I do,' the fair-haired woman says. 'There has to be a God to make some sense of this.'

'Why?' the slight woman asks. 'Why does this have to make sense? I never understood it when people said that and I still don't.'

'Because there are no answers in chaos.'

'Why do you expect answers to everything?'

'There is an answer to every question.'

'Except the chicken and the egg,' the girl laughs.

'To every serious question – about life and death and faith and hope.'

'No, no, no, no, that's waffle,' the slight woman says quickly. 'That's aspiration. That's the kind of stuff you hear on radio breakfast shows, new-age bullshit, crap they throw out at half-six in the morning when you're too tired or hung over to understand, let alone contradict. Nothing has to be.'

'If there's no God, how are we here, in this place, now, talking, continuing to exist?'

The slight woman shakes her head, genuinely amazed.

'You think us being here, in this fucking field, having this poxy conversation is proof of the existence of God?'

'Not if you don't want to believe. But if you have faith, there are answers. To everything.'

'Ah, so I'm a second class sinner travelling in the last train to Graceland because I don't believe? But you're up there in first class with the Communion of Saints and Scholars? Is that it?'

'I wouldn't put it that way.'

'And just how would you put it?' the slight woman says, standing up and leaning into the fair-haired woman's face. 'Pope Whatever Your Name Is? You haven't really said anything definite about any of this, have you? You just think it should make sense because you've always believed in your gossamer, spirity little life that it should. But none of it has to. We don't have to know where we are or why we're here or any of that stuff. Like your man said, "We can see no reasons, cause there are no reasons." Just like there didn't have to be reasons for any of us to be killed. It was circumstances, that's all. Wrong time, wrong place, wrong turn, wrong bed, wrong house, wrong road. That's all it amounts to in the end – situations, details. That's all, no master plan, no all-seeing eye. Nothing.'

'I didn't realise Bob Geldof was a theologian too.'

'Oh yeah, and a great ride too, I'd say,' the slight woman sniggers, stepping and turning away.

'I believe what I believe.'

'Won't get you anywhere, won't solve anything, won't help you find heaven's gate. And even if you do, you'll find the paint is peeling and the hinges have fallen off and there ain't nobody at home. This is it – we go on existing and nobody knows and every now and then we'll stumble across one another and that'll be it. Human contact in an inhuman somewhere or other.'

The young girl swings on the gatepost, looking to the red-haired woman for reassurance, but she just smiles wanly and shrugs. The slight woman turns to face the other three, her face set and earnest.

'Do you know what I remember most clearly from life? A winter morning at three on Leeson Street, and a guy I knew who was tall and attractive and a big black car with that shiny, new look and a smell of someone else's perfume in the front seat and Indian music playing and a pleasant conversation about the party we were going to and what this guy would like to do to me and laughter. There's my life, the last hour of it anyway. No blinding flash, no Saviour coming down off his cross to show the bad guys who's really the boss. Nothing, just losing breath, losing consciousness, being rolled into a hole, being covered, being afraid, being breathless, being dead, being here. That's what it comes to, that's what I remember. That and the Halloween night my dad dressed up in women's clothes and did a striptease and I laughed. And the day my dog died. And the day my sister was knocked down. And that's about it. That's the fucking all of it.'

'When I was nine, my dog was run over,' the young girl says quickly. 'I had a picture of him that I drew. I kept it under my pillow for months. I won a prize for it.'

The slight woman laughs. 'Angel-Arse, you never cease to amaze me with the profound way you link one thing to another, completely unrelated matter.'

The girl smiles.

'If I could go back now, I'd sit on the side of my brother's bed, and I'd sing and I'd say: "I love you so much, scallywallywallywag."'

For a moment she is silent, taking in the field and its lengthening shadows, gazing along the empty roadway.

'Do any of you know where we are?'

'We're at the end of the line, Angel-Arse,' the slight woman says. 'Literally and metaphorically. And if you don't know what that means, ask our learned friend there.'

'Are we ghosts?'

'We're the smell of a dead animal on the side of a mountain, that's what we are.'

It's evening. The red-haired woman and the fair-haired woman are watching the last rays of the sun's afterglow. The light in the field is so delicate it might shatter at any moment, a brittle midsummer crystal in the air. Spirals of gnats gyre above the darkening river, where a trout rises into the air and falls again, the water closing over it.

'Funny,' the fair-haired woman says. 'Whenever I thought about dying, I never dreamed I'd be killed.'

'Can't say I ever thought too much about dying.'

'I did. Often.'

'Maybe that's because your father was a doctor, what you were saying about the waiting room and all that stuff.'

'I think it was more than that. It was like something constantly in my head, like, I don't know… like something I was waiting for.'

'Fear?'

'No, not fear. I wasn't afraid of this thing. I don't know how to explain it properly. When I met him, the man, it was morning, a bright, sunny, summer morning. I was walking along the canal bank and I'd taken a book of poems with me. I saw him sitting near one of the lock gates, watching me walking, peering out over the top of these little round glasses. He was wearing a leather jacket and black jeans. From the first time I saw his eyes, it seemed to me that he knew everything I'd ever thought and done. I know that sounds trite, but it's true. And he had a notebook and pen in his hand, which made me think he was OK. I know our friend over there would laugh at that, say I was pretentious, but it's just something we all do, don't we? We see something about someone and we either like or dislike them for it. Do you know what I mean?'

'Yes, I do.'

'He said something like, "Life is too short" but not in any kind of threatening or dark way, more as if it were a natural thing to say, a natural greeting. Anyhow, I sat beside him and we started talking about nature and life and death and God and meaning, serious things. It was as if we knew each other intimately. Like we'd had these discussions before, like we were comfortable with the conversation. We talked for a long time and then he said he'd walk me to the next lock, his car was parked there. And he took my arm while we were walking, which I didn't like. It was the first thing that didn't feel right. But we were still talking, still discussing, and I was enjoying the conversation, so I thought perhaps it was just a natural gesture.'

'And what happened?'

'Just before we reached the lock gate, it started to drizzle. He said he was meeting someone and asked me for directions. I told him how to get where he was going and wished him well, but just then the heavens opened and he started laughing and said, "Get in the car, I'll drop you to a bus stop." I was wearing a tracksuit, and knew I'd be drenched, so I said OK.

'And?'

'He drove past the bus stop. I asked him to let me out. He smiled and told me to relax, said he'd drive me home. Told me to trust him. One part of me did, implicitly. And another part told me I was mad. It had stopped raining. I thought – this'll be OK because people don't get harmed at ten o'clock on a summer morning, broad daylight. It just doesn't happen.

'"Listen," he said. "I'm sorry if I scared you. What about we take a walk in the mountains, solve the problems of the here and the hereafter? I am sorry if you got the wrong impression."

'I looked squarely at him and he was smiling. His eyes met mine and I trusted them.

'"Alright,"' I said.

'I knew anyone hearing me say that would think I was crazy, but I was willing to take the risk because I felt challenged by the things he had said.

'"Good,"' he said. "Thank you."

'He drove up the mountains. Anyone seeing us would have thought – summer morning, couple out for a drive, a walk through the woods and lunch on the way back. And we did walk into the woods, and he kept talking to me about the same things we'd talked about at the canal.'

'You didn't try to talk him round?'

'No. I just nodded or shrugged. And then he said, again: "Life is short." But this time his tone reminded me of one of those judges handing down a sentence in an old black and white film. I was waiting for the gavel to fall somewhere but all I heard were the birds singing. Then he told me to sit down. "You know what I'm going to do," he said. I nodded.'

'And then it happened?'

'No. He beat me. Just that, just violence, simple viciousness, so out of keeping with the conversation we'd had at the canal. But he didn't kill me. He beat me and then he bundled me down into a dyke. I was in pain, I knew my arm was broken, I knew my ribs were broken, but I was conscious. And I think he knew I was conscious. He threw the book in after me. I started to crawl away from him, away from any more pain, away from whatever it was he was going to do next. I kept crawling along the bottom of the dyke. It was full of dry leaves and bits of broken sticks. And each time I looked back he was watching me, standing on the lip of the dyke, watching. And I kept crawling and then I looked back and he was gone. I lay there, waiting for him, thinking he'd gone to get a gun or a stone or a spade. And the sun kept rising through the sky and there were flies around the blood on my face and I heard voices, not all that far away, but I didn't call to them.'

'He'd come back with someone else?'

'No, no, these were younger voices, girls' voices, laughing.'

'And you didn't shout for help?'

'No.'

'Why not, for Christ's sake?'

'I don't know.'

The fair-haired woman pauses for a moment and considers what she has said.

'I do know,' she corrects herself.

'And?'

'It was as if I had made a decision. Not to try to go back, not to leave that wood. Not to try to escape.'

'Why, for fuck's sake? Why?'

'Because all my life I'd been waiting for something, waiting for that darkness that followed the other people into my father's surgery to find me, to fall across my shoulders. Here was the inevitable consequence that had been shadowing me all my life. Here was my destiny and I had no right to interfere with what had been predestined for me. It wasn't unlike when they told us we couldn't have children, after we'd wanted children so badly. But when they told us there was nothing we could do, we went home and we made love every day for a week, sometimes twice or three times a day, as though we might somehow forget, shed the bad news in the sweat and stimulation of love-making. But of course it doesn't work like that, so I finally accepted it. And my husband accepted it. And I somehow accepted that my life was meant to end in that wood. And I knew my husband would accept it, too.'

'But didn't you want to go back?'

'There is no going back – ever. We think there is; we think we can undo what we've done, or explain ourselves away to those we hurt, but we can't. And it's better to accept what's been laid out for us.'

'I think you're wrong.'

'Most people would.'

'Very wrong.'

'I lay there as my body settled into the ground and the pain became something I could manage, and the day ended and the moon came up like a paper lantern, blowing and catching on branches, then blowing higher and catching again. Right up through the tallest trees, and then down again, falling and catching and falling and catching until it was almost dawn. And I thought of a night when I was young, when I was a student. I had driven up the Dublin Mountains with my husband, who was my boyfriend then. It was summer, 1984, a hot summer night in the middle of July. We parked the car and went into the woods and I took off my dress in the moonlight and we made love. I thought about that while I was lying there. I remembered it, tried to be in that time and that place, with my husband, but I couldn't. Like I said, there's no going back. So I waited. I waited for that man to come back. I knew I'd see him again.'

'Fucking hell.'

'The next day he was there, standing above me again. It must have been late in the morning because I couldn't see his face, the sun was behind him. At first I thought I was hallucinating, I was thirsty and hungry, but when he stepped down into the dyke and his shadow fell across me, I knew this was what I'd been waiting for. I saw the blade, but there was no pain. Then he covered me over with leaves and sticks and clay, but I know some day the winter rain running through the dyke will wash all that away.'

Three of the women are standing in the twilit field, looking across the river and up towards the brow of the darkening hill.

The slight woman sits on the low stump of a tree and kicks off her black boots.

'I knew these would cut the feet off me.'

The others are silent. She stands again and looks at them.

'Right, so much for the party spirit! I'm going. I'll see you. See you, Angel-Arse, keep dancing.'

'Yeah,' the young girl says. 'See ya.'

The slight woman walks slowly across the field and steps through a gap in the ditch, disappearing into another field.

'I wonder if we will see her again?' the red-haired woman asks.

No one answers her.

'Strange,' she says. 'The way we all start out so full of high hopes, when we fall in love, like. We meet someone and we think life is going to be everything that it wasn't for our parents or our friends. We see someone and we think they're gorgeous and we get to meet them and we think they're great and they think we're great and everything is going to be fantastic forever. And then it just goes... somewhere...away...gets lost, goes missing and one day you realise it's gone. And it doesn't matter if you meet someone else and you think they're great too, and they don't mind that your breast has been sliced open, they just want to love you, to make love to you, and then that slips away as well. There's nothing that lasts, nothing you can rely on, it's not just people or breathing, it's everything, feelings, even fucking love itself.'

The girl looks at her, frowning.

'That's very sad.'

'Yes, it is, isn't it? Bloody sad.'

She's silent for a moment, watching the young girl's worried face and then she says, smiling, 'Alice and me…we were fourteen…we were on a bus, with all these other kids from the youth club...it was a summer tour…just for the day…and the bus came over the top of a hill and there it was…the sea…the first time I'd ever laid eyes on it…Jesus…this blue sheet from one side of the world to the other…flat, blue. I just wanted that moment to last forever…I couldn't hear anything…none of the singing or shouting or laughing…just me and the sea. I was holding onto Alice's hand, squeezing it without knowing, and she didn't say anything. She realised how special that was to me…the sea…blue…blue and calm, wide, beautiful…the most beautiful thing I ever saw.'

As she finishes, the fair-haired woman moves away into the twilight, becomes something distant and then nothing at all. As the night settles about them, neither the red-haired woman nor the girl speaks, until each sees the other as a darkness on the darkness of night. Finally, the older woman speaks.

'It's time to go.'

'Yeah,' the girl agrees, carelessly kicking off her runners, as if ready for her next adventure. They begin to cross the field, towards the gate, but then the young girl turns and goes back to where they had been standing. She scans the ground until she finds the child's wellington boots in the grass. Hesitating, she kneels and picks them up, holding them in one hand.

The red-haired woman comes back and stands above her.

'I think we should go,' she says.

'What about these?'

'I don't know.'

'My brother loved it when I stayed with him. Imagine being a child, being left on your own, left out somewhere like here where no one will ever find you.'

'No different to ourselves.'

'I know, but we found one another, didn't we? And, anyway, we're big people.'

'True.'

'Imagine whoever owns these, how small they are? What if they come looking for them and there's no one here?'

'We don't know if they will come, or when. Maybe never.'

'But what if they do?'

'I have to go,' the red-haired woman says.

'I know,' the girl says. 'I'll wait…for a while, just for a while…just in case.'